charmingly
yours

ALSO BY LIZ TALLEY

Home in Magnolia Bend

The Sweetest September

Sweet Talking Man

Sweet Southern Nights

New Orleans' Ladies

The Spirit of Christmas

His Uptown Girl

His Brown-Eyed Girl

His Forever Girl

Bayou Bridge

Waters Run Deep

Under the Autumn Sky

The Road to Bayou Bridge

Oak Stand

Vegas Two-Step

The Way to Texas

A Little Texas

A Taste of Texas

A Touch of Scarlet

Novellas and Anthologies

The Nerd Who Loved Me

"Hotter in Atlanta"

"Kiss Me, Cowboy" in Cowboys for Christmas
with Kim Law & Terri Osburn

A Wrong Bed for Christmas
with Kimberly Van Meter

charmingly yours

a morning glory novel

LIZ TALLEY

Montlake
Romance

Published by Montlake Romance, Seattle
www.apub.com

Amazon, the Amazon logo, and Montlake Romance are trademarks of Amazon.com, Inc., or its affiliates.

ISBN-13: 9781503949683
ISBN-10: 1503949680

Cover design by Laura Klynstra

Printed in the United States of America

To the town that made me who I am—Minden, Louisiana. I can't say Morning Glory is exactly like my hometown, but since it's filled with character, warmth, and busybodies, it's not too far off. Thanks for raising me right, Minden.

Chapter One

The last communication of Rosemary Reynolds's oldest friend lay innocently in the center of the table, half resting on torn polka-dotted wrapping paper, addressed to "My Girls" in the same girlish hoop-dee-loop script Lacy Guthrie had perfected on the back cover of her math notebook in the seventh grade.

"So who's gonna open it?" Eden Voorhees asked, swiping at her eyes, smearing the designer mascara she'd borrowed from Rosemary earlier that morning as they dressed for the funeral.

Rosemary sat in the coffee shop with her two remaining best friends, headachy from the tears she'd shed for the past three hours. No. The past three days.

After the last guest had tossed a soggy tissue into the trash at Fulbright's Funeral Parlor, she, Eden, and Jess gave their farewells to Lacy's mother and headed somewhere where they didn't have to fake smile and nod when someone said how good Lacy looked.

How in all that was holy could Lacy look good? She was dead. Could anyone associate "good" with that?

Rosemary glanced over at Jess Culpepper, who stared at the envelope, eyes dry, chin out. Unflappable Jess. Rosemary had wanted to dissolve into great heaving sobs when she'd realized who'd left the wrapped present, but she was slap out of tears. She'd flooded the funeral and graveside service, unable to stop the sobs, snot, and total heartache at the thought Lacy would never call her again to complain about Mr. Sneed's bad breath . . . or slide onto the bench seat of Earline, the Guthries' old Ford truck, flipping down the mirror to fix her lipstick.

Lacy was plain gone.

But with a dramatic flourish that shouldn't have surprised Rosemary, Lacy had left a gift for her three best friends under the counter of the Lazy Frog coffee shop, which sat in the heart of the square of Morning Glory, friendliest city in Mississippi. Or so the sign welcoming visitors into the small town sitting slightly east of Jackson read. The medium-size box had been wrapped in cheerful multicolored polka-dotted paper with an orange satin bow. Orange had always been Lacy's signature color.

"You do it," Eden said, sliding the envelope to Rosemary. Unless she was in the spotlight at the community theater, Eden preferred to take the backseat, bringing little attention to herself.

"Why me?" Rosemary asked, sliding it back.

"Jesus, give it here," Jess said, picking up the envelope, tearing off an end, and blowing into it. Until that moment, Rosemary hadn't known her friend's preferred method of opening letters.

Weird.

As a surgical nurse, Jess was the perfect person to rip off the proverbial bandage. Unfolding the letter within, Jess swiped at her nose with the back of her hand. If they'd not just attended Lacy's funeral, Rosemary might have teased her friend about her lack of sterility, but today wasn't a day for jokes. Today wasn't a day for much of anything. Jess cleared her throat. "Okay. Here goes."

Eden glanced away, her sleek, dark hair falling over half her face, obscuring her emotions. Ever since Eden had lost her older brother in an offshore platform accident, she didn't deal well with death.

Heck, who dealt well with death? Maybe undertakers? Had to be part of the job description. Wanted: a person who doesn't mind death . . . or the smell of carnations.

"Dear Eden, Jess, and Rosemary," Jess read, her voice cracking. The paper trembled as she struggled to maintain her emotional distance.

"I know you're sitting there wondering what in the heck I'm thinking sending you a letter from the great beyond. Great beyond. Sounds spooky, doesn't it? But anyway, I know my mother probably kept y'all out of the hospital room. You know Connie, she's a control freak and probably had some crazy rule about family only."

Eden snorted. "Got that woman pegged, doesn't she?"

Jess grunted, obviously still peeved at Lacy's mother, but continued. "Thing is, Mom never realized family's not about blood. My true family started the day we walked into Mr. Meyer's homeroom at Morning Glory Junior High. Go Mavs!"

Mr. Meyer's homeroom. That's where it had all begun. Rosemary remembered what Lacy had been wearing that morning. She'd laid out her first-day-of-school outfit a week before—new jeans that flared at the ankle, platform flip-flops, and a tight T-shirt that said, LITTLE MISS TROUBLE. Clueless Mr. Meyer had let them sit where they wanted, and somehow the four girls had ended up at the same table.

"I'm Lacy," she'd said, chewing on a piece of hair she'd painted purple with the hair mascara she'd scored when visiting her grandmother that summer. "Both Rosemary and I went to Prestwood Academy, but we're totally not snobby. So don't worry. We won't bite."

That's how Lacy was. She'd never met a stranger.

"I'm Jess," the tall girl said, her stare direct even at age twelve. "This is Eden. We went to Richards Elementary."

"I know," Lacy said, eyeing the obviously cheap shirt Eden wore, but not in a mean way. Just assessing. "I mean, if you didn't go to Prestwood, you had to go to Richards, right? So far I'm not totally impressed with MGJH. You know, we should stick together at lunch."

"You want to eat lunch with us?" Eden asked, looking over at Jess as if to ask permission.

"Sure," Lacy said with a big smile. "I'm so tired of hanging with the same people. Except for Rosemary, of course. She's always been my BFF."

Jess cocked her head. "You don't know us."

Lacy laughed. "But I will. We're going to be lifelong friends. See? We fit one another. Like on *Sex and the City*. Do y'all watch?"

"No," Jess said, shooting a cryptic look at Eden. The two girls were obviously taken aback by Lacy's cheerful determination.

"Oh my God, it's like the coolest show," Lacy said, sliding a glance toward a cute boy who'd walked in late. She smiled at him with her eyes. "It's about four women in NYC. I'm like Samantha. She's super confident and outspoken. Rosemary's prissy like Charlotte, but she has to be because of her mother."

"I do not," Rosemary huffed.

Lacy had merely given her that knowing look.

"Just because she made me wear this," Rosemary said, sweeping a hand down the pristine dress her mother had ordered from the Neiman Marcus catalog. "I didn't want to, you know."

"It's okay, Rose. I *like* Charlotte. She's optimistic. So that leaves Miranda and Carrie. And my powers of deduction tell me you two are a good fit. Yay." Lacy clapped her hands excitedly.

"Isn't that show rated R or something?" Eden asked.

"Of course. My mom thinks I'm recording *Dawson's Creek*, which I totally am. But I also record *SATC*. Y'all can come over and watch. Okay?"

Lacy didn't wait for an answer. She simply started putting contact paper on her notebook, like her decree was final. They'd all be friends, assuming a particular role. They'd balance one another out, wipe one another's tears, celebrate first kisses, and join *NSYNC's fan club.

And they had. Except for Eden. She'd refused to join the fan club.

Jess set the letter down on the table, drawing Rosemary back to the present. Her friend picked up her latte, sloshing some over the side but not bothering to wipe the spill. "Jesus."

The owner of the Lazy Frog, Sassy Grigsby, made a little mewling sound and blew into a paper napkin. She sat behind the counter in a too-tight navy dress, watching them with sad eyes. Just minutes before, Sassy had approached the table the girls had claimed their sophomore year of high school—the day Kyle Hannah broke up with Eden and they all commiserated with brownies and hot chocolate—and set the wrapped box in the center of the table. Sassy had backed away, almost apologetic, retreating to the sanctity of the coffee bar, where she continued to weep.

Picking up the letter again, Jess swallowed and read, "You three were the sisters I never had, and this is probably so strange, but I want to ask something of you."

For a few seconds, Jess read silently.

"Stop doing that," Eden said, tapping the table.

Jess ignored Eden, her lips moving as she read, her eyes widening.

"What?" Rosemary asked.

Jess lowered the letter and pulled the box toward her, rooting inside.

"What are you doing?" Eden asked, pulling one of the box flaps, causing the box to slip from Jess's fingers.

Jess tugged it back, tossing out tissue paper, finally withdrawing a small pouch covered in paisley whorls. She handed the pouch to Rosemary. The weight sank into her curved palm like an omen.

"Do I open it?" Rosemary asked.

Jess shook her head and returned to the letter. "As you know, my biggest dream was to see the world. Ever since I was little, I wanted to see the things I'd read about in picture books. Going to Paris was the highlight of my life and I'd been saving to go to Australia and New Zealand . . . and, well, that won't happen now."

"This is horrible," Eden whispered.

Rosemary nodded, testing the weight of the small jewelry bag in her hand, knowing what it was, hurting all the same.

"But I realized at some point," Jess continued, the letter still quivering in her hand, "that you all have dreams, too, so I decided my last wish would be to help you to have the things you want. I've written each of you a letter and given you a little help to make something good happen in your life. In the bag you'll find the second part of my wish—completing my charm bracelet. Once you have found what you're looking for, choose a charm and attach it to the bracelet. When our bracelet is complete, find someone who has no hope left and give the bracelet to her. I'll take care of the rest."

"What does that even mean?" Eden asked.

Rosemary felt strange butterflies in her stomach. Lacy had set something in motion, something Rosemary couldn't quite get a hold on. The whole thing felt mystical . . . as if Lacy knew something they didn't.

Jess cleared her throat and flipped the letter over. "I believe in magic and happy endings . . . even though I may not have gotten one. And I believe in you. I love each of you and I will be watching. Hopefully from heaven 'cause y'all know I HATE to be hot. Hugs and cute bugs, Lacy."

The letter fell from Jess's fingertips, revealing the small ladybugs drawn around Lacy's signature, the same ones she'd drawn around her name since junior high. "Jesus . . . why did she do this? Only Lacy would be this melodramatic. Only Lacy—" But Jess couldn't finish. She turned away from them, struggling against grief.

This past year had been hard for Jess. In September her husband, Benton, had come home with flowers and news he was leaving her so he could have "experiences"—i.e., sleep with other women. Jess and Benton had been together since freshman year of high school. Always part of a team, Jess found herself living in a new apartment, struggling to find the confident woman she'd once been. Lacy's death had been extraordinarily hard on her.

Rosemary untied the strings of the bag and allowed the contents to slide into her open palm.

Lacy's silver charm bracelet that her grandmother had given her on her tenth birthday lay in her palm. Eight charms were attached, each one oohed and ahhed over by the three girls when Lacy had added it. Rosemary had always loved the alligator Lacy had bought when she visited her cousin in New Orleans. But there was also a cowboy boot from Dallas and the treasured Eiffel Tower from Paris. Lacy had also attached a megaphone from her cheerleading days at Morning Glory High School, claiming that was one of her favorite places to have visited. Several other sentimental charms gleamed in Rosemary's hand, and she brushed the small silver frog Lacy's biological father had sent from Brazil. The man hadn't even come to his daughter's funeral. He'd given up his life in Morning Glory years ago for a younger woman, a beachside apartment, and a new life in South America. Lacy had kept the frog on her bracelet anyway.

What kind of man didn't come to his daughter's funeral? Rosemary didn't have words for someone like him.

"I get why she left us letters—that's so Lacy—but I don't understand why she left us her charm bracelet," Eden said, reaching over and pushing the Eiffel Tower erect. Three empty links remained. "Why should we have to complete it? And how do we find someone with no hope?"

Jess reached in the box and passed out the individual letters. "I guess she explains in these letters."

Rosemary glanced down at the envelope in her hand, her emotions racing from sadness to anger . . . and back again. Why had this happened to Lacy? Why did she have to die and leave them? Nothing made sense today . . . and she had no idea how to feel about this last act by the girl who'd left bite marks on Rosemary's arm the first day of preschool.

"Do we open our letters now?" Eden asked.

Jess shook her head. "I don't want to do it here. I can't."

Rosemary nodded, curling her fingers around the charm bracelet. "That's fine. She separated the letters for a reason."

"But she wanted us to do this . . . whatever *this* is." Eden pulled the strap off the back of her chair and slid the letter into the depths of her purse.

Jess nodded. "Whatever she wanted us to do, we do."

Rosemary knew things weren't as simple as that, because she'd known Lacy longest and best. Lacy saw the world through orange-colored glasses—she'd never liked any shade of pink—and whatever she deemed good and right, she would make happen. Wasn't the four girls' tight friendship a testament to Lacy's determination? Whatever last bequest she'd given her friends would be something spun in fantasy, cut free from the roots of practicality. Like a ballad from days of old, Lacy would send them on a quest.

And as crazy as all this was, Rosemary would do it. Because Lacy couldn't.

Rosemary placed the bracelet back into the cloth bag. "I'll keep the bracelet until we read our letters, and, yeah, if we can do what she wants, we'll do it."

"So meet back tomorrow?" Jess asked arching an eyebrow.

"I can't come until after six. Gary's bitching about my taking the last few days off. He acts like I've been lolling about on a beach or something," Eden grumbled, running a finger under her thick lower eyelashes framing vivid blue eyes.

"He's an ass," Jess muttered . . . the same thing she always said whenever Eden mentioned the regional manager of Penny Pinchers, the discount store where Eden worked.

"Yeah, but he's an ass I have to stare at twice a week. He'll be in tomorrow to go over my inventory reports and 'accidentally' brush against me."

"You should quit," Rosemary said.

"I should do a great many things, Rose, but I have Mama to think about. Managing Penny Pinchers gives me the right hours and health insurance." Eden's face was resigned. As it always was. Eden hadn't gotten what she wanted from life. Instead of heading off to college like her friends, she'd stayed home, working to make ends meet, never complaining as she took care of the mother who'd never been much of a mother to her.

"I know, but it feels good to say it," Rosemary said, scooting her chair back. "I need to check on the shop. Mama's frying chicken for Basil's birthday, if either of you want to come."

Both Eden and Jess shook their heads.

Rosemary didn't blame them. Her older brother, Basil, had a fascination with breasts . . . which would make him like every other heterosexual man on the planet, except Basil wasn't like anyone else. Rosemary's brother suffered from delayed social and mental development, a virtual child in a man's body. Still, his zeroing in on boobs made a gal uncomfortable.

Rosemary knew, 'cause she had them, too.

But still, Basil was sweet and funny in his own way. His childlike wonder reminded Rosemary to slow down and savor the simple things. And really it was easy to do in her small town. Not much going on, unless one counted the weekly bingo game, hot yoga at the Church of Christ and Benton Mason's girlfriend-of-the-week sighting. Jess had already moved out of the restored Craftsman house she had shared with her soon-to-be ex-husband and taken her maiden name back. All she waited on were divorce papers. Fried chicken, with or without Basil, wouldn't entice Jess to ride out to Rosemary's parents' historic plantation when it sat right next to Benton's family home.

"So I'll see y'all tomorrow?" Rosemary asked, pushing her chair in, pausing as she looked at her friends, their faces still etched in grief. "Everything feels so different . . . like we'll never be the same again."

Jess looked up. "We won't. A piece of us is gone. And inside it feels like something's brewing. Like those aches my granny used to get when it was about to storm."

"Barometric pressure," Eden said, twisting a straw paper, "except this is about us . . . and whatever Lacy left us to do."

Rosemary moved around the table, squeezing Eden on the shoulder before giving Jess a tiny smile. "Storms bring life—they blow withered leaves from trees so new life can grow. Storms quench the earth, causing ebb and flow."

Jess managed a smile. "You're such a poet."

Rosemary laughed, not bothering to be embarrassed by her flowery words. These girls knew her. "Just truth."

And then Rosemary left her friends, pushing out the glass door into the normalcy of her life—Morning Glory, with its quaint square surrounded by glass storefronts, including her own fabric design shop, Parsley and Sage. Somehow the same crumbling courthouse and worn brick streets comforted her. No matter how much change came her way, this town was a constant.

Morning Glory was a way of life. It was sweet tea and porch swings. Mayhaw jelly in a mason jar and fireflies dotting the night. Morning Glory was Sunday morning church bells, gossip at Dean's Diner, and traditions that didn't make sense but were carried out regardless because that's the way it was.

Rosemary belonged in Morning Glory . . . even without Lacy.

Chapter Two

One month later

If driving in downtown Jackson, Mississippi, made Rosemary as nervous as long-tailed cat in a roomful of rocking chairs, then climbing the subway stairs to emerge into frenetic Manhattan made her feel like she needed to take shelter. Because a category 5 hurricane swirled around her.

Totally embarrassing to be such a fraidy cat.

But the flop sweat she'd broken into upon emerging from underground was all her mother's fault. Ever since Rosemary's cousin Halle had called and begged Rosemary to come apartment-sit in SoHo, Patsy Reynolds had been collecting news articles headlining all the horrible things that befell residents of New York City and taping them to the fridge. And dang if the thought of being left for dead in an alley somewhere near the Hudson River hadn't wormed its way into Rosemary's head, eroding her confidence in visiting a place she'd only seen in movies.

Of course, Rosemary had fought against the irrationality by doing extensive prep work. She'd driven to Jackson (nervously) in order to purchase the three seasons of *Sex and the City* she didn't already own. She'd watched Lacy's favorite show religiously every single night after she closed her fabric shop—which, of course, made her miss her friend all the more. Then she'd downloaded a map of SoHo, practicing how to say the street names so people (a.k.a. thieves and murderers) would know she wasn't a tourist. Case in point, she knew to say "HOW-ston" instead of "HYU-ston." She'd even borrowed her neighbor Mimi's vintage Chanel cocktail dress, though it was a size too small, just in case she needed to have breakfast outside Tiffany's . . . or go to a glam cocktail party.

New York would be her oyster . . . whatever that meant.

But now, looking down at her cute seersucker sundress and back at the people striding purposefully down the street, she knew she'd never fool anyone. She looked sweet as sugarcane and they looked . . . well, urbane in their somber, sophisticated baggy pants and stomach-skimming halters.

"Oh, excuse me," she breathed, hopping back before a guy wearing a suit and high-tops nearly ran her down. "So sorry."

The man merely jerked his head in acknowledgment and kept plowing toward wherever he was headed. Another woman wearing . . . an odd, sacklike dress? . . . glanced at her in annoyance when Rosemary accidentally stepped in her path. Someone cleared his throat behind her. She turned, realizing she was blocking the stream of traffic coming from the subway stairs.

"Oops," she said to no one in particular, backing up to plaster herself against the cool stone of the building behind her. It felt nice against her sweaty back. She parked the rolling suitcase at her feet, aggravated at her cousin Halle for talking her into taking the subway. She should have gotten a cab—not that she'd ever ridden in one before. They didn't need cabs in Morning Glory. Good heavens, she'd only flown once before, and even then she'd taken the Disney Magical Express bus to her hotel. How did she even hail a cab? In *Sex and the City* the cabs appeared like magic whenever Carrie Bradshaw needed one. Stepping to the corner and trying to flag down the careening taxicabs looked suicidal.

"Okay," she said to herself, sucking in a calming breath as she riffled through the burlap tote with her initials monogrammed on the side. "Why did I let my phone battery die? And where in the name of Jesus did I put the backup map?"

She pulled out a light and water bill and the gate ticket the flight attendant had handed back to her before finding the map she'd laminated for purposes such as this. "Here we go."

Unfolding the map, she ran her finger down the line she'd drawn from the subway station to her cousin's loft on Spring Street. Not too far. She rotated the map. So she needed to head to her left. She flipped it around. No. Her right.

She looked up, trying to find a kind soul who might point her in the right direction, but no one made eye contact. An older man walked his dog, glancing down intermittently at a newspaper, moving at a turtle's pace. Maybe he'd be nice enough to point out the correct way.

She tugged her suitcase and dodged another flood of people coming out of the subway tunnel to reach the gentleman, whose dog lifted its leg on a scrawny tree set into the wide sidewalk. Honking horns and the swoosh of traffic surrounded her, rattling her nerves even more. "Uh, excuse me, sir?"

The man didn't look up. Merely kept his eyes on the folded newspaper in his hand.

"Sir?"

He lifted dark eyes beneath winged eyebrows. His swarthy skin indicated he might not speak English.

"Eh?"

Rosemary clutched her suitcase tightly in case anyone got any bright idea about making off with her undies and the sensible cardigan sweater her mother had forced her to pack in order to fight the chill. As if June in NYC was cool. She held up the map and pointed to the little star indicating her cousin's five-story building, hoping the man understood she asked for directions. "Is this place that way?" She stood facing Prince Street and jabbed her finger toward the right. "Or that way?" Left.

He took the map and turned it. "Dere." He pointed a thick finger straight ahead.

"Oh, so it's straight ahead?"

"Jah," he said, tugging the leash of the dog and handing the map back to Rosemary. He sauntered off without another word.

"Thank you," she called, not really knowing if the man had given her the right direction or not. "Have a good evening."

He lifted his hand and kept trucking.

"Guess I'm going straight," she said to herself. A woman passing with a baby stroller looked at her oddly. Rosemary merely gave her a little wave and a smile, feeling stupid. Probably something she should acquaint herself with.

"You aren't in Kansas anymore, Dorothy," she muttered.

Squaring her shoulders, she set off in the direction the man had pointed, heading east, hoping like mad she'd run into Spring Street. The sun sat hot on her shoulders and trickles of sweat coasted down her back, dampening the back of her dress, but with each step she encouraged herself.

No big deal, Rosemary. You're a competent person taking a little walk. It's still light out. You're perfectly safe. Stop being a ninny. You got this.

Several people stared at her—she was, after all, rolling luggage behind her—but most talked into their phones or stared vacantly ahead, earbuds in place, world tuned out.

After Rosemary had walked three blocks, she knew something was wrong. She pulled over, this time against a glass storefront, and took the map from the pocket of her bag, cursing herself for not charging her phone during the layover in Atlanta. She traced a finger along her current route and saw the issue. She was walking parallel to Spring Street. If she hopped one block over, she'd be on the right street, but would have to double back a few blocks to get to the building where her cousin lived.

"No big deal," she said.

A man carrying a bag of groceries looked over. "Huh?"

"Oh nothing," she said, death grip on her luggage handle. "Just talking to myself."

He made a face before continuing on his way.

Rosemary swiped at the sweat dripping into her eyes and turned down Mulberry Street, hoping her makeup wasn't pooling. Rosemary rarely wore the stuff, but Eden had scored a bargain correction stick to hide the blemish on her chin along with some shimmery eye shadow. So much for being glamorous. She was sweating like a preacher during a July tent revival.

The street she walked down looked cramped, but in a charming way that made her want to sink down at one of the cute bistro tables covered with red-and-white-checked cloths and drink some ice water. The spicy scent of roasted meat tickled her nose, and her stomach growled at the thought of a garlicky red sauce. She'd studied the map of Manhattan enough to realize she was probably walking through Little Italy . . . but she'd obviously not studied it enough to get her to her cousin's apartment.

A man wearing an apron and a gorgeous smile tried to hand her a menu. "Dinner for the lady?"

"Uh, no thanks." She brushed the paper aside and kept walking, trying to pretend she was a businesswoman late for a dinner appointment instead of a lost tourist.

"My grandma makes the best meatballs. You're missing out, *tesoro*."

Her stomach growled again. Loudly. And the guy heard it.

"Ah, your stomach says yes," he teased.

Rosemary turned to deliver a brusque "Mind your own business," but when she caught sight of the friendly smile attached to the handsome face, she bit her lip. This guy was cute with a capital *C*. "Did your grandmother really make the meatballs?"

The man chuckled. "Well, it's her recipe. Close enough, right?"

He wore dark trousers, a white button-down shirt, and an apron, pristine except for the small splatter of red sauce on the left hip. His shaggy, dark hair swept just across his broad forehead, and those dark eyes positively twinkled good humor with a hint of naughtiness. A firm jaw with a five o'clock shadow added to his rakishness, while the nose that had possibly been broken made him approachable.

"I'm not supposed to talk to strangers," she said, halfway meaning it. But his smile broadened, taking her words as flirtation, and darned if his smile wasn't mesmerizing. Rosemary couldn't look away to save her life.

"I'm Sal," he said, moving the stack of flyers to his left hand and extending his right.

She stared at his hand. The manners her mama had instilled in her for twenty-seven years dictated she reach out and take the very masculine hand held out to her. The wariness she'd coated herself in upon climbing out into the Manhattan sunshine told her to get her sweaty rump to her cousin's apartment and forget about sexy Italian guys with flashing white teeth.

He looked down at his hand and then did something utterly adorable. He wiped it on the apron, then extended it again.

And that meant she had to take his hand. No ifs, ands, or buts about it.

"I'm Rosemary," she said, wondering if she should wipe her hand, too. After all, she'd been sweating all the way down Prince Street and half of Mulberry. She decided against it and slid her hand into his.

He had a nice grasp. Firm, smooth, and almost refreshing. Dang it. She should have wiped her own clammy hand. Now he knew just how hot and grimy she was.

"That might be the prettiest name I've heard in forever," he said, holding on to her hand a bit longer than necessary. "Now that we're not strangers, come in and get something cold to drink."

"My palm was sweaty, wasn't it?" she said, blowing out a breath that ruffled her bangs.

That made him laugh, and damned if that didn't make him ten times sexier. Rosemary felt her heart skip a beat. "A little sweat never bothered me. I have some fresh mint tea to cool you down. I'll even put some sugar in it so you feel like you're on your mama's porch in Georgia."

"How did you know I'm from *Mississippi*?"

"Well, I just don't know, dahling," he drawled in a voice that sounded like a drag queen doing a Scarlett O'Hara impersonation . . . badly.

Rosemary made a face. "I don't sound like that."

"Yeah, you do," he said.

She glanced over her shoulder. "I can't stay. I have somewhere to be."

Sal stuck his lip out. "Aww, don't say that. You're the prettiest southern girl who's come by today."

"I'm probably the only southerner who's come by today."

"Yeah, but still," he said, giving her a wink.

"Maybe I'll come by later," she said, wanting to stay but knowing she needed to find her cousin's place, unpack, and call her mother before the woman called NYPD and filed a missing person report.

Someone from inside called his name. He stuck his head through the doorway. "Coming, Pop." Then he turned back to her, folding a flyer. Holding it out to her. "Promise you'll come back tonight. We have a great dinner special, and . . . I wanna get you that iced tea."

Good gravy, the man made iced tea sound positively naughty. Rosemary took the flyer and tucked it into her bag. "Maybe."

"Ah, you're killin' me." Sal shook his head but jabbed a flyer toward another passerby, who promptly threw it on the ground. "Jesus, the tourists are bustin' my balls today."

Rosemary picked the flyer up and handed it back to him. "I'm sorry."

"Make it right by coming back tonight."

Rosemary started easing away, yanking her suitcase. Who did she think she was, flirting with some waiter on the street? For a moment his friendly smile had distracted her, made her feel almost human in a place where she was a fish out of water. She tossed back a smile. "Maybe."

And then she walked away from the cute guy, rolling down Mulberry, looking to make a right on the next street, which should be the one where her cousin had a fancy loft apartment. God willing and the creek don't rise, she'd find it. Maybe then she could think about flirting with cute waiters. After all, she'd be there for two and a half weeks. And she had nothing to do but soak in the scenery, sleep late, eat exotic foods, and forget she was a totally clueless citizen of Morning Glory. She was in NYC to live a little. And by George, she was going to do it, too.

Sal Genovese shoved the stack of Mama Mello's flyers into his brother's hand. "Thank God you're back. Passing out the specials ain't my vibe."

Dominic grinned. "Don't worry. I can bring 'em in. They like my dimples."

"Yeah, well, next time I'll go pick up Brittany. Not a single person came in to eat with me hustling out here." Dominic had clocked out in order to help their sister, who'd gotten a flat on the way to work. Normally, his pop wouldn't let a Genovese shirk his duty, but when it came to his daughters, Big Donnie had a soft spot.

Dominic slapped him on the back as Sal pushed farther inside the restaurant their family had owned for three generations, making his way through the early dinner crowd back to the kitchen, where his father and the staff bustled around filling orders. The place wasn't stuffy, but they had real tablecloths, a nice bar, and on weekends a guy played the piano. A fellow could do worse, as his pop liked to say.

"Dom's back, Pop," Sal said, running water in the big stainless sink in order to scrub the street off his hands. When he was in the kitchen, he felt himself. Ah, sure, he could dial up the charm when needed, but he preferred the menial tasks of chopping onion and garlic over dealing with patrons.

"Grab the scampi and veal for table three and tell Kyle to move his ass. He's spending too much time talking up them chicks at the bar," Sal's father barked, flipping eggplant parmesan onto the new square plates Sal had talked him into ordering.

"Got it," Sal said, dodging Gus, the pastry chef his father had hired recently to replace his mother. Still surprised him sometimes to not find

Natalie Genovese filling cannoli and whipping together award-winning tiramisu for Mama Mello's. She'd been a constant presence in the back for thirty-five years, but after several back surgeries and severe sciatica, she'd finally retired . . . though she often showed up to boss Gus around, tasting his desserts and wrinkling her nose, muttering about the way things were supposed to be done. That was his mama—a ballbuster. But she was good at whatever she did.

An hour and a half later, Sal took a break, sneaking a beer from the ice behind the bar and slipping out back so his pop wouldn't catch him and chew him out for popping a cold one on the job. But nothing was as good as a cold brew after a long day. One beer wouldn't hurt.

He stared into the fading evening, thinking about how unsettled he'd felt lately. Ever since he'd turned thirty last month, he'd been feeling dissatisfied with his life. Like he needed to make a move. Do something different. His mind felt heavy, and it didn't help that his ma had been pushing Angelina Vitale his way for almost two months now.

Yesterday, he'd dropped by Angelina's place to take something wrapped in foil that the woman who endured twenty hours of labor to bring him into this world—he knew 'cause she liked to remind him—swore Angelina needed. Natalie Genovese wasn't fooling him. She wanted Sal squared away.

When Angelina had answered the door in a cloud of perfume, he spotted bridal magazines stacked beside the couch and had nearly broken out in hives. His mama wasn't the only one hearing wedding bells, and something about Angelina in a veil made him want to chain-smoke a whole pack of cigarettes . . . even though he'd quit last April.

He wasn't ready to be headlocked and dragged to the chapel by the "nice" Italian girl his mother had handpicked for him. But it grew harder and harder to escape both women. He felt like they were both beating him with a stick . . . and eventually a guy got numb and accepting of his fate.

His phone vibrated.

Speak of the devil and she calls.

If he didn't answer, Angelina would call back. And then she'd tell his mother he was avoiding her calls again. And then he'd have to listen to what a rude man he was and how he didn't respect family connections, his mother, or Jesus Christ himself. He loved his ma, but he didn't want another lecture. He'd had enough for a lifetime.

"Hey, Angie, what's up?" he said.

"That's how you're gonna talk to me? No hello or nothing?"

Sal swallowed his aggravation. "Sorry. Hello, Angelina. How are you this evening?"

"And now you're a smart-ass," she said. He could hear the clink of glasses and the roar of conversation in the background. Angelina did happy hour with her girls nearly every day . . . which was when she liked to call him, telling them she had to call her man.

He wasn't her man.

But she didn't seem to care. She had the power of Natalie Genovese on her side. "I told Gina I'd come to her grandparents' fiftieth out on the island this weekend."

"Sounds nice."

"You wanna come with me?"

"Can't. I gotta work," he said, knowing he could probably get off but not wanting to move another step closer to something he didn't want. Or didn't think he wanted. Everything was clear as mud at the moment.

"Don't worry. I'll call Big Donnie. He can get one of your brothers to cover."

"Dom's got a new baby and Vincent already covered for me last weekend. I ain't getting out of this."

Her silence said more than anything else.

"Hello?"

"I gotta hang up now, Sal. We'll talk later," she said. Then she hung up.

"Jesus H. Christ," Sal breathed, taking a final draw on his beer. How in the hell could he even entertain the idea of dating Angelina, much less marrying her, when she was such a passive-aggressive nightmare?

He couldn't breathe around her.

When his mother had reintroduced him to Angelina at St. Ann's Cathedral, he'd been pleasantly surprised to find little Angie Vitale all grown up. The last time he'd seen her, she'd been fourteen years old, obsessed with the Black Eyed Peas, and had followed him and Vincent around, playing silly pranks. But now she was full of honey, charming everyone with her devout Catholicism and sleek good looks. So like a good boy, he'd asked for her number. After she tapped it into his phone, she'd offered to go down on him in the church bathroom. He'd thought she was joking.

She wasn't.

What kind of woman did that?

The kind who obviously didn't have a problem with giving blow jobs . . . unlike his friend Tony Pizzaro's wife, who'd told him under no circumstances was she putting anything but food in her mouth. Tony already had a piece on the side, so maybe the blow job thing wasn't such a mark against Angelina. Silver lining and all that.

The day after he turned thirty years old, his mother stopped commiserating with him over his ex-fiancée dumping him and began a campaign designed to get him settled and focused on expanding the Mama Mello's name. Sal knew he'd played a little too hard for the past year, trying to wash the stink of rejection off himself. And he knew he couldn't continue being the black sheep of the family. After all, his other siblings were perfect fluffy white sheep—his older brother Dom was married with his first kid, Vincent was getting married at Christmas, and his two younger sisters, Brit and Frances Anne, had steady guys. So he'd jokingly told his mother he'd let her pick the girl this time.

His mother hadn't taken his words as a joke. Obviously.

Sal set the empty bottle in the dying palm tree someone had pulled out back to give it a fighting chance, and his thoughts flickered back to that tourist chick who'd given him such an easy smile and a maybe earlier that day. He didn't know why he was so intrigued with her.

Probably because she reminded him of Hillary, the woman who had chosen a life in Connecticut playing tennis at the club over sweating in a Brooklyn apartment with an Italian pizza maker. Yeah, Hillary had tossed him out like last week's Chinese takeout three months before their wedding. Sal had been so certain she'd been perfect for him. But she'd been more certain Franklin Thurgood Cohen III had been perfect for her . . . and her bank account.

He'd heard "I told you so" from every member of his family. Okay, they'd bought him a few beers and cast him a few sad smiles. Wasn't like they nanny-nanny-boo-booed him to his face or anything, but he'd been wearing blinders when his sister mentioned how Hillary seemed so wrong for him and he'd flat-out threatened to punch Dom when he called Hillary a spoiled bitch.

Though Rosemary reminded him of his ex, the women weren't exactly alike. They were both soft, with good manners and pretty in a wholesome way. But Hillary had been very polished and put together, all cool sophistication. Whereas Rosemary's cheeks had been flushed from the heat, her bangs damp with sweat. Mississippi looked like money, even if her clear gray eyes and trim little waist made him think of old photographs from the fifties, the ones of his grandmother and her friends at Coney Island, smiling innocently at the camera. Old-fashioned, but in a good way. In a way that made a guy glad he was a man.

Still, wanting high-class broads who threw guys like him under the bus was way off the menu for him. And tourists like Rosemary were a dime a two dozen in this city. Yet, there had been something in the way she'd said what was on her mind. The way she looked so adorably nervous, but at the same time straightforward. Being around Rosemary for only a minute felt like taking a deep breath.

So maybe if she came by, he'd sit with her for a while. Maybe he'd ask her out.

God, that would piss off his ma good.

Somehow staring up at the night sky gave him clarity. Either that or the alcohol content of the beer was off. He couldn't go on like this, connecting the dots on the picture someone else had designed for his life. But did that mean he should jump at the opportunity to spend time with a soft southern beauty when she was likely here for only a few days? And that was even if she showed up again. Eh, had to be better than avoiding Angelina, who had pulled up an article about the best bakeries for wedding cakes the last time she'd shown up to his parents' house for Sunday lunch. Then she'd volunteered to help pick the fabric for the chairs at the new deli. Like she was already part of his life.

He'd kissed the woman only once . . . and that's because she'd asked him to. Strange as it was, Angelina hadn't been a bad kisser. That had scared him. Made him wonder if he'd already started that slide toward accepting someone else's vision for his life.

Sal took one last look at the sliver of moon hanging over his corner of Manhattan.

Maybe.

Eh, it was a good word for his life right now.

Chapter Three

Rosemary zipped the empty suitcase and jammed it under her cousin's bed.

Unpacking done.

She'd made it to her cousin's apartment and huffed up five flights of stairs, learning exactly what a walk-up meant. Essentially, she'd be getting much-needed cardio over the next few weeks. After retrieving the key from a very strange neighbor, she'd opened the door to a loft that could not have cost as much as her cousin said it had. Way too small for almost a million bucks.

Halle was a partner in a shoe design company with some Italian guy whose name Rosemary couldn't pronounce. Her cousin had teamed up with Benny right out of design school when he got pissed at the designer he worked for and quit. They'd lived together in a cracker box apartment in Harlem for almost a decade before finally catching the attention of magazine editors and stylists with their spring line. Their high-end shoes were now worn by starlets everywhere, enabling Halle to get her own place. Several months back B&H had been invited to do a show in Italy. Benny and Halle had left for Florence two days ago to "get inspired" for their 2017 spring line and put together their fall show in Milan . . . and that's why Rosemary was in New York City.

To cat-sit Halle's darlings, who would not tolerate being boarded.

Melbourne and Moscow seemed highly indifferent to their illustrious cat-sitter. Essentially, when Rosemary had burst into the apartment, gulping for air like a fish on a muddy bank, the cats had turned their sleek heads, blinked once, and returned their attention to the fat pigeons lining the eaves of the building next door.

So much for a welcome committee.

"Hey, kitty-kitties," Rosemary had cooed, between horrible sucking noises that affirmed she needed to join a gym. They never even looked at her. "Okay, with that attitude, you'll not be getting any catnip."

They didn't seem to care.

Rosemary shut the door, locked it like she promised her father she'd always do, and found a plug on the stone kitchen counter to charge her dead phone. Then she took a look around at her digs.

The loft looked chic, with a high, open ceiling, industrial lighting, and a modern kitchen featuring a huge stainless steel Viking range that Rosemary would bet a week's pay her cousin never used. The bedroom had been partially partitioned off with a half screen. Privacy for the bathroom was offered by a rolling metal door, and the huge walk-in shower tiled in vintage black and white didn't have a door. The whole place felt strange and far removed from her cozy carriage home behind her parents' sprawling house.

But surprisingly, she liked the feel of the place. Felt sophisticated. Very New York.

Her cell phone rang as she walked back into the living area. She had 10 percent of battery power left, which would last long enough to allay her mother's fears. "Hey, Mama."

"You said you'd call when you got to Halle's. Are you at Halle's?" her mother asked, worry edging her words.

"Lord, I haven't even had time to pee, much less call. Yes, I'm at Halle's."

"Don't be crass. I've been worried sick. You should have been there over an hour ago. I made your father do the calculations so I'd know when you were supposed to be there, and you never called."

Sweet Jesus.

Rosemary flopped onto the white couch. "Well, my phone battery died, and I got a little turned around and went the wrong direction, but I made it safe and sound with all organs intact."

Her mother made a disapproving cluck. "I suppose you think I'm amusing. Well, let me tell you, missy, that whole organ-harvesting thing is real business. I read things."

Rosemary propped her feet on the cement coffee table, not bothering to remove her cute Sam Edelman sandals. She'd scored them in Jackson when she'd ventured there last month. "I'm being serious."

"Fine. Be that way. You didn't talk to anyone, did you?"

"Are you serious, Mama? Of course I talked to people. What do you think I'm here for?"

"I don't have a clue why you're there, but I hope your cousin appreciates what you're doing for her over a bunch of cats. Silliest thing I've ever heard."

Maybe it was absurd, but when Halle had called and asked, Rosemary jumped at the chance. Ever since Lacy passed away, Rosemary had been stuck in a case of doldrums that not even strawberry cake could cure . . . and she loved Mimi's homemade strawberry cake with buttercream frosting. But, of course, she'd known it would be this way. A gal didn't lose her best friend and not feel like crap for months to come. But her mini-depression seemed to be about more than the enormous loss in her life.

It had started with the letter.

Rose—

I already miss you.

I'm pretty sure I'm in heaven, but maybe not. I'm not exactly the poster girl you are. And about that . . . you have to stop being so damn good. Seriously. You're treading water here in this one-horse town. And you know what treading water gets you (besides a pass on water safety at Camp Cedar Cove)? Nothing but a cramp . . . and eventual death, because a person can't tread water forever. When we were at Ole Miss, you broke away from your suffocating mother. You were you. But then you came back to Morning Glory and slipped into being . . . not you. Oh, there are always glimpses, but you never let Rosemary out to play.

I know this probably offends you, and that's why I never said anything until I died. Feel free to give me the silent treatment. LOL. I'm not being mean. I say this because I love you, Rosemary. You can't live beneath your mother's thumb your whole life. Be strong. Be bold. Find something more than sewing costumes for the second-grade play. Don't settle for some man your mama drags in front of you. You deserve more than that. Stop being scared, Rosemary. Stop treading water. There is a big world out there waiting on you to taste it. See it, bathe in it, breathe it in. And if you can't do it for yourself, do it for me.

This money is to help you realize a dream. Dig up one you had long ago. Remember who you are supposed to be. Take care of Jess and Eden, but most of all, take care of yourself. It's okay to be selfish. Oh, and don't be afraid to inhale. LOL.

Hugs and ladybugs,

Lacy

PS. I've enclosed an article from *Cosmo* that I
stole from my mother's magazine after she told me
about sex. Totally works. ;)

Rosemary had pulled out two ragged pages from *Cosmopolitan* magazine, July 2000, titled, "50 Tricks for Outstanding Orgasms," which
Lacy had slipped into the envelope.

Only Lacy would care about Rosemary having outstanding orgasms.
Which was quite touching, since Lacy had been her mortal enemy in
pre-K. Of course since Prestwood Academy was so tiny, they'd had little
choice but to graduate to friendship by the third grade, thanks to their
mothers signing them up for Girl Scouts. They'd bonded over poison
ivy on a campout and had been thick as Mississippi kudzu from then on.

Lacy had been diagnosed with bone cancer when she was three
years old. She'd gone to St. Jude's hospital, and with treatment had gone
into remission. Every year her PET scan was clear . . . until her senior
year at Ole Miss. Ironically, the cervical cancer she'd developed wasn't
related to the earlier bone cancer. As Lacy always said, her body was a
cancer magnet. Wasn't funny then and it wasn't funny now.

But Lacy had gotten the last word with the letter she'd written to
Rosemary, a letter packed in her suitcase serving as a challenge for her life.

Treading water?

When she'd first read the letter, Rosemary had been offended. Was
she treading water because she stayed in Morning Glory? Because she
still ate breakfast with her parents? Because she thought the good ol'
boys who stampeded into town on Friday nights to raise the roof of the
Iron Bull were a bit too dangerous?

Whatever.

But then she'd pulled back and studied her life from a different
vantage point . . . from the vantage point of a woman who'd been facing
the end of her life. She saw what her friend had seen—a woman plain
scared to live, a woman who'd forgotten the things she'd always wanted

to do. What had happened to becoming a fashion designer? Living in a big city for a few years? Learning French?

But she knew the answer—she'd packed them away like the crayon drawings her mother kept in a plastic box. Yes, her mother had saved ALL of Rosemary's drawings from age two through high school. Patsy Reynolds was the ultimate smotherer.

The day after Rosemary had this revelation about her life, her cousin Halle had called and asked her to come to New York City.

Rosemary hadn't thought twice before saying yes.

"I need this trip, Mama," she said into the phone.

"I don't know how New York City is something you need, but if that makes you happy . . ."

"It does." Or at least she hoped it would.

"But that doesn't mean I'm not going to worry."

"I'd never take that away from you, Mama."

"Oh sure, poke fun of me, but one day you'll understand what it is to be a mother, what it feels like to have your baby living in a jungle all alone for over two weeks."

And there was the biggest problem in Rosemary's pathetic life—her two adoring, overprotective parents. From the time Rosemary was a baby, her life had been insulated with quilted down. Rosemary had worn bike helmets on her tricycle and sunscreen every time she stepped outside, and she'd carried an EpiPen even though she wasn't allergic to anything. Her mother had said it was a precaution. She hadn't been allowed to eat junk food because of the preservatives, go swimming without a life jacket, or wear open-toed shoes at the county fair. Nor had she dated, gotten her driver's license, or pierced her ears until she turned eighteen. If a person looked up the word *sheltered* in the dictionary, there'd be a picture of Rosemary wrapped in bubble wrap.

Her friends had tried to break her loose, unwrap her, but Patsy Reynolds was a force to be reckoned with. Lacy, Jess, and Eden knew if they got too close they could be sucked into the undertow. Instead they used selective civil disobedience, sneaking around the behemoth that was Rosemary's mother.

"I'll be fine, Mama. I'm a grown woman."

"I know that. But—"

"My phone's dying. Gotta go. Tell Basil I made it and the buildings *are* really tall."

"Rosemary, be careful. Don't talk to strange me—"

Rosemary clicked the END button, smiling at the 7 percent battery life. So she didn't want to hear all the warnings her mother was sure to review for the umpteenth time?

"I'm free," she said to Moscow, who'd leaped down from his perch and was currently licking his haunch. He looked up with bright green eyes as if he understood exactly what it was to be coddled and smothered.

"Meow," the cat said.

"Right on, brother," Rosemary responded, jumping up to plug her phone on the charger.

With her mother's cutoff warning ringing in her ears, Rosemary walked to the bathroom and turned on the shower. She felt grungy after her sojourn to find the loft apartment. A hot shower would wash the day away, and then she could think about going out for dinner.

Rosemary was hungry to experience all New York City had to offer . . . even if the news clippings kept popping into her mind like little cuckoo clocks chiming out warnings. She wasn't going to sit in the apartment and order takeout when the world lay at her feet. After all, what's the worst that could happen?

Well, she could die.

But was that worse than how she'd been living? At least at her funeral her friends could say that she'd lived for once. Lacy's words kept floating back to her.

Stop being scared, Rosemary. Stop treading water. There is a big world out there waiting on you to taste it. See it, bathe in it, breathe it in. And if you can't do it for yourself, do it for me.

Lacy had known what her friend needed better than anyone else. Rosemary needed to break out of the mold created for her and find out who she really was . . . even if those experiences bought her bumps and bruises. Life wasn't made to be lived in the comfort of bubble wrap. Sometimes you had to do something scary. Something bold.

Like ride the subway. Or have a torrid affair. Or visit that sex museum she'd read about. Or just spend two weeks in a strange, exciting city with only two indifferent cats for company.

Rosemary was ready to jump in with both feet.

But first she needed something to eat, and as she stripped and stepped into the full-body shower spray, the image of a sexy smile appeared.

Maybe she'd start with Italian.

Sal caught sight of the southern girl out of the corner of his eye when he checked to make sure Kyle wasn't still flirting with the group of women clumped at the end of the bar.

She no longer wore a fussy little sundress, but she still looked good as apple pie in a sleeveless silk tank paired with some tight red jeans. She sat alone.

And that was a tragedy.

"Pop, I'm taking a break," he said, untying his apron and jogging toward the small bathroom next to the room where cardboard pizza boxes stacked nearly to the ceiling. She'd come back. Her maybe had turned into definitely.

"You just took a beer break an hour ago," his father called.

Busted.

"I only had one," Sal said, sticking his head out and meeting his father's gaze. Gus, who'd been slicing strips of dough, laughed beneath his handlebar mustache. The rest of the staff pretended they were busy.

Donnie and Sal usually worked well together, but when they butted heads, no one wanted to be within firing range.

His father tapped his nose. "This nose can smell a dog shitting a mile away."

"That's really disgusting, Pop," Sal said.

"Eh, but it's true," his father said, jerking his head toward the dining room. "And I saw that pretty gal sitting by herself. I know my Sal. You ain't supposed to be shopping around no more."

"Says who?"

"Says that gal your ma found for you. That can be a done deal when you say the word."

A done deal. Like he was buying a house. Sal shrugged a shoulder. "Who said Angelina was a done deal? We're not even technically going out."

"Yeah, tell yourself that, but that woman has already named your bambinos. She's like your mother, and that ain't a bad thing, Sal. That gal knows your world, unlike that other one. This one would be good for you."

"You, too, Pop? You gonna be like Ma and try and decide my life?" Sal ducked back in the bathroom and looked at himself in the mirror. He felt like he wore his shoes on the wrong feet. Maybe talking to the pretty girl out front was merely an excuse to pull away from the direction his life was heading. Or maybe her coming back was fate. Or maybe he didn't know anything anymore . . . except he needed something more than what he had now.

He had to stop the slide toward something he didn't want. Dig his heels in fast, or it would be too late. He'd end up like his brothers, locked into life. He knew Dom and Vincent were happy most of the time. Dom's wife wasn't as controlling as his brother made her out to be. Dom liked his life simple—run the Brooklyn restaurant and go home to the little wife. Nothing wrong with that world. Sal just didn't know if it was the world he wanted . . . if it was the world he ever wanted.

Sal smiled, double-checking his teeth. No pepper or oregano lurking. He huffed into his hand and sniffed. Thankfully he'd stayed away from garlic today. He dug a mint out of his pocket and tugged a piece of dark hair out of his eyes. He looked good even with the nose Frankie Pasco had broken during senior year. He'd been working out harder and his arms looked bigger, his stomach tighter, and he felt good from all the water he'd been guzzling lately. He narrowed his eyes. What did the southern chick see when she looked at him?

He hoped she saw a guy who wanted to be something more than what he'd presented to the world thus far. At one time he'd believed in himself. He'd had a plan, a future he'd chosen to blaze on his own. But then Hillary had wiped it away, the way he wiped the daily special from the placard out front each morning. Somewhere inside, he was there, beneath all the expectations everyone heaped on top of him. He wanted Rosemary to see the real Sal, the Sal who wasn't just another Genovese.

He shook his head. What was he doing? Talking to a chick was just talking. No big deal.

He popped the mint in his mouth and slipped out of the bathroom, twirling his baby sister Brittany around when she tried to pass him, leaving her with a grin.

Rosemary sat alone near one of the columns his mother had painted to look like marble. A half-eaten salad sat near her elbow and she looked like she was checking her Facebook status or scrolling down a Twitter feed on her phone.

He pulled out the chair across from her and sank down. "You order the meatballs?"

She dropped the phone, one hand going up to clutch her chest. "Oh God, you scared me to death."

Sal grinned. "Sorry. I thought you looked too good to sit here alone."

"Do I look that pathetic?" she asked, her nose wrinkling adorably as she placed the phone near her elbow.

Rosemary's brownish-red hair had been swept back in a ponytail, but her face was framed by bangs. He knew what bangs were and who could wear them from growing up with sisters. Rosemary wore hers well, reminding him of Emma Stone with the same smattering of freckles, soft lips, and rounded face. Her gray eyes weren't of the stormy variety, more clear and intelligent, and he wondered how they looked when she laughed . . . when she was pissed . . . when she made love.

And he knew he wanted to see all those things in those gray depths.

Damn. The vibe he'd felt earlier when she flirted with him outside the restaurant was back. Not some figment of his imagination, but real. Something pulled them toward each other. Had nothing to do with being attracted to the wrong kind of girls . . . or the fact he was running scared from the woman his mother had handpicked for him. Or maybe it did. At the moment he didn't care.

"I don't think anyone could attach the term *pathetic* to you," he said, picking up a roll from the bread basket and ripping off a piece.

"Are you joining me . . . or feeding me lines you've practiced on a dozen other dumb tourists?"

Sal placed a hand over his chest and mimicked outrage. "You think I'd treat you like any other tourist? Please."

Rosemary grinned. "I think you see opportunity."

"Yeah?"

"To talk me into spending an obscene amount of money on this delicious food. God, it's so good."

He glanced down at the half-finished salad and hooked an eyebrow.

"So I'm not a salad girl," she said.

And that's when he knew this girl was the kind of girl he needed at that moment. She didn't waste time on salads. Didn't wear low-cut shirts that showed her tits. Didn't play with a guy. Honesty was like an aphrodisiac to him. That and the sensual base of her throat that had to smell like—he sniffed—lavender? "I could tell this about you. You don't dillydally with useless stuff, do you?"

"Dillydally?" She choked down a laugh but her eyes danced. "You sound like my gram."

He almost blushed. "Eh, my grandmother likes that term, too."

"Of course I got the meatballs. They came highly recommended," she said, lifting her wineglass, which had pink stuff in it.

"What are you drinking?"

"White zinfandel."

He tried not to make a face. "You need a good red."

Rosemary's cheeks pinked. "I know, but I like this wine. It's sweet."

She was so not Italian. "Okay, Mississippi girl, what brings you to our bright, noisy city . . . by yourself?"

Rosemary leaned back. "My mother told me—"

"We're not strangers anymore. Remember? I'm Sal. You're Rosemary. We're old friends."

"For all of two hours," she said, waving Kyle away when he approached with a fresh bread basket.

At that moment, old man Weingarten rose from his regular table and ambled over with the assistance of his ivory-handled cane. "This schmuck giving you the what for, Rosemary?"

Sal made a face at the old man, wondering how he'd already managed to hit on Rosemary. The old man didn't miss any opportunities but usually he'd lay off the tourists.

Elijah Weingarten had been dining at Mama Mello's three times a week ever since his wife had passed away. The elderly pipe fitter ordered the same pesto linguini every meal before practicing his rather ancient moves on any ladies under the age of eighty. He never let his stooped posture, caterpillar eyebrows, and untrimmed whiskers deter him from even the youngest of patrons. Both of Sal's sisters knew to be quick in setting down Mr. Weingarten's plate and to give wide berth around his wandering hands.

Rosemary gave Mr. Weingarten a sugarcoated smile. "Well, look at you, Mr. Eli, being so sweet and protective of me."

"Actually Rosemary and I are old friends," Sal said.

"Yes. *Very* old friends," she said, patting the older gentleman on the arm. "Mr. Eli was so sweet to invite me to join him for dinner, but he was already finished. And everyone says New Yorkers aren't friendly."

"He's friendly, all right," Sal said, trying to maintain a straight face.

"If you're sure you're okay, my dear," the older man said, his beady black eyes fastened on Rosemary, his gnarled hand lifting her hand and cradling it. "A girl such as you can't be too careful. I wouldn't trust Sal with my cousin Ethel, and she's a vegetable in the nursing home."

"Oh, I'm sorry about your cousin, but I can handle Sal."

"*Guten abend,* beautiful." He lifted her hand to his lips, lingering a second too long before moving at a turtle's pace toward the door.

Rosemary looked at her hand and then sheepishly wiped it on her napkin.

"Oh, you can handle me, huh?" Sal teased.

Rosemary arched her brows comically. "Well, I couldn't have the old guy trying to defend my honor." She rose and dropped her napkin beside her plate.

"Where you going?"

"Someone needs to help that sweet old gentleman to his cab," she said, her gaze following old man Weingarten's progress. He'd not even made it halfway to the door.

"I don't think you want to do that," he said.

"Where I live we see our elderly out the door and make sure they get home safely." She didn't exactly frown when she imparted that tidbit of information, but she looked a bit self-righteous. Like only southerners had manners.

"Suit yourself," he said.

"I always do," she said with a quasi-smile that made him think perhaps she rarely suited herself. A woman who would leave bad wine, delicious food, and a man who had all his shiny teeth to escort an old rascal who probably hadn't seen his real pearly whites in over three decades to his cab probably rarely thought only of herself.

So she definitely wasn't like Hillary.

He watched Rosemary hurry to catch up with Mr. Weingarten before rising. The poor woman didn't know what she'd gotten herself into. Eli had once cornered Brittany and copped a feel before Big Donnie had come out and threatened to toss him out the door. Eli hadn't accosted anyone since, but the gleam in his dark eyes at the attention paid to him by southern belle served as a harbinger.

Sal watched Rosemary take Mr. Weingarten's arm as he crossed the threshold. The old devil pretended to stumble and wrapped a steadying arm about Rosemary's trim waist.

"Are you okay?" she asked.

"Jeez," Sal muttered under his breath, shooting a grin at Kyle, who stood with Rosemary's meatballs and Italian gravy.

Kyle shook his head. "Want me to save her from the octopus?"

"I got it," Sal said, following them out, grinning when he saw Mr. Weingarten's hand slide south toward a very appetizing derriere.

Rosemary quickly reached around and tugged his hand up. "Here we go."

"You're such a nice girl," Mr. Weingarten said, sliding his hand back down and giving her a pat on her backside.

Rosemary spun and caught the older man's hand. "Thank you, sir. I'm sure my father would appreciate your kind words on my upbringing."

Nicely played. Not only had she prevented old Weingarten from copping a cheap feel, but she'd brought her father into the equation. Mr. Weingarten looked frustrated if not slightly guilty as he stared at the cab.

"You have a good evening, Mr. Eli. I have those meatballs waiting," she said, opening the door for the older man, careful to sidestep another roving hand.

Nothing for Weingarten to do but climb inside and accept defeat. Rosemary closed the door and gave the older man a cheerful wave as the cab pulled away from the curb. She squeaked as another car roared into the spot, nearly falling back over the curb. Sal clasped her elbows, preventing her from stumbling any farther.

"Whoops," she said, regaining her balance.

He didn't want to pull away. He'd been dying to touch her again, but he dropped his hands from her smooth skin because she'd spent the past few minutes dodging the advances of an old dude. No need to creep her out.

Rosemary brushed her bangs out of her face.

"Good?" he asked.

"Yeah," she said, moving back toward the restaurant. Twilight softened the garishness of Mulberry Street, making Little Italy look softer in the glow of the moon. Rosemary turned to him and gave him a crooked grin that made his insides gelatinous. "You totally knew he was going to feel me up."

"Yeah, he's all hands," Sal said, opening the door for her, proving that southern dudes didn't have anything on a guy from Brooklyn. "But I was going to make sure it didn't get out of control."

"A knight in shining armor?"

"Only if I were still wearing my apron and carrying a spatula. You don't want to know how I can mess a guy up with a spatula."

Rosemary laughed and he reveled in those gray eyes shining with delight. Sal had accomplished the first of the things he wanted to see in her eyes. But there were more . . . and something compelled him to say, "Let's go dancing."

Rosemary's eyes widened. "Dancing?"

"I know this place on a rooftop where you can dance to Sinatra and Bennett. Let's go tonight."

"Together?" she asked, her face puzzled.

Asking her out had been simmering on the back burner of his mind all evening. And why not? He might never lay eyes on Rosemary again. So he couldn't let her go on her way without spending a little more time with her. "We could go separately and meet there, but we might as well walk over together."

"You know what I mean. You want to go with me? Dancing?"

"I'd be willing to bet you my grandma's Italian gravy recipe you're the perfect girl to take dancing."

She looked at him as if he were deranged.

Part of him wanted to rewind and snatch the offer off the table, because it *was* crazy, but something stronger inside pushed him toward this girl who'd come back to try the meatballs, this girl who'd wryly admitted to having sweaty hands, this girl who knew how to sidestep an old lecher's hands while still smiling sweetly. Hell, maybe he was crazy. Or maybe it was the way she twisted the pearls at her neck. Most probably it was those blessed eyes that showed her every thought.

He could get lost in those eyes while dancing at the Morey Hotel beneath the twinkling sky.

"But I don't know you," she said, looking skittish. "Not really. My mo—" She snapped her mouth shut.

"You know me. I'm Sal. You're Rosemary. And I'm asking you to dance with me. Nothing more."

Her gaze shifted, softening, and it was as if she slipped somewhere else in her thoughts. Swallowing, she looked back at him. Determined. "Dancing sounds like a great way to meet New York City. Am I dressed nice enough for it?"

"You're dressed perfectly." He waved her inside the restaurant he worked in nearly every day of every week, the family business he was expected to expand like his brother had in Brooklyn. "Now you go try my grandmother's meatballs and gravy while I finish up. Can't leave my pops shorthanded."

Wait.

Maybe he was doing this as a sort of slap in the face to his parents. For some reason he couldn't seem to fall in line with what was reasonable. Maybe he should give in and plod down the path cleared for him, even if it meant an Italian wedding, a mortgage, and, if his mother had her way, Angelina sporting a layer of cold cream lying beside him every night. Didn't sound fun, but maybe life wasn't supposed to be fun. Maybe life was supposed to be endured.

Don't fight the inevitable. Wave the white flag. Be a good boy. Embrace who you are . . . and say good-night to the Dixieland delight.

"You sure about this?" Rosemary asked, jarring him out of his reverie.

He looked at her again. At the gray eyes, cute nose, sensuous lips. Something inside him reached toward her. "I've never been more certain."

"Okay," Rosemary said, sliding back inside the restaurant, sucking in a deep breath. He caught a whiff of her perfume again, earthy and floral. Made him think of lazy days in his grandmother's garden. Made him think of licking his way down to her navel, breathing in her goodness.

He couldn't wait to hold this woman in his arms, to feel her move against him to the same songs he'd danced to in his parents' kitchen every New Year's Eve when he was a boy. Rosemary felt like a tap from the past . . . and a shove into a different place. Like some crazy movie where a guy met someone he knew in a past life. Like something meant to be.

Which was dog-assed crazy.

A man didn't fall in love on a random Thursday while handing out the midweek specials. But, of course, this wasn't love. It was a hunch, a rabbit chase of youth, an opportunity to feel a *what if* pounding through his blood, maybe for the last time. Taking Rosemary dancing was an inexplicable twist of fate.

After all, only a fool would believe such romantic destiny truly existed.

Chapter Four

Rosemary could never, ever, ever tell her mother that she'd agreed to go dancing with a man the night she arrived. Dancing. With a stranger. In flipping New York City.

Her mother would disown her.

Or lock her in a padded cell.

With a chastity belt in place.

Even so, walking beside Sal felt pretty darn good. Like she was doing what she'd set out to do. Grab life with both hands.

"I can't believe I'm doing this," she whispered to herself, sidestepping a garbage bag someone had dragged out to the curb.

Sal overheard. "Hey, you gotta live a little. Nothing wrong with cocktails and slow dancing. You're gonna love this place. Cross my heart and hope to die if you don't."

"I know I will, but I'm rusty on the dancing. Don't think I've danced since my senior prom. That was, like, ten years ago," she said.

Sal clasped a hand against his chest. "That's a travesty. Truly. What pretty girl doesn't get taken out dancing every now and again?"

"The kind of girl who lives in Morning Glory, Mississippi."

He came to a dead stop. "Are you telling me they don't dance in your hometown? Like in *Footloose*?"

Rosemary laughed, tugging his arm forward. "Don't be silly. We dance. When the minister's not looking."

His eyes widened.

"I'm kidding. We have some honky-tonks where people go dancing. I think they line dance, but I wouldn't know."

Sal started walking again, tucking her hand into the crook of his elbow. Something in the old-fashioned gesture made her heart swell . . . or maybe it was the fact she could feel the heat of his body through the cotton button-down he wore. Her stomach trembled at the feel of him beneath her arm. It had been a long time since she'd been with a guy. Probably way too long, which had led to this insanity she'd embarked on.

Hopefully, she wouldn't end up with her head on a platter and her liver served up with fava beans. Her mother would never forgive her for being served with a side dish she detested.

"So you don't do honky-tonks?" Sal asked. "I've always thought those places sounded cool. Or maybe I wanted an excuse to wear a pair of cowboy boots."

Would he think she was nerdy if she said she'd rather spend a quiet evening with a book or a movie night with her friends? "Guess honky-tonks aren't my scene. But you'd look good in cowboy boots."

"Oh yeah?" he said, mimicking the tip of a pretend cowboy hat. "Howdy, ma'am."

His redneck accent was as bad as his Scarlett O'Hara. "But you should keep the New York accent."

He looked resigned. "So you don't do honky-tonks but you will go to a rooftop joint with a guy with a Brooklyn accent?"

Rosemary thought about that for a moment. She'd always been unwilling to pull on tight jeans and head to the Iron Bull on Friday nights. Loud country music and guys she'd seen eat paste in kindergarten didn't really float her boat. But dancing on a rooftop in the city that never sleeps? A gal didn't turn down an opportunity like that, especially when she'd been lying in a proverbial ditch for the past four years. Treading water. Yeah. Rosemary Reynolds needed some crazy in her life the way a sinner needed prayer. "Guess I'm not into guys who dip tobacco. You don't dip, do you? Because I'm going to turn around if you say yes."

Sal made a face. "No, but I used to smoke. Does that count?"

"I don't think so . . . unless you unrolled them, packed them in your lip, and proceeded to spit every few seconds." She shuddered.

"You're safe," he said.

For a few minutes they moved silently down the busy street. It was nearly ten o'clock and the city felt alive. In Morning Glory a single car out and about after ten was a rarity. On weekends local high school kids careened around the square in their big trucks, heading out to someone's farm to sneak booze, but otherwise, after midnight nothing happened in her sleepy little town but . . . sleep.

After they crossed the third intersection, she turned to him. "So your family runs Mama Mello's?"

"Been in our family for generations. My grandfather's pop came over from Sicily back at the beginning of last century."

"Sicily?"

He laughed. "You hearing the theme from *The Godfather*?"

"Maybe."

"Why? You need someone to sleep with the fishes?"

Rosemary swallowed the unease that crept up inside her. She watched crime shows and knew that meant taking someone out. Dear Lord, was she going out with a Mafia guy? She hadn't even thought about that. Suddenly she felt very Diane Keaton. "Uh, I—"

"I'm kidding, you know," Sal said, his white teeth flashing in the darkness. He patted the hand tucked against his side. "There's some wise guys somewhere in the family tree, but I ain't it. Just a guy who makes pizzas and a damn good marinara. You're safe."

She allowed a breath to escape.

That made Sal chuckle. "You were worried, huh? You've seen too many movies, but I feel a little more macho knowing you were willing to believe I'm that tough." He puffed his chest out and swaggered a bit, making Rosemary laugh.

Laughing felt good.

Being with Sal felt good.

"You're silly," she said, punching his arm halfheartedly.

"Not too many people would say that about me, but I guess pretty Mississippi girls make me feel a little goofy," he said, looking down at her. His brown eyes seemed to gleam in the neon lights reflected off the building they passed. Her heart skipped a beat as he gave her a wink. "But I like it. This night's a . . . gift? Something. I've been waiting on someone who makes me feel something more than . . . I don't know . . . panicked? Here lately I've been feeling like my life is on tracks heading somewhere I never bought a ticket for."

For a second he paused, looking aghast. "Guess that might have been TMI."

"No, I know what you mean. My life has been more like waiting at the station. Or maybe running the same track back and forth with no switches. But that's why I'm here. I jumped track . . . at least for a few weeks."

"Jumped track, huh? I like that. Guess I jumped track, too."

She arched an eyebrow.

"Well, I asked a perfect stranger to go dancing."

"So you're saying I'm perfect?" she teased, elbowing him in the ribs.

"I'll say."

Rosemary couldn't help but wonder about his honesty. If he'd jumped track to go with her, what was his regular circuit? And why was he waiting for someone to make him feel different? "So I'm a departure from the norm? I would have pegged you as a professional track jumper."

"I've jumped a few tracks. Maybe too many. But these days I feel like I'm being sucked down a drain. All those things I once thought would happen have disappeared, leaving me with the inevitable. So yeah, you feel like a risk."

"Who would have ever thought Rosemary Reynolds was risky." Rosemary hadn't been the biggest Goody Two-Shoes at Morning Glory High, but she had run a close second.

"Definitely not Mr. Weingarten. But you showed him," Sal said, giving the arm he held a squeeze. "You were something else."

His words were honey poured over her, delicious and needed. She wondered if he felt it too—that zing and zap of something between them. Not sexual, though that was there, but more of a sweetness that ebbed and flowed between them, embedded in the teasing and the honest words. She felt alive with him. "Well, down in Mississippi we have plenty of old tomcats with loud meows and quick paws."

Sal shook his head. "Guess quick paws aren't exclusive to feeble German pipe fitters."

They kept steady progress toward a hotel flying several different flags outside where bellmen assisted patrons from cabs and limos. She turned to him. "Have you ever been down South?"

"Do you consider Orlando part of the South? We went there once. Once. Pops said he'd rather eat glass than go back again."

"Really? I went to Disney World a few years ago and I loved it."

He hooked a dark eyebrow. "I can see that. You're the kind of girl who believes in magic."

Rosemary thought about that. "Well, yeah. Believing in something is what makes life worth living. I had forgotten that but a friend recently reminded me how important it is to reach for the magic in life." She tried to keep her voice light but sorrow leaked into her words.

"You sound sad, *passerotta*."

"Maybe a little. So what's passa—whatever you just said?"

"It's an endearment. Means 'little sparrow,'" he said with a soft smile. "My grandmother used to call my sisters that."

"Oh," Rosemary said, pressing her lips together, shoving her grief back into the space where she kept it locked. She didn't want sadness tonight. Not when romance pushed them toward a canvas of stars above a glittering city. Lacy would be so proud of her . . . and aghast at allowing even a drop of grief to destroy the mood. "Well, this sparrow is glad to be here in this moment. With you."

Wow. She'd said those words out loud.

He reached over and slapped the button on the streetlight in order to get the light. "Best idea I've had in forever."

Seconds later they entered the elegant lobby of the historic Morey Hotel, with its huge shimmering chandelier and bellmen clad in cherry-red coats. A bank of elevators led to the rooftop bar thirty stories up. Several older couples crowded into the elevator with her and Sal, making Rosemary step closer to her sexy Italian. Ah, the perks of a crowded elevator.

Sal topped out at six foot, but his broad shoulders and strong jaw made him seem taller. He smelled a bit like warm Italian bread with a hint of woodsy cologne. He still wore the black trousers he'd worn earlier but had rolled up the sleeves of his button-down shirt, revealing tanned forearms. A swirl of ink peeked out at her, teasing her imagination.

She'd never gone out with a guy who had a tattoo.

The other couples were dressed more formally. The women wore jewels and the men custom jackets. Suddenly Rosemary felt under-dressed. She plucked at the neck of her blouse, winding her fingers around her grandmother's pearls.

"You look fine," Sal said, curving an arm around her waist.

She gave him a grateful smile, appreciating how intuitive he was. Most guys she knew wouldn't have sensed her discomfort. Maybe this was why she had done something her mother and half of Morning Glory would say was dangerous as hell.

"Your pearls are lovely," one of the older ladies said, eyeing the strand she twisted.

"Thank you. They've been in my family for generations."

The woman smiled. "I've always wanted a pair. My mother never liked them. She was a diamond sort of girl."

"Well, diamonds *are* a girl's best friend," Rosemary said, finding herself relaxing against Sal's solid presence.

"So what are pearls?" the diamond-bedecked woman asked as the elevator doors opened.

Rosemary tilted her head before smiling softly. "They're a girl's link to who she is."

"Quite right," the woman said.

Sal's hand rested lightly on her waist as he steered her into the entrance of Luna. Black-and-white-checked floors opened to a foyer of a glass rooftop lounge holding tables with low candlelight. Waitresses in soft blue dresses swirled between the patrons. On the far side of the club, under strings of lights stretched from one end to the other, lay a dance floor. A five-piece band played "Moon River" as a curvy woman crooned into an old-fashioned mic.

"Whoa," Rosemary breathed as she stepped into the foyer, loving that Sal kept his arm around her as he followed.

"Told you," he said, his hand squeezing her waist.

"I wish I had worn a dress. Something swishy." That statement earned her another crooked smile. Lord, she could become addicted to his smile.

A hostess approached. "Table for two?"

"Maybe later," Sal said, nodding toward the dance floor. "We're going to take advantage of your nice hardwood."

The hostess waved her had with a flourish. "Enjoy and let me know when you're ready."

Sal looked down at Rosemary, his chocolate eyes glittering. "This girl hasn't danced in over a decade. We're only sitting if her feet start hurting."

Rosemary lifted her sandaled foot with the flat sole. "Not a chance."

The hostess smiled, because who could not smile when two people were so perfect for each other?

Well, at least perfect for one night.

Rosemary might be floating on a cloud of romance and daring, but she knew what this was—one of those nights that can't be planned, that can never be repeated, only mentioned with a wistful tone years from now when she remembered that one time in New York City . . . under the stars . . . in the arms of a sexy man.

Sal guided her through the tangle of tables, clinking glasses, and laughter to the outer edge of the crowded dance floor and then folded her into his arms.

She refrained from sighing but it felt so right. His arms were warm, strong, and, yeah, safe. She'd never been the sort who felt she needed a man or his protection, but there was something about being wrapped in muscular arms that made a woman feel like, well, a woman.

His five o'clock scruff brushed against her hair as he lifted her hand and clasped it in his. Then he started moving to the music.

"I can't believe this," she whispered again, falling into rhythm with him.

He pulled back and looked down at her. Then he drew her closer so her breasts pressed against his chest, making her mouth dry. He whirled her quickly onto the dance floor, moving his body against hers as the singer's words washed over her. Overhead the twinkle lights did their work, outshining the stars, encapsulating her in a fantasy she'd only dreamed of before.

Rosemary had but one thought—*I could totally fall in love tonight.*

But, of course, she wouldn't. That would be silly upon silly. Still, why not pretend for a few Cinderella hours? No harm in pretending.

Sal adjusted his grip as the band moved into a song he'd never heard before. Rosemary hadn't tried to fill the moment with inane conversation, something he appreciated.

She'd whispered, "I can't believe this," right before he swept her onto the dance floor, folding her into his arms.

If truth be told, he couldn't believe he held her, either.

But damned if it didn't feel so right.

Asking a girl he'd just met—on the sidewalk, no less—to go dancing was something he'd never done before. Sure, he'd picked up girls plenty, but never for dancing. Hell, he didn't really like dancing all that much, but he'd be lying if he said he wanted to be anywhere other than holding her in his arms at that moment.

Song after song, they swayed, the light fragrance of her hair tickling his senses, her warm, firm body moving elegantly. After seven straight songs his feet finally started to ache, along with his back. The thought of an icy beer started sounding better and better.

"Oh, oh," Rosemary said, stumbling into his chest.

An older man dancing behind her turned. "I'm sorry, sweetheart. These old feet don't work so well."

"That's okay," Rosemary said. The man gave her another apologetic shrug and turned back to his partner, moving toward the perimeter of the dance floor.

Rosemary looked down at her foot, which she held aloft. The sandal dangled, one of the straps flopped uselessly. "I think I've been sidelined."

"Want me to beat him up?" Sal joked.

Rosemary's eyes widened.

"Kidding."

"Well, you like playing knight in shining armor. I'm just glad you draw a line when it comes to roughing up the elderly."

"So I have a soft spot for old dudes," he said with a shrug. She looked so forlorn, but really, her blown sandal was a good excuse for a cold beer and some more conversation. He liked talking to her. Another oddity for him. Usually, it was about getting into a woman's pants. Which made him sound shallow. Maybe he was. Or had been. He didn't know, but inside something was changing, evolving, making him want more than what he had even as he ran from the commitment expected of him. "We'll tell everyone you danced your shoes off."

Rosemary smiled, and damn if she wasn't the prettiest—no, sexiest—thing he'd seen in forever. She said, "We won't be lying. But to tell the truth, I'm dying for a drink. Dancing's more of a workout than I remembered."

"Let's grab a table," he said.

Rosemary limped toward the area crowded with tables and chatter. If he'd known her better, he might have teased her more, but she looked a bit embarrassed at the skipping hobble. "How am I going to make it home like this?"

Sal took her hand. "My steed, of course."

"You're taking this gallantry thing seriously, aren't you?"

"Trying to be as courteous as the southerners you're used to."

Rosemary rolled her eyes. "You wanted to nail me for that earlier comment, didn't you?"

Wanting to nail her? Was he that transparent? Maybe. He *was* a dude. "Hey, you threw down the glove. I'm merely picking it up and trying to prove I can be a gentleman. Sometimes."

"I shouldn't have implied only southerners were gracious when I helped Mr. Weingarten to his cab. Not well done of me."

"It's okay. We New Yorkers can be blunt, impervious, and smart-assed. Totally part of our charm." He nodded at the hostess, who gave him a questioning arch of her brow. She jabbed a finger toward a small table sitting next to a window. Sal took Rosemary's elbow and steered her toward the table with the flickering votive. She limped beside him, a flush staining her cheeks. "I feel like such a dork."

"But you're a cute dork," he said.

"Bet you say that to all the girls who break their shoes dancing with you."

The hostess handed him a cocktail menu and disappeared. Sal remembered to pull out her chair. His dating skills were a bit rusty, since they pretty much consisted of buying drinks at the clubs and waiting for a tipsy girl to fall into his lap. He'd forgotten what a date was. He'd forgotten about romance, the art of small talk and subtle flirting.

Rosemary sank into the chair, letting loose a breath. "Made it."

He handed her the menu. "What would you like to drink?"

She stared at the words. "Well, I'm fine with a glass of iced tea."

He couldn't hold back the laugh.

"What?" she asked.

"Nothing. You're just . . . cute."

She blushed again. "You keep saying that. Is 'cute' code for lame?"

He laughed.

"Well, maybe I am," she said. "I don't drink much except for special occasions."

"And this is . . ."

"Right." Rosemary looked back down at the menu. "Hmmm . . . this Ruby Slipper looks good."

He took the menu and eyed the description. "Yeah, that's what me and the guys call a 'panty dropper.'"

"In that case I'll take a glass of white zinfandel."

Laughing had become a habit around Rosemary. Another thing he liked about her. As his laughter died, a waitress appeared. Seconds after he ordered her a glass of wine and a domestic beer for himself, he took her hand. Her fingers were soft, with manicured nails painted the color of the lining of a seashell. Very ladylike.

She looked at him questioningly.

"I'm not feeding you a line when I say this, okay?"

"Okay," she said looking perplexed.

"Thank you for coming with me tonight. I've been waiting for someone like you."

"You said that before. What do you mean by someone like me?"

"You're just different. Lately I've been surrounded by women who seem one thing but then they're not as billed. Thing is, you seem like a person who isn't afraid to be herself."

She made a face. "Well, I don't know who else to be. I'd like to pretend I'm worldly and sophisticated, but we both know I'd fall as flat as I nearly fell out there." She jerked her head toward the dance floor.

"Who needs sophistication? So overrated." His mind flipped to Hillary, to the way she'd ordered drinks with bitters and stalked about in heels that cost as much as a small island. She'd had money and absolute control . . . and she'd never given his broken heart a second glance. Because to her, he'd been something to play with. When it came down to cutting bait, Hillary had chosen to please her Fortune 500 CEO daddy by not slumming with a greaseball from Brooklyn.

Sal watched the guileless Rosemary in the flickering candlelight. Outside the window, Manhattan lay glittering like a backdrop in a movie. Inside he wondered if he'd indeed jumped track. Or was he lying to himself? The conflicting parts of his psyche twisted around each other, each struggling for a foothold. This wasn't about Rosemary. This was about his life.

After a few seconds she said, "Tonight feels surreal, like I'm a different person. I know it sounds like I'm beating a dead horse, but I'm amazed at myself."

"Do you have a boyfriend back in Mississippi?" he asked, not even knowing why that popped into his mind. Maybe because she'd said she felt not herself when all he could see was someone so genuine.

Rosemary shook her head with a wry smile. "My hometown's not exactly wriggling with eligible bachelors."

"You'd like to think NYC would be an easier place to find the right person, but it's not. So what do you do back in—where was it?"

"Morning Glory. We're not too far from Jackson."

He tried to remember where Jackson was.

"It's in Mississippi. That's the state between Louisiana and Alabama," she said, reading his mind.

"I know." Though he didn't. He'd kicked ass in math, but geography was always a weakness. The South was an area he had little cause to know much about. His world consisted of five boroughs. And maybe New Jersey when he wanted to go to the shore.

She grinned. "I'm teasing. I own a fabric shop called Parsley and Sage."

"Like you sell material for sewing?"

"And supplies for knitting, quilting, and crafts."

"My grandmother likes to knit," he said, understanding now why Rosemary seemed old-fashioned. It's because she was. Not in a grand-motherly way, but in a way that made her startlingly unique.

"My grandmother taught me how to knit when I was eight years old. I became obsessed with making things. Still am, I guess." She blushed after she blurted that out. "Jeez, I sound so lame. Hi, my name is Rosemary. I'm a backwoods hick who doesn't dance and sews pillows."

"You're not a hick. Besides, what's lame about loving what you do?"

"I don't know. Most people hate their jobs," she said, giving a little shrug. "Living in Morning Glory can be a pain in the behind, but when it comes down to it, I fit there."

Her words smacked him, leaving behind a sting. *I fit there.* Rosemary knew who she was, but he couldn't say the same. Over the past few months he'd started losing the part of himself that wanted to break away from his world. He hadn't the energy to second-guess his mother's choice for him even though he didn't want Angelina. Nor had he questioned his father buying a deli in the theater district he wanted to hand over to Sal like an inheritance.

So what was his true passion?

Well, he liked making food people came back for time and again. Sal had put several dishes on the menu at Mama Mello's, and his pizzas made must-dine lists across the city. He loved experimenting with different toppings, pairing the unexpected with the traditional. But his pops didn't like anything too different. Donnie was a red sauce kinda guy, and he'd nixed half of Sal's suggestions for the pizza pie menu at the new location they'd open in late fall.

Beyond knowing cooking was his thing, Sal hadn't discovered much else.

Before Hillary broke his heart, he'd vowed never to be like his brothers. Both Dom and Vincent had fallen in line with being part of the business, accepting it the same way they'd done as children when their mother had heaped peas on their plate. *Eat what is given to you.* Sal didn't like peas and he'd been determined not to toe the line for his pop. No living in the city or working for someone else. He'd dreamed of opening his own Italian place in a coastal town or even a place in the mountains. He'd have a house with a yard. Maybe a dog. At night he'd hear crickets, and when he walked outside, the stars would glitter, unfazed by the glow of a city.

"Guess I'm passionate about cooking," he said finally.

"You should be," Rosemary said, accepting the glass the waitress handed her. The light pink wine bubbled on the top and she sighed when she sipped it. "I would have stabbed someone if he'd tried to take one of my meatballs."

He smiled, set a twenty-dollar bill on the tray, and took a long draw on the cold brew. "That's why we don't leave sharp knives out. Too many instances of death by meatball."

Rosemary rolled her eyes then took another sip of the wine. "This is good. Reminds me of home."

"How?"

"Well, my friends Eden, Jess, and La—" She stopped and swallowed hard. "My friends and I drink this when we're hanging out. It's kind of girly and I know hardly any self-respecting wine enthusiast would drink it, but it fits us."

"Bubbly and pink?"

"And sweet as sugah, darlin'." Rosemary tilted her head and batted her long eyelashes.

"God, you're good at that." Sal held his beer aloft, waiting for her to clink her glass to his. Finally, she took the hint. "To a southern girl learning how to be a little bad in New York City."

"Here, here," she said with an impish twinkle in her eye. "And to an Italian guy who's helping her take the plunge."

Chapter Five

Flip-flops had never been her favorite shoe choice. The slap-slap-slap of them against her foot set her teeth on edge. But that was all that was available at the bodega right outside the hotel's back door.

Unfortunately they were a bright yellow with a neon-orange flower. They looked like a nuclear explosion of sunshine.

"They're not that bad. I kinda like them," Sal said as they exited the store, her broken sandals swinging beside her in a plastic bag.

"You either have appalling taste or are color-blind," she said.

"There's an insult hidden in there somewhere. I'm going to plead color-blind . . . even though I'm not," he said, looking around. "You want to go do something else?"

"It's nearly midnight," she countered. She didn't want the night to end, but she could feel exhaustion descending. Flying solo to JFK, surviving the subway, and dancing beneath the Manhattan sky with a hot guy she'd met only hours before was quite an adventure for a gal who went to bed at ten o'clock every night.

"Been a long day for you, I suppose. Probably need to get you home and in bed."

Her stomach flipped over at the thought of bed. And Sal.

He'd look good sprawled on the white sheets her cousin had put on the queen-size bed. The image of his tan skin and inky hair, mussed from a night of lovemaking, made Rosemary swallow. Hard.

She wasn't the kind of girl who picked a guy up for a one-night stand. On the contrary, she'd made Judson Hall, her college boyfriend, wait for three months before she'd even let him slide a hand into her jeans. It had taken six months and a pack of birth control pills before she'd gone all the way with him in his room at the TKE house, door barred and triple locked. Sex was a big deal to her and she didn't need his scuzzy roommate trying to catch a glimpse.

Still, Sal would look really, really, REALLY hot wrapped in those sheets.

"Ugh, yeah, it's been a long one. I flew out of Jackson at six a.m."

"I know. Jackson's in Mississippi."

She smiled, lifting her gaze to his. "Thank you for bringing me here. I'll never forget tonight."

And she wouldn't. When she was on her deathbed, she'd probably remember the way he smelled, the way he held her, and the way they'd talked for hours. The impromptu date had been magical from the moment she'd stepped inside Mama Mello's until the purchase of her ugly flip-flops.

"Yeah, me, too," he said, brushing a piece of hair behind her ear.

Oh God. Was he going to kiss her?

Part of Rosemary wanted to step away, because a woman like her had no business kissing a guy like Sal. The other part wanted to jump into his arms and say to hell with being proper. This was why she'd come to New York City, why she'd gone dancing with a perfect stranger. This was the part of herself she was here to unleash.

Her heart pounded in her throat, and suddenly her mouth went dry. She licked her lips. He watched her lick her lips.

Slowly he leaned toward her.

Time stood still.

He was going to—

Suddenly he pulled back.

"What?" she asked.

"Nothing," he said.

"Weren't you going to kiss me?"

He gave a self-conscious laugh. "Well, I was, but I wasn't sure."

"About what?"

"Whether you wanted me to or not. I mean, you're a nice girl."

Rosemary sighed. "Nice girls like kisses, but if you'd rather not, I under—"

She couldn't finish because his lips had covered hers. Then his arm swept her to him, enveloping her in his total maleness. His other hand cupped her jaw, tilting her head.

The kiss was sweet, nearly innocent, but she felt it all the way down to the toes beneath the orange daisy.

He lifted his head and met her gaze, his dark eyes questioning, revealing a teeny flash of something. Something she wanted to know more about.

But he lowered his head again, capturing her lips, nudging them apart so he could taste her better.

Liquid warmth pooled in her belly, drenching her in sweet instantaneous desire. Maybe it was the wine. Or the fact she'd danced to Etta James and Nat King Cole standards. Or maybe it was the seduction of the city, but she'd never felt such an immediate flash of all-out need.

She needed this man.

His tongue moved against hers, giving her a taste of the yeasty beer he'd drunk earlier.

"Mmm," she murmured, sliding her hands up his shoulders, brushing the dark hair at his collar. His hand cradled her waist then dipped several inches lower to the rounding of her butt, pressing her closer to his hardness.

After a few seconds, he broke the kiss.

If his gaze and kicked-up breathing were any indication, Sal was as turned on as she was.

"Damn, I'm glad nice girls like kissing," he said, still holding her. She wanted to stay in this moment forever.

"Nice girls *love* kissing," she said eyeing his lips again. "In fact, if you want to come—"

"Better get you home," he interrupted.

The invitation she'd been about to extend died on her tongue. Disappointment nudged desire out of the way. Managing a nod, she said, "That's probably a good idea."

He released her, stepping away. He put two fingers against those delicious lips and did that whistle thing she had never mastered, though she'd tried to learn it when she was twelve. A cab pulled up less than ten seconds later. He was as magic as Carrie Bradshaw. Had to be a New Yorker thing.

Sal pulled open the cab door, standing back so she could slide inside.

She hesitated, narrowing her eyes at the idling cab.

"It's easy. Just tell him where you need to go," Sal said.

"You're not coming with me?"

He paused, casting a questioning glance her way.

Oh.

She could see his thoughts. He thought she'd asked him something she wasn't asking. Or rather something she'd decided against asking. Seconds ago it had been a possibility. But it was midnight and her pumpkin idled. Cinderella out. "Are you staying here or something?"

"I live in Brooklyn. It's that way." He pointed over his shoulder.

The cab driver made an impatient noise in the back of his throat and then flicked a bunch of switches on the dashboard, making the meter light up.

"Yeah, of course, I knew that." But she hadn't wanted the evening to end this way. And besides, she'd never ridden in a cab before. Did she pay the driver first or when they arrived at her cousin's walk-up? How much was she supposed to tip? And did Sal want to see her again? Or was this it?

"So I hope you'll come by the restaurant again," Sal said.

To eat? Or for something more?

"I'll try to," she said. What else could she say? *Don't end it this way? Stay with me? I'll forget about being exhausted and we'll keep the night going?*

He'd kissed her and she'd thought it had been good. But maybe she'd been wrong. Maybe she sucked at kissing. She sat down in the cab a little too hard.

Sal watched her before he leaned in. His kiss was short, sweet, yet somehow a balm to her torn thoughts. "You're beautiful. I want to see you again, but I don't want to freak you out or make you feel pressured. The ball is in your court, southern girl."

Then he closed the door and thumped the cab on the top twice. The cabbie pulled away from the curb. Rosemary turned her head and watched as Sal stood on the corner lifting his hand in silent farewell.

She lifted her hand, her heart clenching at the sight of him fading behind her.

"Where to?" the man said in a guttural accent she couldn't place.

"Uh, SoHo. Um, it's the red building on Spring Street. Think the number starts with a five. Five twenty . . . no, maybe twelve? Oh crap, I can't remember." Panic tore at her. How could she forget the address?

The man glanced up at her, meeting her eyes in the mirror. "I drop you off at corner. Good?"

"Sure," she said, taking a deep breath and pulling the seat belt across her body, chancing one last glance back. Sal and the Hotel Morey had been obscured by other cars and the corner of the adjacent building. Like a dream, her night faded behind her.

But it didn't have to.

Sal wanted to see her again.

That piece of knowledge settled inside her, hollowing out a warm place. As buildings ricocheted by, she realized what Sal had done. He'd given her an out, allowing her to make the decision whether to see him again or not. He'd given her room to trust him, to know he wouldn't treat her like a random hookup. And lastly, he'd given her privacy, allaying the 0.0001 percent chance he was a psychotic stalker who wanted to eat her liver with fava beans.

She issued a happy sigh.

"Yes?" the cab driver asked, his bushy brows high on his balding head.

"Nothing."

"You not from here?"

"Nope. You?" she asked.

"Nope," he said.

And that was her first cabbie conversation. Her cousin's building appeared like a prayer granted, and she instructed the driver to drop her off in front rather the corner. She managed to use her credit card to pay the fare and make it inside the building with no incident.

She trudged up the five stories, calves and lungs screaming equally in protest, and unlocked the door to her cousin's loft. When she pushed into the foyer, she found it pitch-black, which was confusing because she was certain she'd left a lamp on. But maybe not. It had been light outside when she'd left earlier. Moscow curled around her legs, issuing a yowl.

"Oh, so now you're acknowledging me?" she asked, bending over to pet him after locking the door. Then, after double-checking the lock just like she promised her father she'd do each night, she set her hand against the wall and inched toward the opening to the loft.

"Meow, meow," Moscow cried, twining around her legs, nearly tripping her. She kicked off the flip-flops, dropping the plastic bag with her broken sandals. Then she shuffled toward where she thought the lamp was, thankfully finding it before the cat managed to send her sprawling.

She switched on the lamp and then nearly wet herself. A scream caught in her throat as a very naked man tumbled out of her cousin's bed, cupping his genitals.

"What the fuck?" He blinked against the light.

Rosemary's first thought was to grab the pepper spray her mother had bought her for the trip.

But it was in her purse, which sat on the shelf under the kitchen bar. She'd taken only her key, driver's license, and a credit card in her pocket when she left earlier.

He advanced and she backed away, scrambling to her left, heart beating in her ears, legs threatening to buckle.

"Oh God, stay away from me," she screeched, tripping over the fluffy shearling ottoman. She caught herself from falling and froze, crouching like a cornered animal.

The naked man stopped, rubbed a hand across his eyes like he could make everything clear before jabbing it through his inky hair. "Hold on. I'm Marco. Halle's fiancé."

"Halle doesn't have a fiancé," Rosemary said, scooting toward her burlap purse. She'd tucked the spray in an easy-to-reach pocket. Just seven more feet and she could clear it and douse the . . . burglar or whatever he was.

She couldn't believe this was happening. Her mother had been right. She didn't belong here and now she'd die . . . or be raped . . . or burgled . . . or . . .

"Okay, not yet, but I'm proposing when she gets back from Italy," he said before holding up a hand. "Look, let me grab my pants. Okay?"

Rosemary swallowed and pressed herself against the stucco wall, trying to think what she should do. Her heart beat in her ears but she managed to say, "That would be a good idea."

He turned, presenting an ass tight enough to bounce a quarter on. He looked like a model—too pretty for her bohemian cousin who'd always liked guys a little rough around the edges.

Halle hadn't said anything about a boyfriend.

But Rosemary knew she'd locked the door when she'd left that evening. She'd checked it twice before leaving, and since the lock hadn't been busted, this very naked and very nice-looking guy had to have used a key to get inside.

She relaxed a millimeter.

Marco walked over to the rumpled bed and picked up a pair of dark slacks; turning away from her, he stepped inside, hitching them up.

"Look, I'm sorry I scared you. I'm assuming you're Halle's cousin. I got here earlier and I was so beat I went to bed," he said, rubbing his bared chest before shrugging back his shoulders like he worked out a kink. He liked to touch himself. A lot.

Rosemary still hadn't moved an inch. Fading adrenaline made her thighs warm and woozy though her heart still beat a million times a minute. "So why didn't she tell me about you? Why would—"

"I'm in special forces. Heading out for a training mission tomorrow. Halle probably got the dates mixed up and thought I wouldn't be here. And I wouldn't have, but I was in the city with friends and came here to sleep off the buzz I'd worked up. Honestly, I forgot you were here until I saw this." He lifted the cardigan sweater her mother had bought her. It looked so weird in his hand. Like a little old lady's sweater dangling in the paw of a cheetah.

Rosemary peeled herself from the wall but still eyeballed him with suspicion. "Okay, so do you have identification or something?"

He cracked a lethal smile. "And how's that going to help?"

"I don't know. They do that on TV," she said feeling like a moron.

So far since stepping out of the subway, she'd gotten lost, danced with a hot Italian guy, and acquainted herself with her cousin's soon-to-be fiancé a bit too intimately.

Wait. Presumed soon-to-be fiancé. She wasn't a hundred percent on that one.

"Look, trust me, I'm her guy. See?" He picked up a photograph from the table beside the sofa and walked toward her. "This is when we went to Niagara Falls this past summer. That's me." He thumped the glass.

Rosemary hadn't noticed the framed picture earlier, but then again, she'd not spent much time poking around. She'd been hungry and tempted by Sal. She glanced at the picture showing her cousin with Marco. They wore rain ponchos. "Okay, so . . . are you going to leave?"

He made a face. "Do I have to? We're practically family."

"I can't stay here with a stranger. I mean, there's only one bed." She gestured toward the rumpled bed. The privacy screen had been rolled aside. Thank God . . . because if the light hadn't woken him and she'd climbed into bed with the guy? Uh, total heart attack waiting to happen.

"I'll sleep on the sofa. I'll be gone before you even wake up tomorrow morning," he said.

Rosemary glanced around the loft. A metal door rolled into place to cover the bathroom and shower area, but that was the only other door in the place. Even with the screen rolled into place, she'd be able to hear him move while he slept. And at the right angle he'd be able to watch her. The whole thing felt super creepy, but if she pitched a fit she'd look like the bumpkin she was. "Uh, I guess that's okay. You take the bed since you're already there."

Rude of him to plop in the bed in the first place. He knew she was staying there, but whatever. Wasn't like she was going to sleep on sheets some naked guy had rolled around in. Future cousin-in-law or not.

"You sure?" he asked, his eyebrows tenting. "Halle would be pissed if I was rude to you."

"It's fine. You're already, uh, comfortable there. I'll grab a blanket and take the couch. No problem," she lied, because everything about this situation was a problem. Sleeping in the room with a strange naked man was a good thousand miles away from her comfort zone. And if she were going to do that, she'd rather it be with Sal. Oh, the irony.

"Awesome," Marco said, padding toward the bench at the foot of the bed. Lifting the lid, he pulled out a blanket and extra pillow. Then he returned, handing them to her. Rosemary tried not to look flipped out, but she knew she failed. "Hey, if this is freaking you out, I can go. I'll find a hotel or something."

But he didn't sound like he wanted to.

She glanced over again at the picture. Her cousin smiled goofily, wrapped in the arms of the guy standing in front of Rosemary. "Don't be silly. It's no big deal." She managed a half smile.

Marco shrugged. "Cool."

"Uh, I need to use the restroom. That won't bother you?"

"Nah, I can sleep through a nitroglycerin plant explosion when I want to." He turned and walked back toward the bed, plopping down and punching the feather pillow before pulling the covers over himself.

Rosemary stared at him for a second before setting the blanket on the couch. Switching off the lamp, she tiptoed toward the restroom, carefully sliding the metal door across the entrance, wincing when the wheels creaked. Took her ten minutes to take off her makeup and brush and floss just like Dr. Culpepper, Jess's dad and her dentist, expected. Then she changed into a sports bra, T-shirt, and athletic shorts. No way was she letting the girls loose with a strange naked man sleeping fifteen feet away. Switching off the light, she slipped the door open and stepped out to Fred Flintstone.

Yeah, if curtains had been at the large windows, they would have been sucked in and out by the god-awful snoring coming from her cousin's bed.

Great.

Even if she had felt comfortable sleeping in the same room with a man she didn't know, she wouldn't be able to sleep with the award-winning snorer sawing logs or whatever the heck they called it in the background.

Rosemary sat on the couch, fluffed the pillow behind her and lay back, clutching the soft quilt like a five-year-old listening for monsters.

Shadows flickered on the wall, and outside the loft, New York refused to sleep. Or maybe the city could hear Marco snoring. Either way, horns tooted, lights stayed on, and the occasional shriek of laughter shouldered its way into the tiny loft.

She put her back to the room and snuggled into the sofa. She'd planned to call Eden or Jess and tell them about her first day, but now she couldn't. Not with that snoring.

So she pretended to tell Lacy.

"Did you see what I did?"

Pretend Lacy high-fived her. *"You rocked it, Rosemary. See? I told you underneath the pearls lay a feral wildcat ready to sink her claws into a delicious Italian."*

"I wouldn't go that far."

"True." Pretend Lacy grinned. *"But still, you knocked it out of the park. He's cornea burning. So now what?"*

"I don't know. Should I go to his restaurant tomorrow? Or is that too forward? Wait a few days?"

"Tomorrow. But make it afternoon . . . or even evening. You're gorgeous, wonderful, and totally not desperate. Oh, and by the way, you don't have to whistle to get a cab. Just jut out that hip and do your pageant wave."

"I've never been in a pageant."

Pretend Lacy rolled her eyes. *"You don't have to be Miss Morning Glory to do the pageant wave, sugar."*

"This conversation is ridiculous. You're not real."

Pretend Lacy shook her head. *"Sure I am. Didn't I tell you the last time I saw you that I would always be here? I'm your guardian angel, chickadee. You can count on me."* Pretend Lacy hopped on a cloud and floated away to the sound of . . . snoring.

Fresh pain flooded Rosemary's heart at the thought of her vivacious friend. Lacy would have loved dancing on a rooftop, and she wouldn't have said only two or three words to the cabbie. By the end of the ride, Lacy would have known about his kids and the tiny village he'd been born into. Her friend had been like that—easy to talk to. Rosemary swiped the wetness from her lashes, thinking about the last words her friend had said to her.

You gotta get out of here, Rose. Life is too short to spend it eating pancakes at Dean's Diner or shopping for dresses at The Fashion. Promise me you'll go somewhere fun. That you'll wear ridiculously high heels and drink gin straight up. Meet a guy and kiss him without knowing his name. Take a chance. Skydive. Snorkel. Bike. Swim. Dance. Laugh. Make love.

Lacy had been lying in her hospital bed, hair unbrushed, eyes sunken when she'd uttered those words. The happy blonde had been but a shadow of her former self, no longer bothering with the irreverent blue wig she'd sported just to bug her mother. Still the fire had burned in her eyes. So much living left to do. No body left to do it in.

Rosemary clutched her chest, stamping down the infernal sob that was always ready to rise when she thought about her late friend and all the missed memories they'd never share.

Rosemary was doing her damned best to bust out of the straitjacket of her life. Of course, not even Lacy would likely approve of sleeping on the couch while a naked stranger snored nearby.

But Sal?

Sal was something Lacy would have stamped with a giant check mark. Which meant Rosemary was going back to Mama Mello's. Not for Lacy . . . but for herself.

Chapter Six

Sal blearily regarded his cup of coffee. He'd gotten home at one o'clock that morning, forgetting he'd traded out the lunch shift with his brother a week ago. His niece had inoculations or something that morning, and Dominic wasn't missing a single fart given by his newborn daughter, much less a doctor appointment. So Sal had to hoof it back to Mama Mello's, fighting the morning commute.

"Why you look like something the dog barfed this morning? You left early last night," his father said, refilling Sal's coffee cup before tying an apron around his waist. The tiny office/storage room off the kitchen housed a messy desk, a rickety table with a coffeepot, and shelves of stuff his father refused to toss out in case they needed it one day.

"I went out."

"With who? That girl you talked to last night? Sally, Sally, that girl's not for you. She'll be back whistling 'Dixie' by the end of the week."

"You don't know that. Besides, I'm a single guy. Not tied down. Yet." He sipped the coffee his father bought special for his staff. Good stuff. Hearty Italian roast.

Big Donnie Genovese made a face. "Now don't you go screwing things up with Angelina. She's a good girl. From a good family. I went to school with her uncle Mikey, and they're a stand-up bunch. Good jobs. Own a lotta rental property in the Bronx. You could do worse."

"Do worse? That's a crappy way to look at falling in love, Pop." Sal cradled his cup and wondered if he should sneak up front and add a shot of booze. This conversation called for something stronger. Course, it hadn't even hit eight o'clock yet.

His father drew his bushy eyebrows together. "Eh, love, what a crock. All them card people got us believing in magic and butterflies."

"You're blaming the greeting card industry?" Sal snorted, watching his old man as he bumbled around. Big Donnie had a lot of opinions his boys ragged him about. Blaming Hallmark for heightened romantic expectations just got added to the list.

"Sure. Them and others. And look what happened with Hillary. She was like this girl. She didn't know you or your world. Looks fade," his father said, turning and jabbing a finger at Sal.

"Just because things with me and Hillary didn't work doesn't mean I stop looking for love, Pops. I can't pick a girl based on her ethnicity, family connections and—"

"Why not?" Big Donnie interrupted. "'Cause if you want to know the truth of it, that's what I did with your ma. I looked at her and she looked good, you know? And then I tasted her cooking, met her family, took her to church. That's all it took. Love comes after nursing a sick babe through the night, after getting the crap scared out of you with that heart thing I had, after living your life together. All this romantic stuff? Bah. Choose a girl who suits you. A girl who suits your life."

Sal stared at his father. "Are you telling me you weren't in love with Ma when you married her?"

The older man shrugged. "Eh, more like I loved the thought of her. But the most important thing was I knew we would work. I had this place to run. I needed someone to stand here with me."

"You make it sound like a business arrangement," Sal said. He knew his parents loved each other. No doubt about that. He'd seen his mother's careworn hands wrapped in prayer at his pop's bedside, tears streaking her cheeks. He'd seen his father carrying breakfast to his ma's bed when her back was so bad she could hardly move. They were devoted to each other.

"I'm not saying it is or isn't. All I'm saying is be careful about chasing a feeling. Being practical about who you're supposed to be with isn't a bad thing. Now that's it. I'm outta advice. We got a kitchen to run. Hungry people will be banging at the door in a bit."

Sal sighed and drained the last of his coffee. Rising from the banged-up stool, he looped a clean apron over his head.

His father believed what he said, and part of Sal understood. Finding someone who fit you was pretty damned important, but what if *he* didn't fit the world he lived in? That was the thing that kept pirouetting through his mind like a tipsy ballerina.

Shit, most of the guys he knew would kill to have the life his parents were handing him—a new deli located near the theater district with a ready-made name? Why was he balking? Why was he being so stubborn about falling into line?

Sal walked out and looked around the kitchen with its gleaming stainless steel prep area, large pots awaiting savory sauces, and Gus's crack as he bent over to grab a can of shortening. And it hit him—this was his world and would always be. He'd tried to break out with Hillary, allowing her to fill his head with ideas, with the thought he could be more than Big Donnie Genovese's youngest boy.

So he should shut up and put his foot in the shoes handed to him like he'd shoved his foot into the lace-up oxford shoes his mother had bought him for Easter when he was nine years old. *Stick your foot in and shut up. This is what you're wearing. Got it?*

Christ, he'd hated those shoes. They pinched his toes, and the slick bottom made them hard to run in. Too bad. He hadn't had a say-so.

But he wasn't nine years old anymore.

He didn't have to wear shoes that didn't fit, did he?

"Hey, Sal. Start the vodka sauce. We're making Mama's special today," his father called from the front.

"Got it. And Pop?" Sal called.

"Yeah?"

"I'm not chasing love. I'm just not hiding from it." Sal tied his apron on and started grabbing the ingredients he'd need to make his grandmother's sauce. He loved feeling connected to his family through the old recipe handed down through generations. Nothing wrong with following the recipe. Lots of people stuck to the step-by-step directives.

His father didn't answer. No need to. Sal was, if anything, hardheaded. But in the matter of Rosemary, it didn't matter. He didn't have her number. Didn't know where she was staying. Putting her in that cab last night after she'd suggested they continue the night had been the hardest thing he'd done. But a sixth sense had told him to give her space. Deep sadness and determination shaded her laughter, etched in her face. This was a girl who didn't do one-night stands. This was a girl who didn't know the score like the chicks in the clubs did. So he'd left it up to Rosemary.

If she wanted him, she'd come to Mama Mello's.

If not, he'd take it as a sign and jab his foot into the hard-soled shoe. He'd live the life handed to him rather than looking for something different. Not everyone got what they wanted. He'd learned that hard lesson at the hands of a stuck-up bitch who'd gotten married over Christmas and honeymooned in Saint Bart's.

As he lifted the strainer full of tomatoes fresh from the market, he said a little prayer.

Please let Rosemary come save me.

Rosemary woke to a silent loft and the smell of coffee.

Blinking, she rubbed her eyes and looked around. No Marco. The bed had been stripped of sheets—if the bundle sitting on the end was any indication—and remade with military precision. A half-full pot of coffee sat on the Carrara marble counter with what looked to be a note.

She'd actually fallen asleep at some point.

Miracle of miracles.

Reaching for her phone, she checked the time—9:25 a.m. Good Lord. She never slept past seven. In fact, her friends always teased her about rising before the infernal rooster her next-door neighbor kept. Stretching, she rose, wincing when her thighs protested. Then she remembered the dancing. The dog-ugly yellow flip-flops in the small entryway proved she'd twirled about a rooftop dance floor with Sal last night.

Her phone vibrated in her hand, and for the slightest moment she thought it might be him. But then she remembered they hadn't shared contact information. Just one perfect night.

She glanced at the ugly flip-flops she'd kicked off.

Okay, maybe not a total Cinderella fantasy.

"Hi, Mama," she said into the phone after pushing the ANSWER button.

"Oh good. You're still alive," her mother said.

Rosemary laughed. "Very funny, Mama."

"I'm not being funny. I'm serious. Being worried sick is not good for my stomach. Just ask your father. I was up all night with acid indigestion."

"She was, honey," her father chimed in. He probably sat next to her mother in the sunroom. No doubt drinking the one and a half cups of coffee Patsy allowed him each morning.

"I wish you wouldn't worry. For heaven's sake, I'm twenty-seven."

"Asking her not to worry is like telling a frog not to croak," her father said. Rosemary was certain she could hear him turning the pages of the morning paper.

"A frog not to croak? That's ridiculous, and I don't care for being compared to a frog, Harold."

Her father made no other sound. No doubt he'd tuned his wife out. Silence was her father's greatest defense.

"I'm fine, Mama. Just got up and about to have some coffee."

"Just now getting up? My goodness. It's after nine there." Unspoken censure. Patsy Reynolds embraced early to bed and early to rise. As a renowned horticulturist, Rosemary's mother rose before the sun awoke each day, pausing to have coffee when her husband got up later.

"I'm on a much-needed vacation," Rosemary reminded her mother. Not that she needed to. Like Patsy forgot for a moment her precious daughter was on the mean streets of New York City.

"So what did you do last night?" her mother asked.

Tell the truth? Or lie like a dog? "I went out for Italian." Rosemary clapped a hand over her mouth so she wouldn't laugh.

"By yourself?"

"Who else was I going to go with, Mother?"

"It seems odd to be alone in such a big city. Why didn't you take one of your friends? Much safer that way."

"I would have. But Eden and Jess had work."

"But you didn't ask me to go with you," her mother said.

And that was the issue. Her mother was miffed Rosemary hadn't asked her to come with her. They'd gone to Memphis and Graceland last year together, and Rosemary swore she'd never repeat the experience. Her mother had brought her own sheets to stay at the Peabody Hotel and complained about every nitpicking thing, including the decor in Elvis's residence. Rosemary was surprised she hadn't suggested a decorator to the tour guide. "Mom, we went over this. I needed a break from my regular life. I—"

"And what's so wrong with your life, missy? You have a family who loves you, friends at your fingertips, and a successful business. Not to mention, Margaret Haven's son just moved back to work at the bank as a loan officer. He's very attractive."

"Chris moved back to Morning Glory? When did this happen?" Rosemary struggled from the depths of the couch and went into the kitchen. Moscow jumped onto the counter and yowled.

"What's that? Halle's cats? They sound feral," her mother said.

"Just hungry."

"Well, I saw Margaret yesterday at our circle meeting, and she said he was moving back. Got laid off by that oil and gas firm in New Orleans. Poor man. But he got in with Jansen Peters at the bank and he'll be moving back this weekend. There you go."

"Mother, Chris is gay."

"He *is* not. Just because a man takes pride in his appearance and doesn't date every slut from here to Meridian doesn't mean he's gay. Now don't go spreading those sorts of rumors, Rosemary Marie. It's very unladylike."

Rosemary rolled her eyes. "Yes, ma'am. I would never want to be unladylike."

"Sarcasm does not become you, dear."

"Look, I'm not interested in the impeccably dressed Chris, and I'm doing fine here. I've already met a nice man who took me dancing last night." Yep. She laid it out there.

"What? You went dancing last night? Have you lost every bit of sense the good Lord gave you? Harry, did you hear that? She went out with a man last night. A perfect stranger!"

"How could I have missed it, Patsy Lee? You're yelling in my ear." She heard the phone crackle as her father no doubt took the receiver. "Now, Rosemary, I want you take the pepper spray with you wherever you go. Oh, and make sure you lock your doors."

Rosemary didn't know whether to laugh at her parents or be offended they thought she was a complete idiot. "I'll do that, Daddy. I need to go. The cats are demanding food, and I'm planning on going out for some of those famous New York bagels."

Another crackle and she heard her mother sniff before saying, "Oh no. You wait a second, missy. We haven't talked about the absolutely irresponsible, not to mention dangerous, thing you did last night. This is why I didn't think it was a good idea to have you going off to that . . . that . . . hellhole. Too much could go wrong up—"

"Mama, stop. You're being ridiculous and I don't want to argue with you. I appreciate you're concerned, but I'm a grown woman. Let me repeat that—*grown* woman."

Silence on the line.

"Mama?"

"Whatever you want, honey. I want you to be happy. That's all I ever wanted. Got to go. Shorty's here to prune the roses in the south garden." The cold words were spoken like a true passive-aggressive southern mama. But the one thing Patsy Reynolds had gotten right was that Sal Genovese was a perfect stranger. Emphasis on *perfect*.

"'Bye, Mama. Give Daddy my love." Rosemary hung up. Looking at Melbourne, who leaped to join his friend on the counter, she sighed. "Guess I shouldn't have poked a stick at her by telling the truth. Should have told her I stayed in and watched *Little House on the Prairie* reruns."

Moscow yowled again.

"Okay, I'm getting it," she said, pulling the bag of cat food from beneath the counter, noting once again how much more expensive the cat food was in NYC than in Mississippi. Her dad would flip out at the sticker shock. The man claimed cats didn't need fancy store-bought food, not when they came equipped to find their own dinner.

After pouring a cup of coffee and figuring out how to work the fancy convection microwave, Rosemary propped up her feet and got out her travel guides. So much to do in NYC, she didn't know where to start.

Should she buy a ticket for the on-again, off-again bus? Someone had told her it was the best way to get a feel for the city, but that seemed so touristy. But . . . she *was* a tourist.

Or she could wander around SoHo and the surrounding neighborhoods, letting the day take her where she should go. Like she had last night.

Sal laughing as she tried on flip-flops in the twenty-four-hour convenience store popped into her mind. He'd looked so incredibly handsome, his dark hair falling over his brow, brushing past his eyebrows. Her father would say he needed a decent haircut, but Rosemary liked the way it lazily skimmed his brows. She also liked his crooked nose and his toothy smile. And the five o'clock shadow had made him more approachable. But the thing she loved almost as much as the kiss he'd given her was the way he'd sung the lyrics from the old standards in her ear as they moved against each other on the dance floor. Nothing was sexier than a man who knew all the words to "At Last" and "In the Wee Small Hours of the Morning."

Snapping the travel book shut, she made a snap decision. She'd go by Mama Mello's first and leave Sal a note with her number. Maybe even ask him out. In her other life it would have felt too forward, but after enduring her mother's rant, she felt even more determined to be the other half of herself—the half who wanted to lock her ankles around Sal's neck . . . the half who wasn't about to let the boy get away.

"Good enough, Lacy?" she asked the empty room.

No response, but Rosemary smiled anyway. She already knew the answer.

Today Rosemary would take the next step toward being a modern woman. She was going to be bold and forward. But she'd do it wearing her pearls like a good southern girl. Of that, her mother could at l east approve.

An hour later, she sat outside a small café eating a bagel that wasn't too different from the ones she bought at the Lazy Frog—Sassy must be doing something right. Fifteen minutes after smiling hello at a dozen strangers who looked uncomfortable smiling back, striking up a conversation with an older woman who walked a poodle with matching bows on her ears—the poodle, not the woman—and refraining from licking the cream cheese off her plate, Rosemary headed toward Mulberry Street and Mama Mello's.

She felt good. The day wasn't as humid, so she wore her hair down and pulled on a new Katherine Way tunic dress she'd found in a boutique in Jackson on the not so ill-fated but still knuckle-gripping trip. In her crossover bag she carried a thank-you note for Sal. Thankfully, she'd stashed a monogrammed note in the side pocket before she left home so she had personal stationery on which to write her number.

And the last line stated very plainly that she wanted to see him again.

Applying a coat of lip gloss, she congratulated herself on finding the restaurant without getting turned around. A good sense of direction wasn't on her short list of talents, so she'd studied the map of SoHo, Little Italy, and Nolita that morning.

The tables that had sat outside Mama Mello's yesterday were noticeably absent, and the sign in the window told her in fancy cursive that the place was closed.

Huh. She hadn't thought about that.

Rosemary tried the door but it was locked.

So . . . what to do?

The old Rosemary would have chalked it up to fate or slid the note under the door hoping for the best. She glanced down at the flush threshold where the note would never fit. But no matter. Because the *new* Rosemary had long tired of playing the role of shrinking violet. She wasn't about to be thwarted by a **Closed** sign.

So she knocked on the glass, cupped her hands around her face, and peered inside.

A young woman stopped setting cutlery on the tables and squinted at Rosemary. Making an annoyed face, she headed toward the front and unlocked the door, pushing it open. "Deliveries over there." She jabbed a finger to the right.

Rosemary leaned back and noted the door. "I'm, ah, not here for a delivery."

"Then we don't want any," the younger woman said, pulling the door toward her.

Rosemary caught the handle before it closed. "Wait."

"What? We open at eleven. Come back then."

"No." Rosemary jerked the door open. "If you'd let me speak, I'll tell you why I'm here."

The woman looked about Rosemary's age. Maybe younger. She wore a white shirt and trim black pants, and her dark hair hung in a low ponytail. Her chin was pointed, eyes dark, and the curve of her face looked familiar. Rosemary would bet her new Tory Burch flats that this girl was Sal's sister.

"So what's this about?"

"Sal," Rosemary said. "Is he here?"

The woman broke into laughter. "Oh God. You're joking, right?"

"No," Rosemary said, feeling the heat rise in her cheeks.

"Let me guess, you left your panties at his place," the woman asked.

"What? No." Rosemary let go of the door, shocked the woman would even think something like that.

Sal's sister or cousin or whoever she was lowered her eyes and took in Rosemary. Then she arched her eyebrows. "Never mind. I can see that probably didn't happen. But, hey, don't fault me. It's happened before. The last chick was adamant she was going to get her Agent Provocateur undies back."

Rosemary didn't know what to say, so she pulled the thank-you note from her bag. "So if you're done telling me about Sal's intimate past, I'd appreciate your giving this to him."

The woman looked at the heavy vellum envelope with Rosemary's initials engraved on the back as if it were a loaded gun. "You want me to give him an invitation or something?"

"Actually it's a—"

"Rosemary?" a voice called behind the woman. Sal appeared, sticking his head around the door. He looked even better than she remembered. This time his hair had been tamed by a brush and a small pinprick of red sauce dotted his white apron. Just like the day before. Like a trademark. "Hey, you came by."

The woman holding the door turned her head, shrinking back, looking flabbergasted. "You know *this* chick?"

"Yeah, so let her in, Fran," Sal said, pulling the door back, annoyance on his face as evident as the scent of garlic permeating the air. He jerked his head toward the woman still looking confused. "This is Frances Anne, my sister."

Rosemary's hands sweated again, but she used her best committee smile when she turned to the woman. "Hi, I'm Rosemary. I, uh, came to the restaurant last night. The meatballs were really good."

Frances Anne reacted like a unicorn had tap-danced into the restaurant. "Oh. Uh, thanks."

"What's this?" Sal interrupted, plucking the note Rosemary had been about to hand his sister from her hand.

"It's a thank-you note. I didn't have your address," Rosemary said lamely, wishing she'd forgotten the whole thing. She felt about as comfortable as a nun in a whorehouse.

"A thank-you note?" Frances Anne repeated.

"You know, Pop needs you in the back," Sal said, jerking his head toward the kitchen, narrowing his eyes in that age-old suggestion of *get lost*.

"He can wait," Frances Anne said, shifting her gaze between Rosemary and Sal. Obviously Frances Anne felt vested in the interaction.

"No. He can't. Vamoose," Sal said, jerking a thumb this time. "I can handle this."

Frances Anne dropped her gaze and looked pointedly at Rosemary. "You sure? 'Cause I have a feeling you need help here, bro. It's like déjà vu all over again."

Rosemary was polite, but she wasn't mealymouthed. Frances Anne seemed way too protective over a thirtysomething brother. "I came to thank your brother for being so kind to me last night. He made sure I had a nice introduction to New York City and was a perfect gentleman."

She expected her somewhat uppity tone to wither Frances Anne. No such luck—Sal's sister crossed her arms and studied Rosemary as if she were bread mold. "He was *kind* to you, huh?"

So Rosemary looked at Sal, who seemed at a loss for how to handle his sister baring her teeth.

Rosemary might be dorky for showing up with engraved vellum, but she wasn't a whore. "I didn't sleep with your brother, if that's what you're implying. And I'm not sure why a thank-you note threatens you."

Sal gave his sister a less than polite shove, angling her back toward the kitchen. "Frances Anne needs to apologize and finish what she was doing."

"Should I apologize to the last one you got hung up on? I mean, man, you so have a type, don't you?" Frances Anne said, ignoring her brother, digging in her heels.

"If we're playing connect the dots, I'm missing a few," Rosemary said.

Sal glared at his sister, his lips a thin line, his posture at least as stubborn as his sister's.

Finally, France Anne gave a one-shouldered shrug, turned to Rosemary, and said, "Sorry if I implied something untrue. Sal can be a blockhead at times. We have to save him from himself when it comes to women. Nice to meet you."

Rosemary didn't know how to respond to that admission. Something bubbled beneath the surface, but she wasn't going fishing. Wasn't any of her business. She barely knew the man. "'Bye."

Frances Anne gave her brother a look and then made for the tables and silverware she'd abandoned.

Sal held out his hands. "Sorry about that. Frances Anne is naturally suspicious and jumps to too many conclusions." He said the last bit loud enough for everyone working inside to hear him.

"What did she mean about me being a type?"

"Nothing," he said, fingering the envelope he'd taken from her. "She's being pissy because she got in a fight with her boyfriend or something. Everyone's a target for her this morning."

"Oh," Rosemary said, not exactly believing that excuse but, again, not familiar enough with the family dynamics to press him further.

"Rosemary, I'm so happy you came by," he said giving her the smile she'd dreamed about last night—the one that made her girl parts tingly. All doubts about the words Frances Anne had flung at him disappeared. This was why she'd come to Mama Mello's.

"I wanted to thank you for last night but I didn't know your number or address."

"So you hauled it all the way here to give me this?" he teased. His lips curled sensuously, reminding her of Elvis Presley. That was a huge plus, because she'd always had a thing for the King of Rock and Roll. She'd thought Graceland perfectly decorated. Even the Jungle Room.

Heat flooded into her cheeks. "It wasn't *that* far. And it's just a lame note. I was going to leave it, but there was no place to put it and I didn't have tape, so . . ." She made a little shrug.

He didn't say anything. Just kept a knowing smile in place.

"Okay, fine. You said you dropped the ball in my court. How in the heck was I supposed to lob it back to you without your digits? This note"—she tapped it—"was my best attempt at a backhand shot. I wanted to see you again."

Sal slid a finger under the seal and tore the paper open. His lips moved as he read and after a few seconds he looked up. "You have lovely handwriting."

Rosemary's blush increased. She felt so stupid giving a guy like him a thank-you note. So, so stupid. Of course, she didn't know what else she was to do. He'd dropped a possibility in her lap and left without telling her what it meant. "You can thank Mrs. Gunch for that. She went Nazi on us if we didn't slant our handwriting to the right or make the proper curlicue on our *Ls*."

Sal folded the notecard and slid it in his back pocket. "I get off early today, so I'll take you up on coffee."

"Or tea if you'd rather have that."

"Of course a sweet southern girl like you would bring up tea." He grinned before leaning toward her and tucking an errant strand of hair behind her ear. "Damn, you're pretty."

She couldn't stop her heart from galloping at his words. "I might have meant Long Island iced tea, you know."

"Pardon my presumptuousness," he said, tugging the strand of hair. His eyes dropped to her lips, and she could see in the chocolate depths of his gaze that he wanted to kiss her. And God help her, she wanted that more than she wanted anything at that moment. Except maybe world peace. She could bear the sacrifice for world peace only. Everything else was off the table.

"Sal," a man called from the back of the restaurant. In the shadows beyond Sal's shoulder Rosemary saw Frances Anne wrapping silverware and vague figures moving around the kitchen. The sound of clinking glasses and the rich scent of Italian red sauce filled the air. "You gotta tend the sauce."

"Oh damn." Sal slapped his hands together. "I gotta go, but I'll call you later. Okay?"

"Okay."

He started toward the back, jabbing a finger. "Don't go finding anything better to do than me."

She laughed. "Is that an offer?"

"You better believe it is," he said, teeth flashing a grin as someone yelled his name again. He hollered back, "Hey, I'm coming!"

"Is that an offer, too?" Rosemary called.

Sal stopped, put a hand over his heart, and closed his eyes. "Ah, a girl after my own heart."

And then he gave her a devilish smile before ducking into the kitchen, leaving her with only a nosy, disapproving sister who stared at Rosemary with a wrinkly V between her eyes.

Lord love a duck, Rosemary had pretty much propositioned Sal in front of his sister . . . after the woman had implied she was a slut. So much for vellum and monograms. She'd gone from a polite thank-you note with an invitation for coffee straight to orgasm. But that's what this man did to her—he unwrapped the person she'd always been beneath the Ralph Lauren dresses and subdued makeup. Sal brought out the saucy Rosemary she'd been before she'd moved back home from college. The woman she'd always wanted to be but never allowed herself.

And why was that?

Because she couldn't be herself in Morning Glory? Perhaps when she returned after college and opened her shop, it had been easier to be what everyone expected her to be . . . what her mother had expected her to be. With Patsy shadowing her every move, she'd accepted the fact she'd wear tasteful clothing, shop at certain places, always write a thank-you note, and chair important events. She'd never smoke, get a tattoo, drink before five o'clock, or date a man who didn't have a good family name. The only rebellion Rosemary had shown since moving back to Morning Glory was clinging to her friends, a few of whom Patsy did not approve.

Obviously when she packed for NYC, she'd found her long-lost courage and zest for being bold hidden in the liner of her suitcase.

So Rosemary was seizing the effing day like a boss. Yeah, she said *like a boss*, a phrase she'd never, ever used before. All these firsts put a spring in her step. "I'll let myself out," Rosemary called to Sal's sister, enjoying the double entendre.

Frances Anne merely nodded, still looking cranky. Rosemary had no clue why Frances Anne acted disapproving. Maybe Italian families were like that, though she'd put her own French Creole/Scottish/Cherokee family up against anyone on the protective spectrum. No one could beat Patsy Reynolds when it came to being a mama bear.

No one.

Ever.

Rosemary pushed out the door into the late-morning sunshine. Around her the city moved like a breathing thing, well-oiled and on schedule. Traffic lights blinked, people strode with purpose, and doors opened and closed like the ticking of a clock. Gone were words like *mosey* and *lollygag*. Absent were the lazy stroll and daydream. Mississippi seemed fathoms upon fathoms away.

She slid on a pair of sunglasses that covered half her face and started walking toward Midtown.

Today she'd be a tourist.

And tonight she'd be Sal's girl.

Chapter Seven

Sal stared at Angelina.

She stared back.

It was a stare-off of epic proportions with his life hanging in the balance.

Okay, so his life wasn't really hanging in the balance. More like one more toe into a pool he didn't wish to swim in. Or maybe he felt more like he stood on a precipice, balancing on uncertainty, ground shifting beneath him.

And right now he wasn't letting go so he could jump toward Angelina.

No frickin' way.

Not yet.

So he stood, toes gripping hard, refusing to tip forward.

Finally, Angelina tossed her dark hair over a shoulder and sighed. "Why not?"

"Because I'm not interested."

"Who's not interested in Maroon 5? That's sacrilege." She pouted pretty lips and crossed her thin arms.

"Color me sacrilegious."

"But I already asked your father if you could have the day off," she said, running a long polished nail along the edge of the bar. Around them the early dinner crowd chatted, glasses clinked, gray heads bobbed. A few young guys, shirtsleeves rolled after a long day, analyzed Yankees stats at the other end of the bar.

"I'm sorry, Angelina. I'm not interested in going to the concert with you, but I appreciate you inviting me first," he said, wiping his hands on a bar towel while checking out his watch. Nearly five thirty. His shift had ended an hour ago, and he champed at the bit to get out the door. Rosemary said she'd meet him at the Empire State Building at six o'clock. But first he had to get rid of Angelina.

"How do you know you were first?" Angelina quipped.

Sal shrugged. "Guess I don't."

"Of course you were first," she said, brushing his arm with her long nails. She cast a look at the Wall Street guys, noting their interest. "Your mother said you liked them. I paid a lot for the tickets."

"See, that's the problem. You're relying on my mother. She wouldn't know Adam Levine if he walked up and kissed her on the mouth."

"Well, I sure the hell would," she laughed, with another slide of her eyes toward the guys watching her. "You know, I'd know what you liked more if you would open up. I thought we had something, you know?"

"Look, Angelina, you know I have a lot of respect for you and the friendship between our families, but I'm not sure you got the right idea."

"What idea did I not get when your tongue was down my throat? Don't act like you didn't like it. I know what a turned-on guy feels like, Sal."

"I'm a guy and you're a beautiful woman, but this isn't about attraction, Angie."

Her brow lowered and her mouth flattened. "What is it then?"

He didn't know. Wasn't like he could tell her about Rosemary, because Rosemary wasn't going to be around next week. Or maybe she was. He wasn't sure. But he knew Rosemary was temporary. Would there be another girl like her down the road? Or was this a onetime ships-passing-in-the-night sort of thing? After Rosemary left and he faced his inevitable future, he might find Angelina to be part of it. Maybe when he signed the contract his father had attorneys drawing up regarding Mama Mello's deli, he'd succumb to Angelina, too. Just marry her, go to work every day, and accept his lot in life. Go the easy way. "How about we work on being friends?"

"Are you joking?" her voice rose. A few diners paused mid-bite and craned their heads.

"Shh," he said, pressing his hands in the air.

"Don't you shush me, Salvatore Genovese. I've been doing all the work here and you've been leading me on a merry chase, but I'm getting sick and tired of running after you," she said, folding her arms across generous breasts he happened to know she still made payments on.

"Look, Angie, I'm not leading you anywhere. I'm trying to be up front with you. I'm not sure we're in the same place."

Her dark eyes flashed hot enough to melt paint off the walls before she blinked it away, donning a smile. Then she lifted a finger to his chin and tipped it up. "We'll see about that, Sal. There's one thing I always get, and that's the man I want. I know who you are and what you need. And your family wants what I want—a man who'll grow up and stop playing at being a petulant boy."

She dropped her finger and stepped around him, following the bar down to the three suits who had eyed her earlier. Sliding onto a stool, she tossed back her long hair. "So what's a girl gotta do to get a drink around here?"

"Look as good as you," one of the men said, smiling like an alligator as he slid onto the stool next to her.

Angelina tossed Sal a triumphant look. "Well, I suppose I'm going to get that drink, aren't I?" She turned her attention back to the businessman, leaning forward so he received a view to her belly button before trailing her fingers along his wrist, tapping the expensive-looking watch. Making her point.

It was a point Sal didn't care about. He had a date with a woman who made him feel like he wasn't a shell of a man.

Saying nothing more to Angelina, he pulled his apron overhead, weaving through the diners, heading to the back. "I'm outta here, Pops," he said to his father, who sat in the office, tapping at a calculator.

"Oh, you got plans or something? I saw your girl out there," his father said, lifting his head and squinting at Sal through his readers.

"She's not my girl, and I don't have plans with her."

His father made a face. "Don't tell me you're still chasing that southern piece of ass?"

"Really, Pop?"

Donnie shrugged. "I'm not saying she's a loose girl, Sally. I'm just saying. What's wrong with Angelina? She's a good girl."

"Oh yeah? Right now your good girl's out there showing those suits from Barney's her tits and angling for free drinks. It's my punishment for not being into her. Thing is, Pop, I don't give a good goddamn what she does, because I'm not ready for that kind of trouble."

"Eh," his father said, shaking his head. "Your sister said something earlier. She's right. That girl you're chasin' in her pearls and fancy purse ain't your speed. You tried that and spent four months moping around acting like you was dying or something. You want things you can't have 'cause you're not made for them. It's that square peg and round hole thing."

"You give me the same ol' song and dance every time, Pop. You should get a record."

"I should, 'cause I can see the painting on the wall."

"You mean the writing," Sal said, shaking his head. He didn't understand why his pop and the rest of his family wanted to trim his wings. This wasn't what a family was supposed to do. They were supposed to cheer you on when you jumped from the nest.

"Whichever. All I know is you are who you are. Just like I was who I was. What's wrong with that?"

Sal didn't want to have this conversation. Again. For his parents, life began and ended in the five boroughs. They never saw life beyond . . . except on television. To them everything outside NYC was a vacation spot, not a place to live. Their sense of belonging to Mama Mello's and the several miles' radius around the restaurant was profound. The thought of any of their kids moving away from their world was beyond them. So telling his pop he didn't feel the same way was banging his head on a cinder block. Nothing moved, and it gave him a helluva headache.

"Nothing. Nothing's wrong with what you believe." And Sal meant that, but he wasn't sure he believed it for himself. "I'm out."

His father waved a tired hand. "Do what you must, Sally. Do what you must."

So he did. Hurrying from the restaurant, Sal jogged to the subway, swiped his MetroCard, and slid into the train just as the doors shut. Ten minutes later he emerged with a crush of people into the blinding late-afternoon sun. Five minutes later he stood on the block of one of the most iconic American landmarks.

He hadn't been in the Empire State Building since his great-aunt Lena had come down from Boston to visit when he was in high school. They'd stood in line to pay what his father considered the price of a kidney to ride the elevator to the viewing deck. He remembered his parents getting into an argument over his pop being so cheap. Aunt Lena had stomped to the counter, plopped down money, and said, "For Christ's sake, Donnie, shut your piehole and get in the damn elevator. I'm too old to wait another forty years to do this."

The incident still lived in the memory of the Genovese children, who loved to mimic their eccentric late aunt who didn't take crap off her grumbly nephew. Big Donnie wasn't too fond of the ribbing, but he'd managed a smile in honor of the woman who'd paid for him to go to business school.

Sal sidestepped a gaggle of tourists holding a map and waved away the man who sold some kind of ride experience at an IMAX and parked himself beside the heavy doors of the building. He waited for nearly ten minutes, watching interesting and not-so-interesting people stroll by.

Then he saw Rosemary.

She looked like a tourist, carrying a brown paper shopping bag, glancing about her as if she'd stepped off a spacecraft onto Mars. She looked down at her phone and then squinted at the street signs. Someone jostled her and she gave an apologetic smile to the creep, who didn't even bother to excuse his rudeness.

Rosemary licked her lips, and then her gaze met his.

Her smile made his heart thump.

Damn. Such power in that smile.

Waving, she moved toward him. The light turned red and she kept coming. His face must have portrayed alarm because she paused. A taxi hurtled across the intersection, and Rosemary leaped back just as the bumper cleared his range of vision.

Her face registered shock and then embarrassment, almost matching the exact shade of pink in her bright dress. Her hand rose to clasp her pearls, a nervous habit he'd noticed. A group of college-age kids next to her noted the near miss. One girl reached out and patted her shoulder, giving her no doubt comforting words. Rosemary's response was something no New Yorker would ever do—she hugged the stranger.

Her actions reminded him how different she was from any other girl he'd ever dated.

Had his dad and sister been right? Was he always chasing a woman he couldn't have, setting himself up for heartbreak as some sort of self-flagellation? And if that was true, why in the hell would he want to do something like that?

The light changed, and Rosemary set her pace to match the crowd's.

"Hey," he said when she reached him. "Glad you're still here. We almost got to play *An Affair to Remember*." He leaned down to kiss her cheek.

"We don't have to worry about cabs in Morning Glory." Fresh roses bloomed in her cheeks. "And you know that movie?"

He shrugged. "I've never watched it. I watched *Sleepless in Seattle*."

"Is that why you chose to meet at the Empire State Building?" she asked, stepping closer to him so the streaming crowd could flow around her.

"Why? You want to be my Meg Ryan?"

Rosemary grinned. "Only if you're my Tom Hanks."

"I'm much better-looking than Tom Hanks," he joked.

"But not nearly as humble," she teased.

"True," he said, tilting his head toward the entrance. "You want to go up and pretend to meet at the top?"

"Yeah," she said, adjusting the bag she carried. "Is it true that if you spit off the building the velocity could make your saliva a weapon and kill someone?"

"I don't know. Let's try it. Look around and pick someone you want to take out," he said, stepping back so she could enter first.

"That can't be true, can it?" she said, laughing.

"No. Some kid made that up. But I thought it was a penny," he said, pulling his wallet from his back pocket.

"You don't have to pay for me," she said, before pointing to the sign that contained the rules for going to the observation deck. "And we aren't allowed to throw anything."

"Darn. I was set on showing off my spitting abilities," he joked, pulling several twenties from his wallet. "And this is my treat. I picked the place."

She gave a lift of her shoulders. "If you insist."

"I do," he said, stepping into a queue. "Looks long."

"I'm game if you are. I have nothing better to do than—"

"Me?" he finished for her.

"You were waiting for that, weren't you?" she said.

"I like to watch you turn red. Besides, it was either that or waiting to use an innuendo when you said you were coming," he said, curling an arm around her waist, enjoying the way she felt beside him. Last night hadn't been an anomaly. The teasing banter and long looks between them made him happy. How long had it been since he'd truly felt happy?

Easy answer—last night.

"You're a dirty boy," she said, laughter in her voice.

"Damn straight. I figured that's why you agreed to go out with me in the first place. Every flower needs dirt."

"You calling me a flower? 'Cause I'm an herb."

He looked down at her. "Huh?"

"Rosemary's an herb. My brother's name is Basil."

He moved them forward. "Your parents sound interesting."

"Not really. My dad has a strange sense of humor. He had a friend who died in Vietnam and insisted they name my brother after him. Then when my mother had my sister, he suggested Sage. Said herb names were trippy—his words, not mine. Now he's just an old goat who putters about the grounds helping my mother with her gardens. They have a huge antebellum home surrounded by heritage roses that daffy old ladies across the South pay to see on church trips."

"People pay to see your parents' house?"

"It's on the historic register. Living in an old house is all I've ever known."

"So, like, there are tours through your house and stuff?"

"Not so much the house as the grounds, though we do serve high tea in the parlor." She waved her hand. "It's an experience type of thing."

An image of the grand old South like he'd seen on Turner Classic Movies paraded through his mind. He saw an older woman in a hoop skirt with Rosemary standing next to her holding a teapot and wearing those damn pearls. "Do you work there, too?"

"Not anymore. When I was in high school, my friends and I gave tours and helped with serving tea. I own my own shop, remember?"

she said, wiggling a finger at a small girl who sucked on her thumb and clung to her mother's bare legs in the line next to them. "That's what these are for." She opened her shopping bag and tugged out a faded pillowcase. Little satin flowers dotted the edge.

"You sell pillowcases?" he asked.

"No, but I use them along with other vintage fabrics to make decorative pillows. I love taking fabrics and trimmings and piecing them together to make something new. Old lace and embroidery are perfect for shabby-chic pieces. There's something so soft and timeless about things from the past," she said, stroking a hand across the pillowcase before tucking it back into her bag. He noticed at that moment how different her hands were from Angelina's. Angie had long fingers with viperous nails, but Rosemary's slender fingers and short, rounded nails seemed elegant.

He imagined Rosemary's hands on him, hesitant but eager. She'd not be as practiced as some women, but she'd be passionate. Like an enigma—untouchable, yet at the same time so approachable. Ageless, timeless . . . beauty and elegance. She was a Rod Stewart song, and he wanted her so much he could hardly stop himself from tossing her over his shoulder and sprinting for the nearest exit.

Instead, he said, "I can see you love what you do."

"That's why I was excited about coming to New York. Y'all have a plethora of vintage thrift shops. I order online, but nothing is better than putting your hands on the fabric and seeing the colors."

They purchased the tickets and waited for the elevator.

"So tell me about your family. Your sister was . . . interesting," Rosemary said, making a silly face at the toddler who'd been flirting with her the entire time they stood in the queue.

"Sorry about her attitude. Frannie is the hard one to deal with," he said.

"Every family has one. Ours is Baz. He's special needs."

Sal didn't want to talk about his family. Or hers. Somehow it poked the bubble of happiness he'd conjured around them. They had a connection and he was unwilling to let it be broken by the reality check of his family. "That's hard, I'm sure, but if it's okay with you, I don't want to talk about my family. They've been difficult lately."

Rosemary nodded. "Preaching to the choir. This little vacation is my break from reality."

He nudged her toward the elevator that opened. "Is that what this is? A break from reality?"

Rosemary stepped into the elevator and held out her hand as if asking him to take a journey with her. "Isn't that what it is for you, too?"

The question seemed rhetorical . . . or more like a statement of what this was between them. This wasn't about building toward something. It was about being in the now.

He took her hand and stepped into the elevator beside her. Others crowded in and the attendant clad in a smart uniform said, "Everyone ready for the experience of a lifetime?"

His gaze met Rosemary's, and something profound moved.

"I'm ready," Rosemary said, her gaze moving toward the cheerful attendant.

"Me, too," Sal said.

The Empire State Building had over a hundred stories, with two observation decks, and Rosemary planned on going to the tip-top, but after ten seconds on the lower observation deck, she decided eighty-six floors was high enough.

The wind blew her hair into her face as she clasped the railing and wagged her head, taking in the sight of half of Manhattan laid out below her. Sal placed a hand on the small of her back, making her feel both protected and excited at the same time. "Look over there."

She followed the line of his finger with her gaze.

"Brooklyn. See, there's the Brooklyn Bridge."

"Oh, I've seen it in so many movies," she said, noting it seemed so romantic . . . even from hundreds of feet in the air. "Where's Central Park?"

He tugged her elbow and took her to the other side.

"I always wanted to ride in one of those carriages," she said, smiling at the huge green space in the middle of the concrete jungle.

"Then we'll do it," he said.

Rosemary couldn't believe she stood here at the top of the world with a sexy man promising to take her on a carriage ride. She almost pinched herself but decided she'd forgo looking like a fruit loop.

A week ago she'd feared going to the city alone. She'd begged Eden to take a much-needed vacation and come up for at least a few days, but with her mother being ill and having taken off a week when Lacy passed away, she couldn't get away. Jess's finances were stretched after the divorce, and she was in the middle of looking for a better job. She'd contemplated asking her older next-door neighbor, Mimi, but knew it would be a burr under her mother's saddle. Yet, today, she'd had a wonderful time alone.

Alone.

Not something Rosemary was unaccustomed to being. Even though she lived in the carriage house in back of her parents' estate, she was seldom by herself. Her parents' plantation home was a busy place nearly every month of the year thanks to her mother's creative horticulture displays and themed teas. And when people weren't poking about the grounds of Meadowlark, her parents had a constant influx of neighbors and friends who came for coffee, cocktails, and gossip. Not to mention her fabric shop was situated on Morning Glory's town square, which meant a constant coming and going of friends, relatives, and customers.

So wandering around Manhattan, poking into small shops and riffling through thrift stores had been exactly what she needed. No one poked his nose into her business suggesting she eat lunch because it wasn't good for her to go so long without food. No one suggested she buy shoes that were sensible. No one pointed out the right way to fold a pair of pants when she'd tried some on at a boutique. Her mother's nagging voice had faded away under the bustle now sprawled out beneath her feet.

"I had forgotten how cool it was to see the city this way," Sal said, his hand stroking her back ever so lightly.

"It's almost too much to take in," she said, noting the way the fading sun turned everything a softer gold.

She felt his whiskers catch her hair and so she turned to him.

People moved all around them, laughing, pointing, complaining about someone taking too long at the binocular things that dotted the perimeter. Yet it all went away when she looked up at Sal.

His thick hair rippled at the tips like grasses waving in a pasture, which was a not-so-romantic image, but dang if the man didn't make her heart go thumpety-thump and her palms itch to run her fingers through those inky locks. And his mouth. Oh man, was it a study in sensuality. Dramatic arch on the top and just a hint of plumpness on the lower. His jaw was angular and a small crevice graced his chin. Total bedroom eyes beneath dark slashing eyebrows. If he had been wearing a white linen shirt, a riding coat, and breeches, she might have thought him her own Mr. Darcy. As it was, she'd take him for her own Sal Genovese.

At that moment he was looking at her lips like a starving man eyes a T-bone steak. Again, not romantic. But true. Totally true.

"You're so pretty, Rosemary."

"And you have such pretty words," she said, her voice growing soft. She lifted her hand to touch his white shirt, to draw a finger along the seam at his shoulder, to feel the warmth of him.

"Only the truth," he said, tilting her chin to redirect her attention back to his gaze.

Then he kissed her.

If kisses were food, this one would be a slice of Italian cream cake—sweet, substantial, and layered with promise.

She let her lips soften against his and kept her eyes open, because she wanted to recall this moment for the rest of her life. The way she felt atop the iconic building, kissing a man who made her heart drum, her toes curl in her sandals, and her stomach flood with warmth. If ever a moment needed capturing, it was this one.

Sal broke the kiss and said, "Wow."

Rosemary giggled.

"What?" he asked, smiling at her.

"I had been trying to think of a word to describe how I felt this very moment and I think 'wow' is really the only way."

"Yeah, that's all I had, too," he said, stepping back, keeping his arm curled around her waist.

Sliding her hand underneath, she wrapped her arm around his waist so they stood facing the northeast, the glow of the sinking sun warm on their shoulders. With her hair tickling her shoulders, Sal's warm presence beside her, and a new world spread before her, the moment stilled. Life rarely slowed down enough for a person to think, *This is the stuff that makes life worthwhile*, but at that precise second, Rosemary knew the profundity of being right where she was.

"Excuse me, ma'am," someone said.

Rosemary turned to find a harried-looking woman clutching the hand of a boy. "Yes?"

"Would you mind taking a picture of us?" The woman held out a phone.

Moment over.

"Sure," Rosemary said, taking the phone from her and stepping back. Sal didn't seem to want to let go, but he did.

"Thank you so much," the woman said, tugging her kid to her and demanding that he "smile big." The boy managed a cheesy grin, and Rosemary clicked several for them.

The woman took the phone, tapping to make sure the pics were good enough, and then said, "I'll be happy to take one for you."

Rosemary glanced at Sal.

"Sure," he said, digging his phone out of his back pocket.

He and Rosemary angled so the city lay behind them. He wrapped his arm around her and they tilted their heads together. Right when the woman took the pic, Sal looked down at her, grinning like a naughty boy. She jabbed him in the ribs, and he straightened for the second one, giving the camera his smile.

"Wow, y'all are a gorgeous couple," the woman said, handing the phone back to Sal.

"Oh, she's my sister," Sal said, pointing to Rosemary.

The woman's eyes popped. "But I saw you kissing."

"We're from Mississippi," Sal said, looking dead serious.

Rosemary pinched him.

"Yeow," he yipped, twisting away, laughing like a lunatic.

Rosemary looked at the woman. "He's joking. I'm from Mississippi, where we *do not* kiss our siblings like that." She gave Sal a withering look, her lips twitching despite her fussing.

The woman laughed; the kid stuck his tongue out. "Well, thanks for the picture. Come on, Joshua. Are you sticking your tongue out? Cut that out. You know . . ." She wandered away, sounding like every mother of an eight-year-old boy, and Rosemary turned to Sal, crossing her arms. "Very funny."

"I thought so." He grinned and pulled her back into his arms, dropping a kiss on her nose. "Let's go grab some grub, southern belle. I'm starving."

"I'm not a southern belle," she protested.

"Oh, baby, you are, and let me just say, I totally dig it." He lifted her pearls and then pressed a soft kiss against her lips. "I'm seriously digging it. Never knew I had a thing for *y'all.*"

Chapter Eight

Sal took her to one of his favorite places in the Flatiron District. Eataly was one of those hybrid places that was both marketplace and restaurant, serving products both from Italy and from the farms surrounding the city. The food was fresh, creative, and a bit trendy for his tastes, but fantastic. He purchased some of his favorite olive oils here, and the Italian coffee was the best in the city.

"Oh my gosh, I love this place," Rosemary said, dipping her focaccia into the red pepper oil before plucking another piece of prosciutto from his plate. "It's so modern and traditional at the same time."

"I knew you'd like it. And they have a bottle shop around the corner. We can grab some wine for later."

She hooked an eyebrow, popping the last of the bread into her mouth. True to form, she'd skipped the salads in favor of the meats and cheeses, further proof she was absolutely what he looked for in a woman. "Where are we going later?"

He wanted to say, "Back to your place," but she might not be ready for that. Still, the knowledge Rosemary would only be in Manhattan for another two weeks knocked on the door of his mind. If they both wanted each other, which he assumed they did, they'd have to settle for a microwave relationship rather than the oven.

A crappy way to start.

But better than not starting at all. He wasn't willing to walk away from her at this point. Despite the misgivings expressed by those closest to him, despite the fact he and Rosemary were worlds apart, he couldn't run from the way she made him feel. Like an addict, he edged ever closer to that feeling he'd vowed never to chase again. When he'd jumped into love with Hillary, he'd not looked to see where he might land. Recovering from the ensuing splat had made him cautious, but apparently not nearly careful enough. Because the way he felt with Rosemary made him scared, excited, and free all at the same time. "We can go wherever you want. Carriage ride, stroll, drinks, dancing. Name it, Rosemary."

She picked up the wine he'd suggested. The pinot grigio was slightly sweeter than the dry he preferred but it had a soft finish. Rosemary had smiled her approval when she tasted it. He'd be damned if she ordered sweet tea to pair with the house-made mozzarella served here. Not that he was controlling or anything. Just some things were meant to be done right. "I want to see as much of the city as I can, but honestly, my feet are tired, and I'd love to go somewhere where we can sip wine and talk."

"There's a great lounge in this area, which has the twenties art deco feel and old-fashioned cocktails. We can—"

"What about my place? I mean, my cousin's place?" Rosemary asked.

Something inside surged at the thought but he played it cool. "You sure you don't want to try the Flatiron Lounge? It's upscale but we—"

"You don't want to go back to the loft?" She licked her lips nervously. And it struck him.

She wasn't asking him back so much for drinks as for drinks and something else. But was his sweet small town girl ready to get down and dirty in the city? "You sure?"

"Unless you don't want me that way?" She looked surprised at herself for asking . . . but not regretful.

"Are you fucking kidding me? I've wanted you since I first laid eyes on you," he said.

And of course her cheeks bloomed. "Okay, but I've been thinking all day about something."

He quirked an eyebrow.

"Well, we both said we were looking for something to pull us away from reality for a little while. So I suggest for the next two weeks, we do that. We go where whatever this is between us goes, but when I leave, we're over."

"Like a clean break?"

She nodded. "We're from two different worlds. I'm going home to Mississippi, and your life is here. It will be like summer camp or something. You know—good, sweet, and temporary."

"You have a contract or something I have to sign?"

Rosemary gave a nervous giggle, but he liked that she wanted parameters. She liked things nice and neat. Probably made her comfortable. "We can call it a verbal agreement. A two-week love affair, mutually beneficial for both parties. We can shake on it." She put out her hand.

"Hell, no," he said, leaning forward. "We kiss on it."

He kissed her, tasting the saltiness of the prosciutto mixed with the sweet grapefruit of the wine. Then he slid off the brushed metal stool parked at the stand-up counter table they'd claimed in the busy restaurant. The white marble and gold art deco surroundings paired with the contemporary metal and large, round lampshade chandeliers made a statement . . . almost as strong as the one Rosemary had made when she had invited him back to her cousin's place. "Let's go."

"What about dessert?" she asked, a twinkle in those gray eyes.

"We'll grab some chocolates at the pastry bar to have with the wine." He glanced over to where decadent chocolates and other confections could be purchased.

Rosemary stood and drained the wine left in her glass. "Sounds perfect."

Fifteen minutes after sampling hazelnut candies and debating wines, they headed to SoHo, snagging the subway since they were now in a hurry. Seeing the metro through her wide eyes was actually cool. When people moved through the car, she studied them, her body language betraying her anxiety.

"Do you think someone's going to mug you or something?" he leaned over and whispered in her ear.

She gave a nervous laugh. "You cannot imagine how many guidelines my mother sent me on safety in New York City. She even clipped articles and taped them to the fridge."

"Seriously?"

"She has issues," Rosemary said, leaning against him but keeping her arm hooked through her shopping bag. He inhaled the scent of her hair. It smelled like something he couldn't place, but he'd be happy to be buried in. "It's not really her fault, though."

"What do you mean?" he asked.

"Remember I told you how my brother is special needs? Well, there were complications during birth that caused developmental issues." Rosemary quieted, her fingers knotting together. "And a few years later my sister, Sage, circumnavigated the childproof lock on the back door and ended up in the swimming pool. She drowned. Both were accidents that my parents had no control over and happened before I came along, but those tragedies molded them into super overprotective parents." Those words given so matter-of-factly, as if she'd said them a hundred times, but the fingers she twisted, the slight edge in her voice, told him her childhood had not been easy.

"Whoa, that's really heavy," he said, hating that the mood had shifted to something serious but now understanding Rosemary's situation better. "I'm so sorry about your sister."

"Thank you, and I wouldn't bring it up other than I've spent my whole life being the thing my mother had to control so nothing bad would happen to me. Just some context. Not trying to ruin the mood."

Sal shook his head at the pain Rosemary's parents had endured. Now he understood why Rosemary seemed cautious and hyperaware of situations. The woman had been smothered her entire life.

And like the proverbial penny dropped from the top of the Empire State Building, something struck him.

Was Rosemary a virgin?

He couldn't imagine a woman in this day and age being . . .

"How old are you?" he asked.

"Twenty-seven. I'll turn twenty-eight in November. How old are you?"

"Thirty."

"When's your birthday?"

"March ninth."

"I'm not a virgin," she said.

He jerked his gaze back to hers. "I didn't—"

"But you were thinking it. I could totally see it in your whole demeanor," Rosemary said, her hand stroking his thigh in a nonsexual way. But it still revved him, reminding him how much he still wanted to get her naked.

"That talk about your mother's apron strings made me a little nervous. I imagined you locked in your room or something."

Rosemary smiled. "She's not that bad. Well, she can be. She's like a bull terrier, latching on and shaking until you go limp. But I manage to pry those teeth apart sometimes. Like now."

"What do you mean?" he asked.

"Mama was against me going away to college, against me moving in with a male roommate even though it was totally platonic, and she was emphatically against me coming to New York City alone. Her tight grip on me has been the biggest obstacle in our relationship since I went through puberty." Rosemary brushed her hair back and sighed. "I love my mother, but sometimes I need to be away from her. And that's why I'm here."

He pulled her to him, dropping a kiss on her temple. "Odd that both of us are running from our families."

Rosemary turned, her eyes questioning. "You, too?"

Might as well be honest about what he had been facing for the last six months. "My pop's pushing me to run the deli he's opening in the theater district, and my ma's breathing down my neck about getting married. Parading good Italian girls in front of me."

"Married? Like she wants to pick out your wife?"

"Natalie Genovese is an Italian mother who gives the Jewish ones a run for their money. She wants all of us paired up and popping out babies for her to feed *pan di Spagna* to. My family seems to think they know what is best for me."

Rosemary picked up his hand and stroked it. "Is that why your sister acted the way she did? She thinks I'm a road bump or something."

He curled his hand around hers and tugged her up. Their stop approached and he didn't want to talk about the reality they were avoiding. Their families didn't matter. At least not at that moment. "You're the sexiest damn road bump I've ever seen."

"Never been called a sexy road bump before, but I'll take it," she said, leaning up to brush a kiss across his jaw.

The doors swooshed open and they spilled from the car, hurrying up the steps into the warm June night. They held hands like two teenagers in love, years falling away the way they do when something feels so good, so right . . . so perfectly designed in the stars.

"Which way?" she asked, her breath coming faster from her jog up the stairs.

"What street again?"

"Spring."

"You realize Spring runs through lots of neighborhoods?" he said, spinning her around and pulling her into a kiss. The bag she held bumped his leg making the wine clink against the side of the building he pressed her to. He kissed her until they were both breathless.

"Uh, what were we talking about?" she asked, her eyes hazy, her breathing ragged.

"I don't remember," he said, kissing her again before grabbing her hand and walking toward the intersection. "I think it's something to do with getting back to your place before we start leaving our clothes all over SoHo."

She gave him the address.

"How did you manage to get to Little Italy the other day? Your cousin's place is eight blocks away," he asked.

"I asked a man who didn't speak English very well for directions."

Sal couldn't help it. He started laughing.

"What? My town has only six thousand people living in it. We know where everything is."

He looked over at her as they jogged to make the light. Her hair bounced on her shoulders, a bit frizzy from the humidity rolling in with the night air. Her light makeup had long since worn off, making her look even younger. He thought about her embroidered pillows and the way she only drank sweet wine . . . oh, and tea. She made him ache for her. "You're killing me, Rosemary."

"Why? 'Cause I'm a goober?" she laughed.

"Because you're freakin' incredible. Because you make me feel like I'm a teenager again. It's crazy."

She stopped walking, suddenly sober. "It is. Totally crazy, but I've never wanted to do crazy more." Her eyes glittered beneath the streetlights.

Sal paused beside her. Nothing like refreshing honesty. It's what had attracted him in the first place. It's what made him more determined than ever to take the moments he had with her. "I know the verbal agreement back there sounded good, but can we handle this?" Not you, but *we*. Because moments ago he'd stopped sliding toward complacency and embraced something that could be dangerous, something that dragged his heart along for the ride.

He gave himself a mental shake. No, he wouldn't risk his heart again. That was why they needed the agreement. At the end of two weeks, Rosemary would go back to her world and he'd be stuck in his.

This woman, a beauty who'd wholly captured him, turned, her features softened by the darkness. "If we walk away from each other right now, we might miss two weeks of something wonderful. I don't want to give that up because I'm scared of . . . you know."

He knew. The big *L* word.

"But we know this going in, right?" he asked, begging his mind to take a memo, because he tilted dangerously close to going in that direction. He'd been there. Knew all the signs. The euphoria, the horniness, the invincibility.

Treacherous waters to tread.

He didn't want to believe his sister was right—that he had a type—but he couldn't deny he'd gone as eagerly to Hillary. And that crash and burn had rendered him heartbroken for a good couple of months. His ego had been pancaked, his confidence shaken. So if Rosemary said it was only a two-week love affair, he would guard his heart.

"Right. That's why I brought it up earlier," she said, reaching up to stroke his cheek. "I don't want to do the safe thing, Sal. I've spent my whole life going the speed limit, wearing my seat belt, sticking to the safest route. I need these two weeks to be . . . off-road. I need thrilling daredevilry and adventure. I promised someone I loved that I would live big because she couldn't. Help me live big."

He looked deep into those pretty eyes and saw the need there. Slowly she rose on her tiptoes and kissed him.

It wasn't sweet the way he'd expected from her.

No, her kiss mimicked her words. Open, hot, and determined.

And when the tip of her tongue traced his bottom lip and then she nipped it with her teeth, his mind felt officially blown.

"Oh, Rosemary," he breathed.

"That's right," she said with a smile. Taking his hand, she pulled him toward the next block, which housed her cousin's place. She wasn't taking no for an answer.

They didn't talk as they walked, hands joined, convicted in conducting their own affair to remember. Perhaps it was selfish, reckless, and stupid, but Sal didn't care. Not when gratification was so close.

Rosemary dug a key from the small bag she'd looped over her shoulder and unlocked the door. When they stepped inside the apartment building foyer, she pulled the door shut, making sure it clicked. Then she double-checked it . . . which made him smile. No doubt another bit of paranoia given her by her mother. The neighbors would definitely appreciate such conscientiousness.

"Hate to tell you, but it's on the top floor," she said, looking up the stairwell.

"Then we'll have to reward ourselves after each flight."

She smiled wickedly. "What did you have in mind?"

He kissed her, sliding a hand up the back of her thigh. "You'll find out on the second floor." Then he turned and jogged up the first set of stairs before ducking his head under the floor and grinning at her.

He heard the slap of her sandals fast behind him.

Rosemary had never had more fun going up stairs before in her life. Sal decided an article of clothing had to come off on each landing.

"I'm not taking my sandals off. The floor doesn't look clean," she said after he announced the kinky little game.

"As if I were interested in the sandals coming off," he said, leering at her.

"But I'm not wearing anything else but my dress, undies, and bra. That's only three things, and if you think I'm getting totally naked on the fourth floor, you're nuts. I've seen the guy who lives in 4C. He probably doesn't need much encouragement to join in."

Sal kissed her and then started unbuttoning his shirt. "We'll take turns. I'll go first."

"Okay." She ran a hand over the undershirt that appeared when shrugged off the white oxford button-down. She could feel how flat his stomach was and there were small ridges that screamed *I work out*. And then there was the tattoo on his left shoulder—a cross and some other things she didn't have time to contemplate. Sweet niblets, he was going to burn her corneas when he pulled that undershirt off.

"Third floor," he called out, tossing the shirt over his arm as he jogged up the next flight.

Rosemary squeaked and followed him, reveling in the euphoric feeling of being young, crazy, and . . . well, not in love. But she felt something she'd not felt since she'd drunk too much jungle juice and participated in wet T-shirt contest on Panama Beach her freshman year of college.

He caught her as she came off the last step, wrapping her in his arms, nibbling a path up her neck. His breath was hot and her stomach flopped over as his hands slid up the back of her thighs again. "Your turn."

Rosemary stepped back and stuck her purse in the bag she carried. Through her dress, she unhooked her bra. Quick as a cat, she wriggled and pulled her arm through the sleeve the way she'd done changing into her dance costumes as a girl. The bra dropped on one side and then she pulled it out of her corresponding sleeve like it was a magic trick. "Ta-da!"

Sal frowned. "Wait a minute. I didn't get to see anything."

"Fourth floor," she said, slapping him lightly with her lacy bra and jogging up the next flight. She tucked the bra inside the shopping bag, glad she'd gone to Victoria's Secret before coming to NYC. Her old bras weren't nearly as pretty or as polka-dotted.

"Vixen," he called, making her smile.

Her breath came faster now. Not from jogging stairs, but from being completely turned on. She *was* a vixen, a naughty seductress ready to toss out good sense for a shot at the sort of man she would never forget. Ever.

She turned and waited. Of course she didn't have to wait long. Like last time, he swept her into his arms, his hand cupping her breast through the material. "If I can't see, I'll touch."

"Oh," she said, her mouth falling open. Sal took advantage, giving her a punishing kiss. Her blood sang, her body hungered, and she felt daring. Oh, so daring.

Pulling back, she plucked at the hem of his undershirt. "Off."

Sal gave a throaty laugh. "Demanding, aren't you?"

Her hands move to his waistband, sliding underneath the undershirt, stroking his firm belly. His stomach contracted and he ground his pelvis against hers, letting her know how much he wanted her. The hardness against her softness ratcheted the desire level up a notch. "Yes, now I need this off you. Play fair."

Sal grabbed the hem and wrenched it overhead to reveal a drool-worthy set of abs and span of chest. Dark hair gathered between his pecs, trailing deliciously downward. He made his pecs dance. "You likey?"

Rosemary gave a light laugh and then ran a hand across his chest, then trailed her finger down to the clasp of his black pants. He had a tattoo of an eagle covering part of his chest; a ribbon with some words curled down his biceps and forearm. The bird looked as fierce as she felt. "I would say that's a yes."

He kissed her hard, then swooped down, snagging his shirts and tossing them over his bared shoulder. He had another tattoo on his back. She'd never thought tattoos were all that sexy. She'd been so wrong. "Follow me to the finish line."

And he ran up the last set of stairs.

Rosemary followed, pausing five steps from the top. She waited for him to notice she wasn't right behind him, then she set her shopping bag on the step next to her.

"What are you doing?" he asked, his gaze devilish.

Rosemary hiked her dress to the top of her thighs and reached under to snag the waistband of her thong panties. "Getting more comfortable."

"You haven't made it to the top yet," he said, his gaze sliding down, watching as she shimmied the turquoise lace down her thighs.

"You complaining?" she asked, stepping out of them.

"Only about the fact you're out of reach right now," he said with a laugh.

He looked so damn fine standing atop those steps, shirts thrown over his broad shoulders, bare skin beckoning for her touch, his smile an encouragement.

She stood and twirled her panties around her finger. She was outrageous at that moment. She hadn't won second prize in that wet T-shirt contest for nothing.

"Such a tease," he said.

Rosemary made a slingshot out of her panties and launched them toward him. He reached up to grab them but missed. They hit the door to the loft and fell harmlessly to the floor. She laughed and jogged up the remaining steps to his waiting arms.

Sal pulled her to him, kissing her along her jaw, peppering her face with silly kisses as his hands started at her thighs and moved up. "Let's see what you unwrapped for me," he teased.

She wriggled away, slapping at his hands. "Now wait just a minute, mister. We're out here in the hallway and I'm not the kind of girl who lets a man put his hands just anywhere on her body."

"So you're saying there are places I can touch and places I can't touch?"

She didn't know what had gotten into her. Wasn't the wine. She'd had only one and a half glasses. Like that tattoo, she was bold, free, doing what she damned well pleased in this city teeming with so many people she didn't have to worry about anyone knowing just how naughty Rosemary Marie Reynolds was. "You seem to like games. Maybe we'll play—"

"No," he interrupted. "I'm going to touch every inch of your delectable body." She tilted her head and pretended to think about it. "Hmm. Every inch?"

He nodded, his dark eyes intense.

Rosemary smiled. "Well, okay."

Then she launched herself at him again, wrapping her arms about his neck, not even caring her new panties lay on the scuffed tile outside her cousin's door. She had better things to do.

Sal turned her, pinning her to the wall next to the loft door. His lips moved hungrily over hers and his hands weren't idle, stroking down her sides, grazing the sides of her breasts before meandering down to tease her thighs. Rosemary wrapped her arms around him, kissing him with every ounce of desire she had, giving back what he gave, tongue meeting tongue, teeth nipping, as desire spun out of control.

No more teasing. No more games.

Like an uppercut from a prize fighter, need belted her. Long-forgotten warmth uncurled in her stomach, sinking into her pelvis and coating her with deliciousness.

"Mmm," she groaned, tilting her head as his mouth moved down the column of her neck. "You're driving me crazy."

"Good," he said, one hand rising to cup her breast through the material. His thumb brushed over the hardened nipple, strumming her, making liquid heat flood her again.

"Oh, that's nice," she groaned, arching her back, offering herself to him.

Vaguely in the back recesses of her mind she felt the door beside her open. Desire had her in its grip, but still the squeak, the rush of air, the concept of a presence registered.

"Rosemary Marie!"

She froze. Then pushed Sal back.

Turning, she registered two things at once—the pink rollers and her turquoise undies dangling from fingertips.

"Mama?"

Chapter Nine

Standing in a SoHo hallway sans panties and bra with her mother looking at her like she'd lost her mind was so not the way her evening was supposed to end.

"What are you doing here?" Rosemary asked, scurrying so Sal stood behind her. She gaped at the older woman framed in the doorway of her cousin's loft. Her mother wore metallic Daniel Green slippers and held Rosemary's panties between the thumb and finger. They dangled like a surrender flag . . . only turquoise with lace.

"Obviously I'm saving you from a horrible decision," her mother said, closing the gap in the fluffy pink robe Rosemary had given her for Christmas two years ago. It matched the pink foam rollers perfectly.

Her mother's gaze flicked to Sal, who stood bare chested, looking like a kid who'd been caught flipping through a dirty magazine. She lifted both eyebrows. "I'm assuming this is your new . . . friend?"

Her mother hadn't dropped the undies, so Rosemary snatched them from her fingertips, looking around for her bag before realizing she'd left it on the steps. Crazy desire made people do things like that. No doubt shopping bags sat orphaned all over the world because making out with a hot guy took precedence over a new blouse or a bottle of peach body lotion. Or maybe that was just Rosemary. After all, she'd suffered a drought of sexy men for the past five years. Unless one counted the sheriff's son Teddy Grantham as a drink of water. Which many did not.

Sal swallowed, blinked, and then looked from Rosemary back to Patsy. "Uh, is this your *mother*?"

Rosemary turned to Patsy Reynolds and asked again, "What are you doing here?"

"I was worried about you up here alone. Thought I'd come give you some needed company," Patsy said, arching an eyebrow she'd had tattooed on in a Jackson salon. She dared Rosemary to deny her words.

"Well, you thought wrong," Rosemary said, doing just that as the shock of her mother standing in the loft doorway dissipated. Outrage replaced it. "When did you get here? Wait, how did you get inside?"

"I flew on an airplane," her mother said, giving Rosemary the same look she'd given her when her dog Pretzel had dug up the prized rose in the west garden. Needless to say, her dachshund had found a new home down the street within the week. "As to getting inside, you did not answer the many calls I made to your cell phone, which forced me to phone your cousin, waking her. She called the building superintendent, and he let me inside."

Rosemary's thoughts grappled, trying to gain a foothold, to cling to reason and make sense of what had just happened to disrupt making love with Sal. Her mother stood there in a bathrobe. She'd come to New York City. She wasn't a figment of Rosemary's imagination. Her mother was real. Her emotions unwound like a reel of old film pooling onto the floor.

For a few seconds no one said anything.

Finally, Sal said, "I should probably go."

Good thinking. Wasn't like they could ask Patsy to stand in the hall while they got busy in the loft. Night over.

Regret prickled in her gut, fueling hot anger. "I'm so sorry about this, Sal. I had no idea."

His brown eyes looked soft with understanding. "Me, too. I'll talk to you later, okay?"

"Yes. I'll call you." She reached out and touched his forearm. "Thank you. I had a great time tonight."

Her mother looked like someone had given her a lemon to suck. "Nice to have met you, Mister . . . ?"

"Genovese. Sal Genovese," he said, stepping away. "I'll leave you two to . . . catch up." Then he started down the stairs, pausing on the fifth one to lift the bag she'd forgotten. Her polka-dotted bra hung drunkenly over the side. He didn't say a word as he turned and handed it up to her.

Rosemary met him halfway and mouthed, "I'm sorry."

He stepped up and kissed her. Hard. Like he meant it. "Later."

She pressed a hand to her mouth as she watched him jog down the steps. He glanced up at her when he turned the corner and she waved. Then she turned back to her mother.

"Really, Rosemary?" her mother said, eyeing the dangling bra. "This is exactly why I didn't think it a good idea for you to come here alone. You've always had self-control issues."

"Are you joking?" Rosemary said, stooping to pick up the bag Sal had been carrying. The bottle of wine sat inside, looking lonely. They'd had such plans for it and the chocolates nestled at its side.

"I am most certainly not. What nearly happened here is proof enough you shouldn't be left unsupervised." Her mother stepped back so Rosemary could pass through the doorway.

Rosemary set the package on the bar and turned to study her mother as she dead-bolted the door. "I don't want you here."

Patsy Reynolds wasn't a woman who cared what her daughter wanted. And that was the true problem. "I'm sorry you feel that way. I came to keep you company."

"I don't want company."

Her mother arched an eyebrow.

"I don't want *your* company." Rosemary felt something inside her break loose. She was done with her mother running roughshod over her. For years she'd let things slide. She'd convinced herself Patsy meant well. That it was easier to overlook her interference. But no more. "I didn't want you to come with me for a reason, Mother. I need to be away from you."

The hurt in her mother's eyes allowed guilt to rear its sneaky head. But Rosemary stamped it down quickly. Her entire life had been lived this way—her wants and dreams sidelined by her mother's insistence of what was appropriate. The whole fact she'd allowed her mother to manipulate her for so long embarrassed her. She should have put a stop to this long ago. Why had she lived this way? So resigned.

Lacy had been right.

Patsy drew herself up. "You were about to have sex with a man you've known less than forty-eight hours. And you're mad because I busted up your kinky little night of irresponsibility? Too darn bad, Rosemary."

"You know what? That's exactly what I'm angry about. I'm a grown woman, Mother, who wanted to screw the brains out of that very available, very willing man. I don't care if you think it was irresponsible or crazy. I *want* irresponsible and crazy. I deserve it for putting up with you. So I don't need you to—"

"Care about you?" Patsy asked, bringing out the big guns. Her mother had an arsenal full of guilt, shame, and indebtedness she carried with her, and she wasn't afraid to employ any one of them at the exact right time. Patsy was an excellent marksman.

"Don't do that. Don't make this about you and your love for me. This is about you trying to control me . . . as usual."

"I've never tried to control you. Just because I have more life experience and know a girl like you shouldn't be on her own in New York City doesn't mean I'm trying to control you. I'm merely helping you see the danger in it. And that"—she jabbed a finger toward the door—"right there proved my point. What do you know about that man? He could have an STD. He could have a criminal past. He could be physically or verbally abusive. Have you ever heard of date rape?"

Rosemary gave an incredulous laugh. "I can't believe you. You've painted him into a criminal because I wanted to invite him in for a drink?"

Her mother sniffed and tossed her head. "You can have a drink with your drawers on, Rosemary Marie."

That made her laugh. "Oh, come on, Mother, it's just sex."

"Don't be crass, Rosemary. I know what sex is, but I've always considered it something to be shared between two committed people. Not with some horny man you picked up God only knows where. Have some pride, dear."

"No," Rosemary said, barely refraining from stamping her foot. "I don't need him to be medically tested or take a lie detector test or want commitment. I need *him* to give me a no-strings-attached, headboard-knocking fucking. And I need *you* to call the airport and rearrange your flight out tomorrow."

Rosemary's breath came hard and emotion made her legs tremble, but she crossed her arms. Like she meant it. 'Cause she did.

On the other hand, her mother deflated like a balloon at the hands of a six-year-old boy. Her plump shoulders sagged and her blue eyes looked weepy. "So you really want me to leave? That's really how you feel? Choosing sordidness over your own mother?"

Another zinger of guilt. This time it missed its mark.

"I'm not trying to hurt you, Mother. I love you, but I need to do this. I know you don't understand. Just trust me on this. Okay?"

"Is 'all this' merely having sex with a stranger? You could have done that in Jackson and saved yourself the plane ticket."

"No, it's not about sex. It's about making my own decisions. It's about falling down. Getting hurt. I need to live messy and dirty and . . . just different. For a little while."

"I *don't* understand," her mother said, sinking onto the sofa, self-consciously checking the pink rollers in order to rein in any escapees.

"You don't have to." Rosemary said, unfolding her arms but keeping her jaw flinty. "A few months ago I lost my best friend. Before she passed, Lacy reminded me of all the things I haven't done with my life. I've been content to stay put, and while some people may think that's okay—you included—I don't. The life I have is not the life I want. Or maybe it is, but I needed to have other experiences in order to know. I needed a break from everything so I could get perspective."

Her mother said nothing. She studied her with eyes the color of irises, giving nothing away.

Rosemary continued, "I've been living with blinders, but in the past two days my eyes have been opened to a whole new world. And, sure, Sal was a happy surprise. But I need him, too. I need someone who doesn't wear seersucker, have monogrammed luggage, and own a Labrador retriever named Drake."

"So you're indulging yourself in some fantasy?" Patsy eyed her as if she'd never seen her before. Rosemary liked that idea, because her mother had been wearing blinders, too. She still saw Rosemary as a little girl, not as a grown woman hungry for experiences Morning Glory couldn't give her.

"Maybe it is a fantasy, but it's mine to live. If I don't fall down, I won't know how to get back up. You can't protect me from the world, Mama. It's a messy, dangerous, wonderful place I want to dive into."

"I'm not trying to deny you, Rosemary. I just love you and want the best for you," her mother said, hands out, seemingly helpless to understand why her daughter didn't want a rope looped about her neck so she could be dragged to heel.

"And I love you, but you have to stop putting your thumb on me. No other mother would climb on a plane, probably paying a small fortune, to rescue her daughter from . . . going on a date in New York City."

"Well, I always have money tucked away for emergencies such as this."

"This is not an emergency. It's me getting away and being someone different. Don't you understand wanting something more than small-town Mississippi, pruning roses and managing me? Isn't there a tiny piece inside who wishes you would have stepped outside the expectations your mother set for you? Don't you wonder what it would have been like to chase something wonderful?"

Her mother said nothing.

Rosemary sighed. "So this is not an emergency. I don't want you here."

Teardrops perched on her mother's thin lashes. "I see."

"You probably don't, but you don't have to understand. Just call the airport and get a flight back home."

"But I've never visited this city before," her mother said, tucking her robe around her knees. "I can fly back on Sunday. You can give me one of your fantasy days, surely?"

Rosemary didn't want to give up even one day. She'd already missed a night of passion with Sal. But her mother had never been to NYC, and though she was mad as hell at Patsy, she didn't want her to leave with this between them.

But that would be giving in. Letting her mother get what she wanted. "No, you can come back another time."

"Please." Her mother spread her hands, looking so not like typical Patsy Reynolds. Somehow she looked human. "Just a day. It would make me feel better about leaving you here."

"No."

Her mother sighed. "Fine. I'll have your father call and get my ticket rebooked."

Exactly. Her mother clung to old mores—her father dealt with the finances, put gas in her mother's car, and always led them in grace. "Why does Dad have to do it? You have a phone and credit card."

"Because he always deals with the airlines."

Rosemary shook her head. Rome wasn't built in a day and her mother couldn't jump into 2016 with one leap. "I'm going to bed."

"I already put my satin pillowcase on the pillow on the left."

Rosemary glanced at the only bed in the loft. She was *not* going to sleep on the couch another night, especially when she'd already given up wine, chocolate, and a sexy Italian. "I'll take the right side."

Trudging to the bathroom, Rosemary wondered if Sal would bother calling her to pick up where they'd left off. She wouldn't blame him if he ignored her calls or texts. No doubt he'd never had to deal with a crazy woman in rollers interrupting foreplay and asserting he was a bad decision.

She'd text him later and pray he would want to see her again. That he'd want to finish their kinky little stripping game.

Because as soon as she got rid of Patsy, she would jump back in with both feet. Bra and panties optional.

Chapter Ten

Sal sipped the spicy cabernet and prayed a TARDIS would appear so he could go back to Friday night and the kinky stripping game he'd played with Rosemary. Because sitting at the dinner table with his entire family and Angelina had turned into medieval water torture.

Yes, Angelina again.

His mother hadn't been subtle in her attempt to integrate the woman into his life. She'd been at the last two Sunday lunches, charming his family with her silly anecdotes, hoodwinking his grandmother with her devoutness.

"So, Sal, the contractor needs you to go down to the deli and see about the meat display. He needs to know where you want it so he can install the counter. Let's get that checked off," his father said, passing the platter with the pork roast to Brittany, who took a healthy serving. His sister was whip thin and ate like a horse.

Sal craned his neck, because his collar suddenly felt too tight. "It's wherever you want it, Pop."

His father glanced up. "What do I care where you keep the meat? It's yours to decide."

"But it's your place, Pop," Sal said.

Dominic jabbed a finger at him. "Stop playing dumb. You know Pop's gonna retire soon. He's doing that deli for you. I run the main restaurant, Vince is over in Brooklyn, and you got the deli. What's so hard to understand about Pop wanting you to take some interest in something that will be yours?"

Dominic was the oldest, which meant he was the enforcer of his parents' directives. Like Himmler to Hitler, not that his parents were as bad as Hitler. Much. Dom had bought into the Genovese way with nary a thought of any other career. Vincent, on the other hand, had expressed an interest in medicine, even getting accepted into medical school, but once Big Donnie handed him the keys to the Brooklyn restaurant, Vinnie couldn't justify years upon years of schooling when he could marry his high school sweetheart and buy a place in Brooklyn. Sal was always odd man out.

"And what about me and Brit? What, 'cause we're girls we're shut out?" Frances Anne chimed in, her expression showing she wanted a fight. Frances took more interest in the small Mama Mello's empire than anyone else. After attending business school and getting a degree in marketing, she had ideas about social media, advertising, and branding that often pitted her against her too-traditional parents. As much as Frances aggravated him with her overly protective nature, she was the sibling he related most to. They were both frustrated.

"We're not having this discussion today," his father said, glancing over at Angelina. "We have company."

"All I'm saying is I'm not sure running the deli is what I want." Sal took another swig of wine. He didn't want to gulp it but God help him, he needed more booze to deal with the family theatrics that were inevitable around the table. Last week it was over the christening of the new Genovese and who would be the godparents. The week before that it was over the Yankees' midseason trade. Always fireworks at the Genovese table.

"And why don't you?" his mother asked, her fork pausing in midair. Her dark hair had been secured in the familiar bun she always wore, and the diamond loops his father had given her for their thirty-fifth wedding anniversary sparkled beneath the extravagant chandelier. Natalie had insisted they needed the garish light fixture in their formal dining room, but it looked incongruous in the cramped space, which was made even smaller by his boisterous family packed in at the table. "Your father is handing you a future and you treat the opportunity like it's garbage?"

"That's not what I'm doing," Sal said, trying to keep his voice level. *Not another shouting match, please.* His nerves already felt shredded. "I'm just saying running the deli is a big commitment."

His mother looked disgusted and eyed his father. "This one is always so difficult."

Angelina leaned forward. "Don't worry, Mrs. Genovese, once Sal sees how incredible the place is looking, he'll be excited for a new opportunity."

Sal turned his head. "How do you know?"

"Because I went by the Mello deli Friday morning. It's an incredible location. Can't believe you got it for that price." She nodded like a good Realtor should.

He wondered if he'd fallen down a hole . . . in a desert . . . in Mongolia. "You went to the deli on Friday? Why?"

"I had a showing nearby and your mother invited me to drop in and check out the progress. At least *she* appreciates my expert opinion on what works in the neighborhood. I have a lot of experience, you know."

Vincent's gaze met his. His brother grinned. Sal thought about flipping his brother off, but he didn't want to set his mother off again.

"And we appreciate you, Angelina. After all, you were the one who suggested the deli in the first place," Natalie said.

What the hell?

"I thought Mac Terelli suggested the deli?" Sal looked at his father, something hot slithering into his gut. His father had told him Mac, a developer and close friend, had seen opportunity for the Genoveses to expand in the theater district. To find out Angelina was behind the sudden press to buy space and outfit it as a pizza and sub sandwich joint felt manipulative. Like she'd laid his future out for him like a woman setting out a suit of clothes . . . then waited for him to see how indispensable she was. She'd probably already ordered stationery with "Angelina Genovese" scrawled across it.

"Oh, and Angelina had such a good idea for that brick wall where customers line up. She knows a muralist who can paint the Mama Mello's logo on the wall. Maybe a nice pastoral scene, too. Make the customer feel like they're in Italy."

Angelina vibrated with pleasure beside him. "Oh, and don't forget I know a supplier for the tables and chairs. Old world iron would lend authenticity to the space," Angelina said, shoveling around the pasta on her plate. Their conversation last Friday at Mama Mello's hadn't been mentioned and Angelina had been sweet as the cream cake his mother had sitting on the sideboard. Nauseatingly so. "As long as it's okay with Sal, of course."

He didn't say anything.

What could he say? Everyone in his life, except maybe Brittany, who was clueless about everything, had set this new direction for him into motion. Sal was a trained ape. *Come at this time. Stand here. Do this. Do that.*

He pulled at his collar, feeling like he couldn't breathe. He should have pleaded being sick that morning. Sal didn't want to be there. Not even for Grandma Sophie, who looked to be falling asleep in her meatball soup.

"I have to go," he said, dropping his napkin beside his half-eaten lunch.

"You haven't finished your lunch yet," his father said, looking pointedly at Sal's plate. "Your mother and grandmother worked hard to cook this."

"And it was delicious," Sal said, pushing back his chair. "I forgot I have a commitment."

"What commitment?" his mother asked, her brow knitted in discontent.

"Uh, I told some guys I'd meet them at the gym. We have a makeup game for league."

"And you just now remembered?" Angelina asked, pressing her manicured hand on his arm. It felt like a shackle. He pulled away.

"Sorry, but lunch was excellent as always, Mama," he said.

As he rounded the table, heading for the large opening to the foyer, his grandmother extended her cheek so he could kiss it. "So nice to see you, Salvatore. Come visit. The lavender smells lovely and the bee balm brings the butterflies. I miss you."

Guilt pinged him. His grandmother Sophie loved to take tea in her garden. After she quit working in the restaurant, she'd turned her attention to the small courtyard behind her house in the Bronx, filling it with fragrant herbs and lovely blooms. Since Sal lived in Dyker Heights, it was hard for him to get out to see his grandmother, but he always found it restoring to sit with her on the cobbled patio, sipping herbal tea and watching the birds hop on the branches of the cherry tree draped over the privacy fence. A small piece of paradise, a place where he could breathe and think.

Angelina dropped her napkin and made to push back. "I'll go with you. I love basketball," she said.

Sal felt panic rear inside him.

"No," he said, pressing his hands toward her as if it could hold her in place. "You know, the game will be a long one. And that gym smells like sweat and dirty feet had a kid together. Plus, we're going out to a strip club for Jared's bachelor party afterward. It's a guy thing, you know?"

"A strip club?" Angelina repeated, her face growing stony. "Isn't that a bit juvenile?"

"You know guys," he said with a shrug, edging out of the dining room.

"Take me with you," Vincent said.

"Me, too," Dom chirped. "Please."

Both guys got pinched by the women sitting beside them. Two yips of pain accompanied his scramble out of the dining room. As he fled, he heard accusations and laughter from his brothers and their women. The halfhearted fussing distracted everyone from his escape.

Of course the basketball game was total fabrication. He hated lying, but he'd blame it on that infernal woman his mother kept shoving down his throat. Every time he said something to his mother she'd say, "What's not to like? Angelina's beautiful, Catholic, Italian, and has a job. You got a better chance of winning the lotto than finding a good girl like her. Don't be stubborn. And stop chasing girls with their snooty noses in the air. They don't understand the life you lead. Angie is one of us."

And his mother's approval paired with innate confidence had Angelina believing he already belonged to her.

As long as Sal is okay with it.

Ha.

How many times had he heard his mother say the same thing when it came to his father? Hundreds. Natalie always pretended like she included his dad in decision making when she knew she made all the decisions. Big Donnie Genovese might be the face of Mama Mello's, but his wife ruled with an iron fist.

Sal loved and admired his parents, but he'd never wanted the same kind of relationship. And settling for Angelina because it was easy felt like giving up on being the man he dreamed of being. Of course, he didn't have an exact plan for who that man was, but he knew he was a man who made his own way.

Angelina had gone down to Mama Mello's Express to pick out tables, make suggestions, and plan a goddamned mural to cover the wall. And then she'd looked at him with those wide gingery-brown eyes and said *as long as it was okay with him?*

As he walked briskly through the hall, he knew he was drowning. Eventually he'd grow tired of swimming and he'd give over to the current and be washed downstream toward a life planned for him. Maybe it was inevitable. Maybe three years from now he'd be married to Angelina, working at the deli, and oblivious to the mundane life he'd accepted.

But right now he fought to grab on to the southern girl who was his island in the middle of the current. Lush, simple, and untouched by the flotsam and jetsam of his life, Rosemary gave him reprieve. Even if he knew it was short-lived. Eventually the island would disappear, leaving him with only the memory of paradise.

Almost exactly two weeks.

That was all they had.

Then she'd fly back to Mississippi and leave him here to the life designed for him. Postponing the inevitable. That's what if felt like. His life was inevitable.

After all, how could he change it?

Sure, it was easy for someone to suggest he quit the family business, take his meager savings, and move elsewhere to start over. But it was altogether another thing to do it. Rosemary claimed to have been living in a bubble, hungry for experiences. Wasn't he the same? His bubble was just different—bigger, noisier, and smellier. Like her, he'd been content to exist as a Genovese doing what Genoveses had done for almost a century.

He slipped through his parents' parlor with the plastic-covered settee and the wall of photographs, wincing when he saw his geeky confirmation picture. His mother called, "Sal," but he hurried out the door and down the steps of the brownstone he'd been raised in.

Then he pulled out his cell phone and dialed Rosemary's number.

Please let her mother be gone.

Sweet baby Jesus, please.

Rosemary studied her mother over the fluffy stack of lemon-ricotta pancakes on her plate. Patsy hadn't been able to get a flight out until Sunday afternoon. Or so she'd said. Rosemary swallowed the disappointment of not getting to see Sal until then and tried to be a good daughter.

And Patsy had tried to be a good mother, pretty much going along with her daughter's suggestions. Still, her mother had taken to NYC like a duck took to the desert. As in she didn't like it so much.

They'd started the sacrificial day early Saturday morning by purchasing tickets for the on-again, off-again bus. Rosemary had loved hearing about the various neighborhoods they passed through. Her mother had preoccupied herself with hand sanitizer. They'd stopped off at the World Trade Center memorial, visited Battery Park, and taken a tour of Ellis Island. She had a picture on her cell phone of her and her mother at the foot of Lady Liberty. Her mother hadn't been smiling. Saturday evening they'd scored tickets for *Wicked*. Finally, she'd found something her mother loved. Of course, when they pushed through Times Square, her mother had almost needed a paper bag to breathe into. The cheesecake at Junior's had eased the panic.

Then that morning they'd walked in Central Park, visiting several gardens, ending their sightseeing at Sarabeth's with Sunday brunch. The restaurant rambled, making the small, crowded rooms uncomfortable, but the food was delicious, including the famous jams and jellies.

"Well, my veggie frittata was decent," her mother said, wiping her mouth at each corner and folding the napkin beside her plate. "How are your pancakes?"

"Sinful."

"Well, that seems to be your theme these days," her mother said, tempering her comment with a half smile.

Rosemary let it slide. It was the truth. For once in her life, she wanted something a little bit wicked. Nothing wrong with that. Even the Amish had *rumspringa*. That's what this was for her—a time to sow her oats and find out if the life she had was the one she truly wanted.

"I wish you weren't so angry with me," her mother said.

Rosemary had tried over the past day and a half to temper her irritation with her mother. She hadn't done a good enough job. "I can't help the way I feel."

"But I want you to be happy, Rosemary. That's all I've ever wanted."

"But you can't get happiness for me. I have to find it myself. You may not approve of my coming here, or of Sal, but it's what I need right now."

"When I was eighteen I went on spring break with some of my sorority sisters and I met a guy from New Jersey. I understand the appeal of someone different."

Rosemary took a sip of the French roast and said, "You went on spring break? Where?"

"Fort Lauderdale."

"No way," Rosemary said, disbelief edging her words.

Her mother smiled. "I, too, was young once."

She tried to imagine her mother in a bikini lying on the beach covered in iodine and baby oil, humming along to the Beach Boys blaring out of a transistor radio. But she couldn't. For as long as Rosemary could remember, her mother had dressed tastefully, said the right things, and drank only on special occasions.

"What was his name?"

"David. He went to a community college and drove a woody. Do you know what a woody is?"

Rosemary giggled, even though she knew very well what her mother meant.

"Oh, don't be lewd," her mother fussed, but she smiled. "It was a paneled wagon that surfers liked to drive. He had the best body, too. Wore those board shorts and flirted with every girl on the beach."

"And you caught him?"

"For a few days." Her words were wistful, her smile mysterious. "So I can understand the inclination to . . . uh, play with Sal."

Rosemary nearly choked on the bite of pancakes. "What?"

"I may be old and set in my ways, but I have eyes. Sal has a certain attraction."

"Mother."

"What? His torso was very masculine."

Rosemary did choke then. She gulped the water she'd ignored in favor of the coffee. Her mother rose and thumped her on the back.

"I can't believe you said that," Rosemary finally managed, wiping water from her chin.

"As you said, it's only sex." Her mother folded her napkin and lifted her purse. "Now I need to use the little girls' room before we go. I want to get to the airport in plenty of time. They say it takes two hours to go through the security line."

A passing waitress heard her and said, "Are you looking for the restroom?" She pointed toward the back. "To your right."

"Excuse me," her mother said, proper as ever. As if she'd discussed the weather rather than Rosemary having sex with Sal.

Rosemary watched Patsy weave around the small tables, murmuring, "Excuse me," nodding her head and giving a warm smile as she made her way to the powder room.

As her mother disappeared, her phone rang.

Eden.

"Hey, you," she said, answering the phone.

"Oh my God. Your father told Mrs. Daigle that Patsy flew to New York City. Tell me she's lying," Eden said.

"Nope. I mean . . . yes, Patsy's here."

"Oh my Lord," Eden breathed. "Why in the world did she do that?"

"Because she thinks I'm lonely and making bad decisions," Rosemary said, unable to stop her lips from twitching.

"She beats all I've ever seen. I hope you told her to get the hell back down here and to leave you alone," Eden said.

"I'm about to put her in a cab for LaGuardia."

Eden gave a hushed laugh, telling Rosemary she was at work at Penny Pinchers. "Good girl. So I'm on a fifteen-minute break and need to hear something good. Mr. Grabby Hands comes this week to go over reports."

"Well, my bad decision has a killer smile and took me to eat at this cool marketplace called Eataly."

Eden squealed and then caught herself. "You bad girl."

Rosemary laughed. "Well, didn't Lacy want us to kick up our heels, stretch ourselves, and grab on to something good?"

"I'm not sure those were the requirement for me, but for you? Probably."

"I'm grabbing on to something with an amazing six-pack."

"And how would you know that?" Eden's voice went singsong.

"Wouldn't you like to know," Rosemary said, warmth flooding her. She'd not had a good talk with either Eden or Jess beyond a few text messages. It felt good to hear Eden's voice. Something about the much put-upon Eden always soothed Rosemary, putting everything in context. Eden recognized how hard it was for Rosemary to step outside the box since she was trapped in a box herself, with nary a box cutter in sight.

"So you met a guy. Spill the deets."

"Not much to tell other than he's sexy, Italian, and likes to dance to Etta James and Sinatra. He helps run his family restaurant in Little Italy and has incredible puppy dog eyes."

Eden sighed. "He sounds perfect. Seriously."

"Only two weeks' perfect. It's not a forever thing."

Eden was silent for a few seconds. "Why can't it be forever? I mean, what if he's the one?"

"He's not. I mean, he can't be," Rosemary answered before she could latch on to a thought like that. Stay in New York City? No. This wasn't where she belonged or what she wanted. Morning Glory cradled her business, her family, her friends, her entire world in its arms. Being in Manhattan was about living a fantasy. Here she could take chances, play naughty, and live for the moment. Coming to pet-sit in SoHo wasn't the start of a new life. It was a break from her real one. "This isn't about falling in love, Eden."

"Why do you love it here so much?"

"I don't know. I'm happy in Morning Glory."

"So you didn't need Lacy's money or to live a dream?" Eden sounded perturbed.

"No. Look, Lacy was right. I've been treading water even if I've been doing it in a happy place. The problem isn't Morning Glory. It's me. Maybe coming here to NYC will shake me loose again. Maybe when I come back, I'll be ready to find a shore."

"Yeah," Eden said halfheartedly. Rosemary knew what her friend felt. Eden was trapped in Morning Glory. Until her sister came back home, Eden would stay and care for her mother. "Then don't go falling in love then, you hear?"

"In two weeks? That's ridiculous."

Yet Rosemary knew herself to be a hopeless romantic who'd slurped up fairy tales one right after the other . . . and not the original gruesome fairy tales. No, she loved the sanitized ones that nestled happily ever after deep within her heart like a . . . princess tiara in an upswept pile of golden curls. True love was real to her, and she knew falling in love didn't necessarily happen when it was super convenient. No, it was apt to knock the wind out of her, leaving her on the floor gasping for breath.

"Don't worry, E. I won't. This is just sex . . . or will be if I can get my mother on the next plane out," Rosemary said. "Now, how are things there?"

"About as exciting as watching paint dry."

"That much, huh?"

"Well, it *is* Sunday, so someone's slip is bound to show at the Greater Galilee Baptist Church. I'll let you know who as soon as the gossip trickles in."

"Definitely let me know. Have to stay up on the gossip," Rosemary said, acknowledging her mother, who suddenly looked lost. She waved her hand and both Patsy and the waitress headed her way. "Well, I need to go."

"Me, too. I have to mark down some clearance stuff. And Margie's gout is acting up, so I'm shorthanded. Have fun with tall, dark, and Italian."

"I never said he was tall," Rosemary joked as her mother slipped into the chair and took the bill jacket from the waitress. "'Bye, E. I love ya."

"You, too," she said, hanging up.

"Who was that?" Patsy asked, sliding her American Express into the pocket and handing it back.

"Eden."

"Poor child. Having to work at that horrible store."

"Mama, she can't help her situation. At least she's the manager."

"Well, if her mother hadn't been such a whore. We were in the same class, you know. I could tell you stories that would freeze the blood in your veins. Running around with all kinds of men, marrying a common criminal and then leaving her girls alone—"

"Mama." Rosemary lowered her voice in warning. It wasn't as though Eden chose to be born a Voorhees. After all, Eden hadn't robbed a bank at gunpoint and ended up in prison. Her stepfather had. And Eden hadn't twined herself around a stripper pole and fought a heroin addiction. That was her mother. Eden hadn't done anything but fight, scratch, and sacrifice her whole life.

"No, Eden has to pay for her mother's sins. And her father's. I don't know how she manages it. Betty brought all that on them with her loose living."

"Eden's mother had a stroke, Mother."

Patsy gave Rosemary a flat look. "You're more than kind. You and I both know what a burden that poor girl carries in taking care of her mother and working at that dead-end job."

Rosemary didn't want to talk about Eden's issues. As far as Rosemary was concerned, Eden had achieved sainthood in their small town . . . but they didn't have to discuss how terrible Eden's mother was every time her friend's name came up. "Why don't we do a little window shopping? Bergdorf's will be perfect."

"You're changing the subject," Patsy said, patting her ash-blonde bob. Rosemary could see her mother had powdered her nose and reapplied her favorite coral lipstick while in the restroom.

"Of course I am," Rosemary said, starting to rise.

"Just a second, dear," her mother said, reaching over to place a hand on Rosemary's.

"What?"

"I shouldn't have imposed my will on you by coming here. It wasn't fair. I sometimes forget you're a grown woman. That's my fault. Not yours."

Her mother's earnestness took her aback. Was this some new manipulation or was Patsy truly sorry for showing up where she was not wanted? She didn't want to give in so easily, but again, Rosemary didn't want to stack another brick in the wall of blame she'd started long ago with her mother. If she wanted her mother to treat her like an adult, she couldn't hold onto grudges like a child. Even though the anger at her mother's presumptuous stunt still lingered, she didn't want her mother to leave believing Rosemary held the grievance against her.

"Okay. You're my mother and I understand you want what is best for me. But you have to let me make my own decisions—both good and bad—from here on out. If I want your help, I will ask for it."

Her mother took the bill from the waitress. Rosemary plopped down a few bills as tip and her mother started to pick the cash up and hand it back to her. She caught herself and instead stuck the money in the jacket and scrawled her name at the bottom of the receipt. "I'll try very hard. You may have to remind me at times, though. Old dog and all that."

Rosemary nodded. "And you shouldn't call yourself a dog. You're a strong southern lady, a steel magnolia, a—"

"—bossy britches?"

"That, too," Rosemary teased, stepping out into the New York City sunshine.

Just as she turned onto the sidewalk, her phone rang again.

Sal.

"Hey," he said, "I have to see you tonight. I just spent a miserable lunch with my whole family. Only a pretty girl can help me now."

"Where?"

"Uh . . . let me think. Some place that is you. Oh, how about the Rose Club at the Plaza?"

Rosemary smiled. "Absolutely."

"Eight?"

"I'll be there," she said hanging up.

"Was that him?" her mother asked.

"Sal? Yeah. We're going to meet there." She pointed to the sumptuous Plaza, the hotel that had housed her favorite child heroine, Eloise.

"So is that a booty call?" Patsy asked.

"Oh good Lord, Mother."

"What? I watch TV."

Chapter Eleven

Sal didn't feel comfortable standing in the Plaza. He'd been there only two other times. Once when he was drunk with his buddies and they'd decided to go slumming . . . something they thought enormously funny at the time. And once with Hillary for high tea. It should be known that the concierge did not find him and his cohorts the least bit amusing and also that he didn't know the difference between high tea and low tea and thought the whole thing was stupid.

So, no, he wasn't comfortable standing at the sumptuous bar in the Rose Club, sipping a gin and tonic. He didn't really care for gin, but it was an easy enough drink to request. He'd showered and tugged on his best slacks and a button-down shirt that was not white but a nice light purple linen for her. He stood here because of her. Because somehow he knew Rosemary would like this place.

Not because she was ritzy, but more because she had a romantic streak. And meeting at the Plaza and taking a ride in a carriage through Central Park would please her.

And for the second time in his life, he really wanted to step outside his comfort zone in order to make someone happy.

She walked in and a few heads turned.

Rosemary wasn't a bombshell, radiating sex appeal, stalking in too-high heels toward him. On the contrary, she was subtle and pleasing in her beauty. Her light auburn hair brushed shoulders covered by a white blouse that looked like something hippies had worn in the seventies. A smart skirt the same color of his khaki pants hit right above her knee. She wore another pair of sandals, along with a gold necklace with a single pearl nestled in a gilded oyster shell that sat under the hollow of her neck. Of course she wore a pearl.

Spying him, she smiled.

And his heart started thumping.

"Hey," she said, reaching him and setting down a small purse his sisters called a clutch with a fancy gold cross on it. "What are you drinking?"

"Gin and tonic."

She wrinkled her adorable nose and then looked at the bored bartender. "I'll have a white zinfandel."

The bartender raised his eyebrows and his lips might have smirked a bit.

"Yeah, I know. It's the opposite of what a wine aficionado would choose, but I'm a bumpkin from Mississippi, so humor me," she said with a smile.

Sal gave a bark of laughter. "She's very honest."

"So I see." The bartender smiled and poured her a glass of the sweet wine. "And it's what my sister drinks, too. I can't turn her on to anything else. Here ya go, Mississippi."

Rosemary took the glass and held it to his. "Here's to two weeks without my mother."

He tapped his glass to hers. "I'll drink to that."

She took a sip of her wine. "I have to say I'm relieved you wanted to see me again. After that fiasco in the hall of my cousin's place, I wasn't so sure. It was sort of horrifying."

Not want to see her? Not a chance. "It wasn't your fault."

"Yeah, but it *was* embarrassing, and my mother is not the most . . . subtle of women. I was afraid you'd wash your hands of my craziness."

"Are you kidding? That was nothing. Wait until you meet my mother," he said.

"You want me to meet your mother?" Rosemary sipped her wine, looking over her glass at him with gray eyes he couldn't read.

He knew why. He kept forgetting they were like a crazy camp romance or a cross-Atlantic cruise hookup. Because every time he was with Rosemary it felt more like the start of forever instead of a here-and-present sort of thing.

They were from two different worlds . . . incredibly different worlds. Yet he felt so much himself when he was with her. No, he felt true to himself. That was what it was. Being with Rosemary made him feel like the man he wanted to be, the man who longed to blaze his own path, to choose his own life. One in which his father wasn't having walls painted, counters mounted, and a new grill installed in a deli twenty blocks away. One in which his mother hadn't picked out the future mother of her grandchildren. One not in Brooklyn. Or Manhattan.

But that was crazy.

He'd only known Rosemary for a few days. Besides, being impulsive about love hadn't worked out so well last time. So why did he feel like saying the hell with a two-week verbal agreement? Why did he feel like scrubbing away all his family had given him? To prove a point?

Vincent had once berated him for his stubbornness when he'd wanted to spend the money he'd inherited from his grandparents on a truck. The more everyone said the truck was a foolish idea, the more Sal wanted it. On the day he turned eighteen and received the lump sum, he went to the DMV and got a driver's license. Then he went to a used lot and bought a Ford F-150 with shiny chrome and leather seats. But six months, a fortune in parking, and two fender-benders later, he admitted he'd made an unwise decision. His family was good at told-ya-sos.

"What are you thinking so hard about?" Rosemary asked, jarring him back to the Plaza and the gin and tonic paused at his lips.

"That you're like a truck I once bought," he said.

"You bought a truck? Like a pickup truck?"

He nodded. "Had her for six months before I realized parking in New York City comes with consequences—dinged doors, parking tickets, and a big-ass monthly garage bill."

"So you're saying I'm dinged? Or that I'm going to run up a steep bill?" She laughed but her forehead crinkled.

"Nah, I'm just thinking about how much I want you."

Rosemary's cheeks pinked and she gave a nervous laugh. "Says he who was denied the final article of clothing."

"Damn straight."

"Well, maybe I can skip a few steps for you." Her cheeks turned persimmon but her eyes sparkled. Her embarrassment was so cute it made him want to say all sorts of dirty things to her.

Hell, made him want to do all sorts of dirty things to her.

"Will you really?" he drawled, lowering his gaze to her breasts, which looked encapsulated in rayon or spandex or whatever bras were made out of. Going braless might be too in-your-face for Rosemary, but . . . "You have something in mind?"

He ran a finger along the skin showing at her skirt hem.

Rosemary's intake of breath made him smile wider. He arched an eyebrow. "Yes?"

"Maybe," she said, mischief skipping across her face.

He set his half-full glass on the bar. "So you need to go to the bathroom?"

She looked confused.

He looked pointedly at her skirt.

"Oh," she said, her cheeks growing even redder. "You're suggesting . . . oh."

"But of course," he said, once again stroking the sweet flesh of her knee. "You want to be a little bad, don't you? Why not start right now?"

She nodded, swallowing. Picking up the glass of wine, she downed it. "Would you excuse me for a moment?"

⁓

Rosemary locked the stall and then leaned her head against the door. Her pulse skipped and something warm slithered through her belly. Sal liked sexy games, and damned if the man didn't believe in extended foreplay.

She reached beneath her too-tight skirt, cursing the Godiva truffles she'd eaten last month when she drowned her grief in chocolate, and snapped the elastic band of her shapewear. Yeah, she wore a veritable granny girdle beneath the skirt.

What had she been thinking when she got dressed earlier?

Well, she hadn't, because she'd only been thinking of fitting into the skirt, looking sexy and sophisticated. Of course, taking the slimming shapewear off would pretty much save her the mortification of pulling them off later. If there was a later.

But to go without panties . . .

Without any more thought, she peeled the Lycra underwear down and wiggled to get out of it. Then she contemplated what to do with her drawers. The Tory Burch crossover bag had room, but it would look bulky. Why in the heck hadn't she worn the cute thong she'd bought in Jackson?

Taking a deep breath, she wadded up the underwear and shoved them into her purse, making the leather bulge. Stepping out of the stall, she caught sight of herself in the mirror.

Her face was crimson and now the skirt revealed a small belly poof. Darn it. She should have joined a gym and done ab crunches or something. Obviously long walks down the back roads of Yazoo County weren't cutting it. She sucked in her stomach and turned sideways and then nodded. Would have to do. Then she moved the undies to the side and fetched her smoky plum lipstick.

The door opened and a well-dressed woman came in, startling her.

"Oh, hello," Rosemary said to the woman, feeling guilty for some reason. She set the tube of lipstick down so she could adjust the flipped-up hem of her skirt.

The woman gave a quick and confused hello before moving to the nearest stall and slamming the door.

Rosemary washed her hands, straightened her shoulders, and pushed back out the door.

The Rose Club was decadent and red, perfect for seduction. Rosemary dug beneath all her insecurities to pull out her very seldom used inner vamp and sashayed across the room toward where Sal lazed at the bar. He looked dashing and dangerous. Made her feel too warm just by looking at him.

"Ma'am?" someone said behind her.

She turned to find the lady she'd scared with her friendliness in the bathroom.

"I think you left your lipstick," she said, holding out Rosemary's tube of Elizabeth Arden.

"Oh, thank you," she said, taking it from the woman. She took the few more steps she needed to reach Sal, who'd dropped his gaze to her knees. Lifting his eyebrows, he silently asked her.

She merely smiled.

Opening her purse, she jabbed the lipstick in. But her fingers accidentally grabbed the girdle when she lifted the flap of her purse. The nude Lycra flopped out and before she could catch them, they fluttered to the floor, where they landed beside Sal's shoe like a giant beached jellyfish.

"Oh my God," Rosemary hissed, kneeling to snatch them up.

But Sal beat her to them. Lifting them between his thumb and forefinger, he raised his gaze to hers.

She knew she was the color of the velvet banquettes lining the wall. Never should she have tried being naughty. This is what happened when she—

"Kinky," Sal drawled, his dark eyes teasing her as he handed the horrid shaper back to her.

"And it hides flaws, too," she tried to joke.

Leaning toward her, he kissed her on the nose. "So why would you need it?"

Rosemary closed her eyes and stifled a laugh. Only she would walk across a posh bar in the Plaza Hotel and drop her girdle on the floor. Big ol' sexy fail.

Sal downed his drink and pulled her to him. "Wanna go for a carriage ride?"

Rosemary's smile was answer enough.

"I'm not too fond of studying the back end of a horse, but since you did such a nice thing for me, I'll manage. Let's go."

Rosemary took his hand.

The horse's name was Buttercup and he was a gray dapple with a swayback. But Rosemary didn't care. As far as she was concerned, Buttercup was a magnificent steed and the man next to her a dashing Italian prince. Such as fairy tales go.

"Now over across the lake you can just glimpse the Loeb Boathouse, reimagined by Stuart Constable in the 1950s. Here you can rent a rowboat, a one-hundred-fifty-year tradition, or ride in an authentic Venetian gondola. Don't forget to look for the many birds and native butterflies as you row across the lake," Simon said. Simon was the fairy-tale coachman wearing the requisite frock coat and vest.

"I wish he'd stop telling us about every damn stick in the park," Sal whispered in her ear before sliding his lips down to that delicious spot on her neck that made her—

She shivered. "Shh, I'm learning about Central Park."

Simon turned and gave them a look.

"Sorry," Rosemary said, pointing a finger at Sal. "He's being rude."

"And handsy," Simon said with a pointed look at the way Sal stroked her knee. Then the driver turned back around and started his scripted lecture on the flora and fauna occupying the particular section they rolled through.

"Why did you tell him to give us the tour? I wanted him to just drive so I could violate you back here," Sal grumbled and then nuzzled her neck. His hand stroked the side of her knee, making her blood heat.

"Because I'm a tourist. I wanted to know about the dairy and the place where—oh," she said as he slid his hand to the inside, rucking up her skirt.

Sal wiggled his eyebrows. "Mademoiselle, I must request payment for this horrid exercise in patience. I care not about Union forces or blasted orioles."

Rosemary laughed and then said, "Shh! You're going to get us in trouble."

"Did you say something?" Simon asked, cocking his head as he urged Buttercup on.

"No, I merely commented on the lovely lines of the, what's that tree?"

"I don't know," Simon said with a shrug before picking up where he'd left off on his script, seemingly not missing a beat.

Rosemary pinched Sal, who yelped but didn't move his hand, and for that, she was thankful.

She wanted his hands all over her. That was the point of surrendering her girdle, right?

She felt wicked and loved it.

Sal's hand crept farther up her thigh, turning her knees to jelly. Who knew making out in the back of a Central Park carriage was such a turn-on? She'd read about people who got off on having sex in public places and could never imagine how the heck they could concentrate on the task when they could get caught any moment.

But now she understood the thrill.

His fingers stroked her, making her heart pound and liquid warmth pool in her pelvis. The achy want intensified as his other hand wandered up the column of her neck to lightly stroke her ear. It was as if that hand was the decoy for any onlookers who happened upon them . . . while his other hand was up to naughtier business.

"You are wicked," she whispered, sliding her hand onto his thigh.

He swallowed and she knew she'd affected him. "Of course I am. Isn't that what you want? Now help a brother out." He lightly tapped her other thigh.

Rosemary didn't know what came over her. Yeah, she did. It was called being horny. She opened her thighs a little bit more.

"Good girl," Sal whispered.

Rosemary held her breath as he moved his hand higher, tickling the inside of her thigh, making her pant a little.

"Oh my gosh," she breathed, yanking the sweater her mother had insisted she bring with her over her lap. She was fairly certain Patsy would die if she knew how Rosemary was using it.

"Good plan," Sal whispered in her ear, moving his lips toward her mouth. She turned her head and met him, letting his tongue tease her as much as his fingers were beneath the perfectly tasteful summer sweater.

Simon droned on, thankfully unaware of what Sal was doing to Rosemary in the back of his carriage.

And what he did was oh so nice.

Finally, after what seemed like forever, his finger traced her cleft. She knew she was spectacularly wet and might have been embarrassed about how revved she was if Sal hadn't sighed like he'd reached the Promised Land.

"Oh, so sweet," he murmured against her lips. "Just a bit wider, Rose."

As if she'd deny him anything. She opened herself a bit more to him and he moved his fingers so that he finally strummed her clitoris.

"Oh," she panted, her chest heaving as his fingers performed a magical rhumba or fox-trot or . . . sweet mother of . . . she was about to come. "Maybe we better—"

"Shh," he said, dipping his finger lower, entering her briefly before withdrawing and moving back to that sweet aching bud that needed to be . . .

She moved her hips, wanting more. Needing Sal to give her the ecstasy hovering on the edge, waiting to shatter her.

The carriage halted.

Rosemary's eyes flew open and she pushed Sal away while simultaneously slamming her thighs shut.

Holy crap.

"And that concludes your tour of the largest and most famous of New York parks, Central Park," Simon said with flourish.

Sal pulled his hand away. "You've *got* to be kidding me."

Rosemary plastered on a smile as Simon turned and said, "I hope you folks enjoyed learning a bit more about this wonderful national treasure."

"Oh yes," Rosemary said, tugging her skirt over her knees and nodding like a lunatic. "It was so beautiful and very informative."

Sal didn't say anything. Simon looked at him, lifting his bushy white eyebrows, awaiting comment.

"Uh, it ended way too soon," Sal said.

Rosemary coughed to keep from laughing. "It certainly did."

Simon jabbed a finger at the sign attached to the carriage. "You can pay for more time."

Sal looked over at her. "You know, as good as it was, I'm ready for bed."

"It's only nine o'clock, but I guess you have a good reason there," the old driver cackled, winking at Rosemary. "And be glad I'm not giving a test on the tour, because I know you two were back there making out. So you can give me a tip that reflects appreciation for my discretion."

Giving a laugh, Sal reached into his back pocket. "Point well made."

After settling up with Simon, Sal helped her out of her fairy-tale carriage/porno movie set. Simon said, "Hey-ah," and Buttercup obligingly stepped into a trot, heading toward Central Park South and a watering trough.

Rosemary gave a little wave.

"Horses don't wave back," Sal teased.

"Ha, you think I don't know that. Who's the country girl around here, anyway?" Rosemary sassed, sticking her hand on her hip. She still felt wet, turned on, and slightly disappointed she hadn't had an orgasm in a Central Park carriage. Oh, the story she would have had to tell . . . to hardly anyone. Okay, she'd totally tell Eden and Jess. Or at least hint at what had almost happened. A little locker room bragging to her girls.

I didn't see that one on the fifty orgasms list, Lacy. Her thoughts made her smile wider.

Sal set his arms on her shoulders, bringing her to him. "I'd look appalling in Daisy Dukes and a gingham crop top, so I'm going with you as the country girl around here."

"I'm pretty sure I'd look appalling in that outfit, too," she said, wrapping her arms around his neck, twisting the dark hair that kicked up around his neckline.

"I can promise you, you'd look amazing. Any place we might pick those things up?"

Rosemary silenced him with a kiss.

And Sal seemed to like that answer.

But he seemed to like it even more when she said, "Let's go back to the loft and finish what you started."

He swept her into his arms à la Rhett Butler and said, "Frankly, my dear Rosemary, I think that's a fabulous idea."

She looped her arms about his neck, ignoring several people who tittered and pointed. "You've been dying to quote *Gone With the Wind* at some point, haven't you?"

"As if I even know what *Gone With the Wind* is. I'm a Yankee, remember?"

"So I can't scream, 'The Yankees are coming! The Yankees are coming!'" she asked, using her best Prissy voice, still flushed from their earlier naughtiness but loving the romance Sal brought her.

"Are you suggesting a Yankee will be coming tonight?" he asked with a quirk of his eyebrow.

"I think I am," she said nuzzling his neck. "A Yankee coming is a real possibility."

Sal laughed as he walked to the sidewalk and set her down. "Then I suggest we grab a cab. A really fast cab."

"In my experience New York cabs only know one speed—suicidal—so your chances are good." She fit her hand into his as he raised the other one to flag down a cab from the fleet of yellow taxis whizzing down Central Park West. "Thank you for the carriage ride."

As a cab pulled up, Sal glanced down at her. "Don't thank me yet. We have unfinished business."

Chapter Twelve

Rosemary turned on the lamp and set her sweater and purse on the bar. "Well, this is it."

"Whoa, fancy. What does your cousin do? Rob banks?" Sal asked, running a finger over the funky cowhide-covered angular chair. He lifted his eyes to the industrial ceiling before sweeping around to spot original abstract paintings and no doubt expensive furniture.

"More like she robs pocketbooks. Halle's a shoe designer," she said, opening a cabinet and pulling out the bag from Eataly he'd left with her a few nights ago. Setting it on the marble countertop, she walked over to the entertainment center and grabbed a remote control and a laminated piece of paper. After several attempts, soft music flooded the space. Billy Joel. Nice.

"So creativity runs in the family."

Rosemary made a questioning face as she set the clicker down and went back to the kitchen. She pulled out two goblets. Of course they weren't the kind of goblets made for drinking reds, but he wasn't about to point that out. Not when her hands were trembling. "How?"

"You design pillows, right?" he clarified.

"Oh yeah. But that's more a hobby than a career. I'm assuming you want the wine we bought?"

"The rain check wine?" he said before sinking onto the sofa, ever mindful of the plush bed over his shoulder. He wanted to bring back the passionate woman he'd held in the carriage, sweeping her once again into his arms before laying her across the gray bedspread or coverlet or whatever they called the puffy things you covered a bed with. And then he'd show her how a New Yorker took a woman to bed.

"Rain check something, I guess," she said, pouring the wine.

He leaned forward and picked up a design magazine and leafed through it while Rosemary occupied her hands with mundane things. He heard her tear into the bag of Italian crème chocolates they'd purchased with the wine and he slid a gaze over as she clacked through a stack of plates. He noticed she kept casting glances his way, reminding him of a bunny ready to hop away at the first sign of a gun. There was a nasty joke in there somewhere, but he wasn't about to go there.

The vibe had shifted from fun and sexy to . . . strained. And he had no clue why. They'd been teasing, kissing, and daring not ten minutes ago.

Finally, Rosemary walked toward him, setting the plate of chocolates on the concrete coffee table before extending a full-to-the-brim glass to him.

"You're nervous," he said, taking the goblet from her shaking hand. Wine had sloshed over the side and he caught the droplets with his hand before they could splash onto the fluffy white rug. A single rivulet ran down her hand, so he grabbed her hand and licked it. Which was a weird thing to do, so he tried to turn it into something sexy by taking her index finger and sucking it into his mouth. And it didn't work. He'd made an awkward moment ten times more awkward.

"Wow, uh, that's an interesting way to mop up a spill," Rosemary said, watching him as he nipped her index finger with his teeth before dropping it. Feeling like a freak, he grabbed the paper napkin she'd set beneath the plate and wiped the residual dampness from his hand.

"I'd make a crack about being talented with my mouth, but that would make this moment more awkward than it already is." He gave her a sheepish smile before pulling her down next to him. "What's wrong?"

At that moment a cat jumped onto the arm of the couch and nearly scared his socks off. If he'd been wearing any. "Jesus."

"No, that's Moscow," Rosemary said before pointing toward the oddly carved red footstool. Inside sat another cat curled into an *S* shape. "And that's Melbourne. They're my job."

"Cats?"

"My cousin loves them more than apple pie, designer handbags, and her own parents combined. I'm their caregiver for the next two weeks."

Sal didn't like cats. Or maybe he did. He hadn't a clue. So he reached out to give Moscow a pet. The cat hissed and slapped at him.

Yeah. He definitely wasn't a cat person.

"Down, Moscow," Rosemary said, reaching over and sweeping the snarling beast off the arm. "Sorry about that. If it's any consolation, he doesn't like me much, either."

"It's a small one," Sal said, placing his arm on the back of the couch. She reacted, stiffening slightly.

He couldn't figure out what was wrong with her. Less than half an hour ago, she'd been close to an orgasm. But now the vibe between them was tense.

Moving his hand so that it stroked her shoulder, he said, "Relax. We don't have to do anything, okay?"

"But I want to."

"You're way too keyed up right now."

She sighed. "I know. It's strange because all I could think about was, you know, and then the whole carriage thing was wonderful, but now it's like I've built things up too much in my mind and now that we're here, it just feels wrong. I mean not *wrong* wrong, but strange. I'm sorry. I—"

"Shh," he said, pressing his finger against her lips. "Let's just drink some wine and chat."

Rising, he went to the kitchen and grabbed the glass of wine she'd poured herself and brought it back. Taking his own goblet, he took a big gulp, mostly to keep it from sloshing again. "Even though we've been on a few dates, I still don't know a lot about you. So I'm thinking we play twenty questions."

"Twenty questions?"

"Yeah, like . . . what's your favorite color?"

Rosemary took a small sip of wine. "Lilac."

"Is that yellow?" he asked.

"No, it's almost the exact color of your shirt. A sort of light purple. What's yours?"

"Blue," he said.

"Yeah, but what shade? Navy . . . royal . . . or periwinkle?"

"I don't know what those are. Um, the color of the sky on a summer day."

"You're such a poet," she teased.

He felt her relaxing by degrees and congratulated himself on thinking of the silly game he'd always used when he was a camp counselor at Pine Ridge. "Favorite subject in school?"

"Home ec."

"Duh," he said, reaching out to twist a hank of her hair around his finger. "Mine was math. Go figure, huh?"

"Why?" she asked, looking genuinely perplexed.

How could she know he'd struggled with schoolwork? He'd suffered from mild dyslexia and ADD, which made school more than challenging, but something about numbers made sense to him. "Well, I ain't no genius, you know?" he said in his best Rocky voice. "Favorite singer or band?"

"That's easy. Elvis Presley," she said.

"Really? You're not one of those weirdos who have a whole room dedicated to him, are you?"

Rosemary pressed her lips together, her gray eyes dancing. "Uh, maybe. I actually went to his eightieth birthday party at Graceland."

"You know he's dead, right?" Sal joked.

"If you're going to disrespect the King of Rock and Roll, I'm going to have to ask you to leave. He's a fellow Mississippian. Besides, everyone knows Elvis is alive. Let's just say I looked very closely at the party-goers," Rosemary said, wiggling her eyebrows. "And what attracted me most to you was that you resemble him."

"Thank ya. Thank ya very much," Sal said.

"Oh jeez, your Elvis impersonation is as bad as your southern belle," she said. "Okay, what about favorite actor?" she asked.

"That's easy. Robert De Niro."

"Why's that easy?"

"He's the epitome of a New Yorker. 'You talkin' to me?'"

"Much better impression." She settled into his side with a sigh. "Well, I like Vince Vaughn."

"Really?" He'd never have guessed that one. He'd had her pegged for liking stuffy British guys off *Downton Abbey* or *Poldark*. She had that romantic streak he liked so well, but Vince Vaughn?

"He's funny but he also has this sweetness, this lovable loser vulnerability, you know?"

"You're an odd one, Rosemary," he said, turning toward her.

She made a face. "Hey, at least I don't lick people."

He laughed and then grabbed her, hauling her against him. "You complaining about my licking abilities?"

She reached over and set her wine on the coffee table. "I don't know. Maybe you'll have to try again," she said.

And just like that, the sexy factor came back. Sal brushed her hair from her face, loving the clearness in her eyes, the bloom in her cheeks, the way her pretty lips beckoned to be tasted. "Maybe I will."

He gently kissed her, savoring the spicy wine on her lips and the sheer softness of her body pressed against his. One hand slid up to brush the five o'clock shadow on his jaw and her touch inflamed. Just like that. He'd gone from laughter to desire in seconds.

Pulling back, he smiled. "Better?"

She nodded. "Weirdness gone. But we only got to, like, four questions."

"We don't need them anymore," he said, covering her lips with his again. Rosemary opened herself to him, kissing him with more heat this time. Her breasts brushed his chest as she shifted herself, tilting her hips so her butt settled on his thigh. He helped her out by pulling her all the way into his lap, groaning slightly at the friction of her softness against the erection surging against his fly.

Her fingers tangled in the hair at his neck, reminding him why he always ignored his mother's plea to cut his hair. He loved the way a woman's fingers felt running though his hair . . . and that they were Rosemary's fingers scratching that sensitive skin made it even better.

He'd always been a sucker for sweets, and kissing Rosemary was sweeter than honey from a hive. Hit the spot.

And even better, the woman gave as good as she got, abandoning any hesitation.

"Mmm," she sighed against his lips, tilting her head, giving him access to her neck. He took direction well, so he obliged, grazing his lips down the column.

"Nice," she sighed, dropping her hands to his shoulders, stroking, making his blood heat.

He moved the hand resting on her bent knees, loving the smooth length, the softness of her skin. His fingers found her hem and he paused. Lifting his head, he looked down at her.

"What?" she asked, gray eyes dilated, hair spilling onto the sofa arm where the cat had sat minutes ago.

"Want to take this over to the nice soft bed?"

She rose up and looked over his shoulder. "It *does* look nice." Without any warning, she hopped from his lap. Then with a twinkle in her eye, she jerked her shirt over her head and tossed it toward him. As he pulled the shirt off his head, she scooted around the end table and started for the bed.

"You little minx," he said, making her laugh. It was in the flutter of her laughter that he realized why he constantly teased her. He loved the sound.

He chucked her discarded shirt toward the cow chair and jumped to his feet. He managed to grab her and scoop her into his arms before she reached the bed. Her squeal made him grin.

Then he tossed her on the bed.

"You big brute," she said, sitting up and spitting hair out of her mouth, swiping flyaway locks from her eyes before popping up on her elbows. He crossed his arms and stared down at her in her pink lacy bra, breasts heaving, tummy flat, skirt shimmied up her thighs. She still wore the sandals, which needed to be done away with, like, yesterday.

"May I?" he asked like a shoe salesman, lifting her foot onto his thigh.

She nodded, her gaze drawn to his fingers as he tried to unbuckle the sandal. Which was impossible. The damn thing was smaller than a thimble.

After a good thirty seconds of his fumbling, she sighed, brought her foot to her, and pulled it off. "There. Easier."

He grabbed her other foot and gave the sandal the same treatment, tossing it over his shoulder before sliding his hand up the side of her leg all the way to where her thigh joined her body.

She gasped.

"Just reminding myself my naughty girl isn't wearing panties." He climbed onto the bed and captured her lips.

Rosemary's elbows collapsed and she fell back onto the fluffed bedding. Sal covered her body with his, a sigh of pleasure escaping at the full body-on-body contact. All his hard angles fit the soft places of her body the way the good Lord intended.

He broke the kiss, working his way down to those breasts he'd yet to see, touch, or taste. "You're so beautiful."

Rosemary vibrated with pleasure, her fingers stroking over his shoulders. He paused and lifted himself, not bothering to unbutton his shirt before pulling it overhead. He wanted her hands on his bare flesh.

Settling on his side, Sal unhooked the front clasp of her bra. The two cups popped open, spilling out the loveliest of breasts—full, rounded, with an upturned slope. The dusky pink nipples were tight as if aching for him.

"Pretty," he said, cupping the breast farthest away while he lowered his head to capture the delicious peak of the other.

"Oh," Rosemary gasped, and he looked up because he wanted to see her face while he loved her. Her eyes were closed, face a study in absolute pleasure. Something about her enjoying his mouth and hands on her stroked his ego.

He moved his attention from one breast back to the other all the while caressing her thighs, gliding his hand across her stomach, teasing the sensitive inside of her elbow, putting his hands everywhere he could touch. His entire focus was on taking Rosemary's breath away.

He inhaled her essence. Rosemary smelled of summer flowers and something so womanly; her skin was satin beneath his and he felt as if he could devour her. After several minutes of his enjoying the responsive woman beneath him, she lifted herself. Tossing the lacy bra toward the end of the bed, she said, "Okay, my turn."

"But I—" He kissed her, nipping her lips, teasing her with his tongue.

She pressed a hand into his chest. "Stop. I want a turn to touch you," she said, trailing a hand across his chest, threading her fingers in the dark hair covering his chest.

Sal flopped back and brought her with him, trapping her against him. "So you want me at your mercy?"

That thought seemed to sit well with her, because she smiled and nodded. "I think I'd like that."

Lifting herself from him, she sat up, breasts swaying like tantalizing fruits as she moved forward. He didn't mind her touching him, but she hadn't said anything about keeping his hands to himself, so he filled his hand with one. "I have to touch you, too."

"I'm not complaining," she said, her lids lowering as she traced a path across his shoulder. Leaning forward, Rosemary kissed him. It was a simple kiss that turned hot when she tentatively traced her tongue along his lower lip. Her hands stroked his shoulders, lingering on his tat before moving down to his chest. He released the breast now squished between them and surrendered to her ministrations. Rosemary seemed to enjoy putting her mouth and hands on him, because she made soft little sighs against his skin and her hips squirmed, rocking back and forth, giving a little grind even now and then.

She moved her lips down his neck, dropping tiny kisses across his collarbone, biting his shoulder. Her hands skipped lower across his belly, ringing his navel, diving down to the button of his pants.

He held his breath as she dipped lower, then lost his breath when she traced the length of him through the placket. "Rose," he warned.

She gave a throaty laugh and with a quick flick of her wrist, she had him unbuttoned and unzipped. "Whoa, whoa, easy now."

Rosemary looked up with bright, turned-on eyes and said, "Did you just treat me like Buttercup?"

"Buttercup?" Realization dawned. The horse. "No, I'm trying to slow you down."

"Why?" she asked, parting the fabric of his trousers and tracing a finger down the erection straining against his boxers.

He hissed, closing his eyes. "Because I want it to be good for you."

"But what if I want to go fast?" she asked, grasping him through the thin cotton.

"Keep doing that and we'll really slow down. Like, I'll be finished."

She contemplated that, tilting her head. "How soon can you be ready to go again?"

Enough.

He'd been a good boy and let her have her fun, but it was time to get down to business. He sat up, capturing her hand. "We're not going to have the chance to find out yet. Time to lose the skirt, baby."

Rosemary kissed him while fiddling with the zipper on the side of the skirt. He heard the unzipping and broke the kiss so he could watch her shimmy from her last piece of clothing. What was denied to him Friday night was now all his. He quickly made short work of his pants, drawers, and socks. Finally, they lay on the bed completely and splendidly naked.

"Perfect," he said, trailing a hand across the curve of her hip. "Just perfect."

Rosemary had never thought she had a good body. Oh sure, it was mostly trim, but her breasts sloped weirdly and her hips were a bit too big. A bit swaybacked, she'd been constantly pinched for slumping her shoulders in effort to counterbalance. And her belly wasn't exactly flat. But Sal made her feel gorgeous. His dark eyes seemed to consume her, and the heat within the depths told her he found her more than adequate.

"I'm not perfect," she said.

"Oh no, you are," he said, his hands tracing her hip, sliding down to her thigh to brush the delicate skin behind her knee. Then his hand returned to her waist, pushing her back.

She let go, falling back onto the bed.

Part of her wished the lights were totally out, but the other half was glad of the lamp's glow. She could see his face as he touched her, and nothing was more of a turn-on than a man enjoying a woman's body.

Her skin felt hot, her breasts tight and achy. And she was utterly drenched between her legs. He dragged his fingers across her belly, making it flutter before ringing her navel.

Sal lay on his side, and she reached up to twine her fingers in his inky hair. "Kiss me."

He obliged with a hot, wet kiss that curled her toes. He broke the kiss and looked down at her. "You're driving me crazy, you know?"

She shook her head. "No, I'm the one about to go over the edge."

Obviously liking that admission, he cupped her sex.

"Oh." Her body silently cheered as he started a slow rocking of his hand, his middle finger teasing the dampness.

"You're so hot and wet. It's addictive," he said, kissing her ear. She swallowed hard as something frantic slammed into her. She needed him inside her. Bucking her hips, she moaned a sigh of pleasure when his finger dipped inside her.

Sal shifted so he slid down her body, dropping a kiss on her belly, settling himself between her legs.

Rosemary shot up to her elbows, eyes wide. She knew what he was about to do. She'd had sex plenty of times before but never had a man go down on her. She wasn't sure she wanted that much intimacy, that much vulnerability. But, of course, she'd imagined what it would be like to have a man make love to her that way while she lay lonely in her bed at home. "You don't have to do that."

He looked up, eyes half-lidded. "Are you fucking kidding me? This is so happening, baby. Let me love you, Rose. I need to taste you."

Rosemary knew he wouldn't if she said the word. "I don't . . . that is to say . . . okay."

Slowly he parted her folds with his hand, opening her, before dragging his tongue through the sensitive folds of her sex.

"Oh my, ah—" Rosemary cried, arching her back, her head falling back. Any protest she had left died on her lips. She'd never felt anything so spectacular . . . until his tongue hit her clit and started moving in a steady rhythm.

Holy crap. The sensation was amazing. No other word for it.

Sal moaned against her, his mouth fastening on her, sucking lightly, as his hands pushed her thighs up, spreading her even more to the most pleasure she'd ever experienced.

Rosemary felt drenched in desire, buckets and buckets of sheer heat. Inside her a delicious pressure built. Sal held her firm when she tried to struggle, the pressure of his mouth and tongue increasing.

She stretched to reach that pinnacle, twisting her head back and forth as she dug her toes into the covers and lifted her hips, reaching toward something, arching until . . . it happened.

Waves of pleasure crashed over her, taking over her body, making her tremble. A cry ripped past her lips, and she fell back, slamming her hands down, gripping the comforter, and holding on.

"Sal," she cried, trying to twist away.

But he held her tight, unrelentingly bringing her more pleasure. She stretched tight once more and then catapulted again, shattering against the delicious torture.

And it was good.

So, so, so damn good.

Finally, as the sensation abated, she pressed her palm against his forehead and panted, "Enough. Please."

He looked up then, eyes triumphant. Rosemary tugged his ears when he tried to lower his head again. "Seriously. I need you. Inside me."

Sal rose and moved backward, groping for something. His pants. He withdrew his wallet and pulled a condom from the depths. She hadn't even thought about protection. That's how crazy he'd driven her. Out of her mind.

As languid as her limbs felt, she still longed for something more, for him to sink inside her, filling her.

Ripping the package with his teeth, he withdrew the thin sheath. She plucked it from his fingers. "Can I?"

He smiled.

She shimmied to her knees and reached for him, admiring his length, the thick hardness she so desired. He was perfect. She placed the condom on the head of his shaft and rolled it down, a tight fit.

He pushed her on her back with a wicked grin, but she sprang back up, meeting him with a kiss. "I want on top."

"Of course you do," he murmured, capturing her lips, his erection wagging against her stomach. Hunger tapped again, and she pushed him to the side so he fell onto the pillows. Then she straddled him. Something about having this big man beneath her emboldened her.

She ran her hand down his torso, following the goody trail to what she needed to feel inside her. She grasped him, lifted herself, and sank down ever so slowly. He filled her completely, and for a moment she didn't move. Merely closed her eyes and leaned her head back.

This was what she needed. Not only to be free in New York City, living a life she'd only imagined, but to have this beautiful closeness with a man who made her feel so alive, so cherished, so damned sexy. With a man who let her be in charge of what she wanted in bed.

Sal's mouth opened almost as if she'd hurt him. "Oh, that's—"

"Incredible?" she asked, cocking one eye open.

He smiled.

Then she started moving, rocking her pelvis, riding him. He went deep and she loved the feeling of control she had over him. His hands clasped her hips, helping her, and she didn't mind because she wanted his hands on her.

Her hair hung in her face and her breasts bounced as she hooked her toes and lifted herself so he went even deeper. Dropping her head back, she increased the tempo.

"Fuck, you're sexy," he groaned, hands coming up to cup her breasts.

She moved faster, feeling the pressure again, wanting to be swept away. Sal lifted his hips in time with her before sitting up and sucking a nipple into his mouth. Lightly he bit down and then he surged forward, dropping her onto her back.

He pinned her knees back and reached a hand under her butt to lift her so he could drive deeper. Rosemary wrapped her arms about his neck as he pumped into her, hitting the sweet spot with delicious friction. The explosive had been lit, and before she could do anything else, she came again.

And Sal joined her, pumping furiously, a rough cry interrupting the sound of her heart beating in her ears.

"So good. Good. Good. Good," he said with each thrust. With a final move, he collapsed on top of her.

He was heavy, but she was beyond caring. Her knees dropped to either side and she panted, trying to catch her breath. Her arms stayed around him, registering the sweatiness, loving that they'd worn each other out. She felt incredibly boneless and euphoric.

After several seconds, Sal withdrew and rolled off her, sprawling on his back. His breath came fast and his chest rose and fell rapidly.

"Shit, that was good," he said to the ceiling.

Rosemary laughed, twisting her knees toward him and rolling to her side. "I'm pretty sure I've never come that many times."

He slid his gaze toward her. "You just needed a New Yorker."

"No, I needed an Italian," she teased.

He lifted his head. "Do all prim and proper southern girls screw like you?"

Rosemary pursed her lips, lifting her eyebrows. "Keep talking like that and I'll have to wash your mouth out, mister."

"Is that foreplay in Mississippi?"

And that made her laugh. Not just because he had a good sense of humor, but because he made her feel like the woman she'd always wanted to be.

An independent, modern one who didn't wear panties under her skirts and could ride a man like he was a . . . well, she wouldn't compare him to Buttercup. This was what her friend had wanted for Rosemary. And she knew Lacy would have approved of Sal.

Because he was a guy a woman could fall in love with.

"Will you stay with me?" she asked, reaching out to feather her fingers through his chest hair.

"Just try and stop me from holding you all night," he said.

Chapter Thirteen

The sound of harps strumming woke Rosemary and for a moment she thought she indeed had died and gone to heaven. But then she remembered she lay in her cousin's comfy bed in a loft in SoHo . . . and Sal lay beside her. The sound intensified.

"Damn it," he whispered, a thumping sound coming from the nightstand. Rosemary lifted her head as Sal grabbed his phone.

She threw an arm around his waist when he tried to roll away. "What're you doing?"

"Trying to"—he punched a button on the phone and the strumming stopped—"turn this alarm off. Sorry I woke you."

He flopped back, pulling her with him. She curled into him, resting her head on his shoulder. "Do you have to go to work this early?"

"No, but I have to get back to my place to change. I didn't think this out very well, so I'm without clean clothes. I didn't want to be presumptuous by packing a bag."

"As in you didn't think you'd score?" She yawned.

"I had hope. I had hope," he said, grazing her forehead with a kiss. "But I do have to get going."

"Don't you want to shower first? That shower is pretty incredible."

He twined his fingers in her hair. "But this bed is so warm."

Her hand stroked his stomach as she snuggled into him. Dipping lower, she found him hard and ready. "And there's this. Would be such a shame to waste this." She curved her hand around his length, making him groan. She loved the sounds he made when she touched him.

"Keep doing that and—"

She moved her hand up and down lazily. "That?"

"Witch," he said, catching her hand. "I have to get out to Dyker before the morning grind."

"I'll take a shower with you. Let's think of it as a time saver," she whispered, kissing the tattoo on his shoulder.

Sal slid from the bed, looking amazing in the pale morning light streaming through the windows. "Deal."

He reached under the cover and snagged her ankle, pulling her across the soft sheets to him.

"Ay," she squealed, flailing, showing him way too much skin. She'd slept naked in his arms, something she'd never done. She was a nightie kind of girl, but it had felt so nice snuggling skin on skin. As she slid toward him, she noted his morning erection had thickened. Fire lapped at her blood.

"You like being a brute, don't you?" she teased as he hauled her against him, wrapping her in his arms, dropping baby kisses on her jaw.

"Me Tarzan, you Jane," he cracked, lifting her and shuffling toward the huge shower with the full body sprays.

His naked body felt solid against hers, and she dipped a hand down to grab his hard butt. "Tarzan has a nice ass."

She felt his smile against her hairline. "Was hard to say ass, wasn't it?"

"I'm trying new things, trying to be a badass New Yorker. I'm thinking of tearing off my shirtsleeves and buying some motorcycle boots.

Maybe I'll do De Niro, too. 'You talking to me?'" She tried an impression but it was pretty terrible so she laughed at herself.

"Nah, I like you in pearls and those tight little prissy skirts," he said, his hands sliding down to cup her butt and bring her against his hard parts. "Especially when you do naughty things like ditching your underwear."

"You liked that, did you?" she asked, slipping from his grasp in order to turn on the vanity light and start the water. Took a while for the hot water to flow, so it gave them time to make out before climbing inside.

Sal's hands seemed to be everywhere at once. And his mouth found hers. "I like that you want to please me. I like that you want to be naughty for me."

She sighed, and when he lifted her from the black-and-white hexagon tile, she wrapped her legs around him, loving every part of their bodies lined up just right. She wriggled her hips, rocking his hardness against her softness.

The spray had warmed and Sal reached over and adjusted the temperature, still holding her aloft. He let her down and she went straight to her knees.

Since she was trying new things, there was still one thing she hadn't done. Okay, yes, she knew there were other things. Sex toys, stuff she'd read about in *Fifty Shades of Grey*, et cetera, but this she was pretty certain she could handle. She'd read an article in *Cosmopolitan* two months ago on how to give the perfect blow job.

"What do you think you're doing?" he asked, looking down at her with a lazy smile.

"Practicing my fellatio skills?" she said with a saucy flashbulb smile.

"Well, never let it be said I held you back from practicing," he said.

And Rosemary went to work, making damn sure he found taking a shower with her very worthwhile.

Ten minutes later, she found herself sprawled wet on her cousin's fluffy living room rug. Ten minutes after that, she had a panting Sal lying beneath her and kitty pitty-pats on her rump.

"I think your cats want to be fed," Sal said, peering around her hips at the cat standing on his thighs.

"They're not my cats."

"Still, I think you should feed them before they swat me again. My balls are sorta out there."

Rosemary climbed off him, reaching for the towel she'd abandoned earlier. She did a quick cleanup, tossing the towel to him before rising and padding toward the kitchen. She was bare-assed naked and didn't care. She'd never walked around the carriage house naked because her brother had a bad habit of sneaking inside at strange times. He'd scared the daylights out of her more than once. So it was freeing to walk around without a stitch of clothing on.

She made coffee in the professional chef's coffeepot that honestly didn't taste any better than a Mr. Coffee, but she wouldn't point that out to Halle. Sal pulled on the clothes he'd abandoned last night and used Rosemary's brush to comb his hair. She'd found a spare toothbrush in the cabinet and set it out.

She'd just poured a cup of coffee for him when his arm snaked around her waist and his lips found the sweet spot below her ear.

"Mmm, delicious," he said, nuzzling her neck and bringing his hands around to cup her breasts. "Do you always make coffee in the nude?"

"Of course not. I'm not a weirdo, you know." She held a mug out to him. "Want some?"

He took the cup. "And she pours him coffee the morning after? I'm pretty sure you're the perfect woman."

"What can I say? I'm a woman of many talents," she said, parking her hip against the counter, watching him add cream to his coffee. She felt a little silly standing there naked, but he seemed to enjoy it. His gaze felt hot on her.

"No, you're a woman of considerable talents," he said, taking a sip, his eyes closing briefly in appreciation. "Now I know why those

Mississippi boys keep you hostage down there." Her reached out and traced her hip.

"Ha. Guys from down my way only hold a woman in high esteem if she can cook up a mess of peas or help process venison," she said, thinking that if he knew how few Mississippi boys she'd actually been with he'd think her even more backward than she was.

No. Sal didn't think her anything. He didn't seem to be a judgmental sort. He was a what-you-see-is-what-you-get kind of guy. For the second time, she thought about how similar they were. She had little doubt he knew she wasn't very experienced when it came to the bedroom, the same way she could tell he knew his way around a woman's body.

"Wait, you know how to process venison? Bonus!" he joked, giving a fist pump.

"Actually, I don't. But it's highly prized in a southern woman, along with baiting her own hook, baking a pie like his mama, and never mistaking his spit cup for her Diet Dr Pepper."

"Spit cup? I'm not sure I want to know."

Rosemary laughed. "Yeah, Morning Glory is backward on a lot of things, but it's also pretty as a Sunday picnic."

Sal smiled. "Is it?"

"Sure, my town has a lot of colorful folks who walk slower, talk slower, and live slower. Guess slow is not exactly a bad thing these days."

And it wasn't. If anything, being in the fast-paced rat race of New York City, she'd learned to appreciate the time she had to smell the flowers. Like, literally smell the flowers. The town square was overflowing with blooms planted by the horticulture club, of which Rosemary was a member. Oh, make no mistake, she liked Manhattan. Stepping outside onto the hot pavement opened a new world of different cultures, sounds, tastes, and smells. Electric energy sparked in the air, making her feel as if she was drunk on life. But she wouldn't trade the soft summer nights on the porch drinking wine or the way everyone showed up for funerals with a casserole. It might be hard to keep a secret in Morning

Glory, but that was the key to a good small town. People knew and they cared.

Sal's brows knitted together. "I guess you're right. It's not a bad way to live." He looked as if he might say something more but then seemed to think better of it. "What are your plans for today?"

"Go back to bed for another four hours and—"

"You're going back to bed without me?" he asked, poking a lip out comically before giving her ribs a tickle. "You can't do that. Not fair."

"But I need my beauty sleep. You wore me out."

"Me? More like you. You're a sex machine, woman."

"I am not." Rosemary faked outrage but stepped toward him. She looped an arm about his waist and snuggled in to him.

He dropped a kiss on her head, his hand immediately sliding down to squeeze her butt. "I'm working early, so I'll be off again tonight."

"Does that mean I should wait here with the handcuffs and whips?" she asked against the buttons of his shirt. She could smell his cologne, the yummy woodsy yet clean scent. She wanted to bathe in it, have his scent on her all day long.

He tipped up her chin. "I've unleashed an insatiable monster."

"Yeah, you have."

"In all seriousness, there isn't a moment I don't want to spend with you. As long as that's good with you."

Then he kissed her, his hands sliding up and down her naked back, lingering on the curve of her breast, patting her rump.

And his kiss tasted like coffee and a promise.

"It's better than good with me," Rosemary said, going up on her tiptoes to kiss his chin. "I want to be with you. So text me later?"

"Yeah. I can get back here by six o'clock. We'll go out."

"Or stay in," she said.

He kissed his way down to her breasts. "Or I can quit my job and stay here all day long. Just me and your tits."

Desire reared its head, twitching its ears as if to ask, *Yes?* But Rosemary tamped it down and stepped away. "Just them? Or is the rest of me not invited? And really, don't start what you can't finish."

"No worries. I can be quick," he said, reaching for her again.

"No, you go on to work. I'll stay here and find something to do," she said, cupping her breasts before sliding her hands down her stomach, teasing him.

Something in his gaze flared and he stilled. "Rosemary, you're killing me."

She pushed him toward the door. "I'm joking. I'm saving it all for you. Now off you go before you have to explain to your family what you've been doing all night." Rosemary walked to the bed and found her nightgown she'd discarded yesterday. Of course, she had to move Melbourne off it first. She didn't know what had gotten into her. Rubbing her hands down her body, going down on a guy, walking around naked, and going back to bed. She'd turned into *that* woman. And she loved it. Why hadn't anyone ever told her how much fun being slutty was?

Sal waited at the door for her, still sipping his coffee, watching her the way a hawk regards the hapless field mouse. "Maybe I want to get fired."

Something in his tone gave her pause. "Do you?"

"I'm thinking about it. I feel bewitched."

"Bothered and bewildered?" she finished for him with a smile. "That's it exactly. My evil plan is now fully realized. When I hopped on my broom and set it for SoHo, I told myself I'd find a sexy Italian and make him my sex slave. Mission accomplished."

He gave her a hard kiss. "If my being your sex slave qualifies as an evil plan, I'm all in."

"Silly slave boy, you now have my permission to go make decadent sauces. Return to me and prepare to be punished . . . exquisitely," she said, unlocking the door and flinging it open with more than a little dramatic flair.

He walked out and paused. "Thank God you have no sense of direction or there might be some other guy under your spell. If I could find the man who pointed you my way, I'd kiss him."

"Hey, now. I'm open to kinkiness but not that much kinky." She laughed, blowing him a kiss. "I guess being directionally challenged was a good thing in this case."

"A very good thing. I'll see you tonight." And then he was gone, hurrying down the stairs. As he turned on the landing, he looked up at her and smiled.

Rosemary felt happiness all the way down to her Pretty in Pink toenail polish. She closed the door, locking it. And then double-checked it the way she'd promised her father she would. But she took Sal's smile and tucked it inside her for an extra glow that would last all day.

She couldn't wait to see him again.

An hour later Sal emerged from his apartment, humming "I've Got You Under My Skin," and nearly bowled Angelina over.

"Holy crap," he said, catching her upper arms so she didn't fly backward.

"Sal," she squeaked, her long fingernails grazing his pristine white button-down as she grappled for something to hold on to.

"You okay?" he asked, righting her. The stairs were dangerously close and she was lucky she didn't take a tumble.

"Yeah," she said, looking up at him. Her brown eyes were ringed red and makeup streaked her cheeks. Something crawly wriggled inside him.

"What's up?" he asked cautiously while locking his door.

"You know what's up. You know how terrible this all is."

He spun toward her, his mind grappling with a million thoughts but centering on one—she'd found out about Rosemary. And the hot-tempered Angelina wouldn't take it well. "What?"

"This whole thing," she said, swiping at fresh tears pooling in her eyes. "How could you—"

"You don't have the—"

"Aunt Louisa always loved you."

"Aunt Louisa?" He stood far back in the dark on this one, but relief that he didn't have to deal with Angelina's jealousy that morning bloomed in him.

"You mean you don't know about Aunt Louisa? Your ma didn't tell you?" Angelina said, placing her hand on his arm. "I can't believe you haven't heard. It's the worst news possible."

He didn't know what in the hell Angelina talked about. "Did something happen to Mrs. Grimaldi?"

"The garbage truck? The wreck?" A fresh wave of emotion seemed to hit her and she pressed a hand to her mouth. "Oh God."

Sal took Angelina's trembling hand. "What happened?"

The Genovese family had been friends with the Vitale family for generations and Angelina's mother, Marianna, had three sisters, one of whom was Louisa Grimaldi, whose husband owned a dry cleaner's. Sal had always liked Louisa with her dimpled smile, good Italian bread, and red cowboy boots. She had a crush on Johnny Cash that surpassed the county singer's death.

"She's dead," Angelina wailed, nearly collapsing. "I thought you knew. Your mother said she tried calling you and you didn't answer. But I assumed she talked to you this morning. I called three times myself."

"Uh, I had my phone on vibrate. Had trouble sleeping last night." Which was not a lie. No way could he tell her about Rosemary now. Not when she was this emotional.

With nothing left to do, he curled an arm around Angelina's thin shoulders and pulled his keys out of his pocket. He didn't want to let Angelina in his apartment, but then again, the death of her aunt had knocked him for a loop. "Here, come sit down. Let me get you some cold water or something."

Angelina nodded, sniffling and swiping at her cheeks. She wore a business suit, dark gray and impeccable with a bright-pink, silky-looking top. Her heels clacked on the old linoleum in the hallway. Opening the door, he stepped back to let her pass, but she reached out for his arm. "I'm glad you're here. She always liked you so much."

Had she? Sal didn't know. He'd been around the woman only a few times. Plus, the only reason he was here for Angelina was because she'd shown up on his doorstep. "Louisa was a nice lady. I'm sorry for your loss, Angelina."

She swallowed hard and then stepped inside his place, which was neither pristine nor posh. While the location was good, he'd never bothered to make much of the place. He'd collected leftover furniture from his parents and brothers and bummed his grandmother's secondhand dishes. The place had always felt temporary to him.

Angelina looked around, her nose wrinkling before she smoothed her face into an accepting one. Tricks of the trade, no doubt. "So this is your place?"

She didn't sound impressed. He hurried to pick up last Sunday's *New York Times* from the end of the couch along with a stack of folded laundry he'd yet to tuck away. "Sorry it's a bit of a mess. I've been busy lately."

"It's fine," she said, sitting down on the cleared spot. She grabbed his arm. "Sit with me?"

What else could he do?

Gingerly he sat next to her, toeing a flip-flop back under the coffee table next to its mate. "Can I get you anything?"

She shook her head, lower lip trembling. "I can't believe what happened to her. The police said it was her fault, so Uncle Joe can't even sue the stupid city. She T-boned a garbage truck and they're checking her blood alcohol. But Aunt Lou didn't drink. Sure, the communion wine and maybe a nip every now and then. Oh God, it's just so horrible." Angelina pressed her hand against her mouth again and then collapsed against him in tears.

Sal patted her awkwardly. "I'm sorry, Angie. She was a good lady."

"I know," Angelina sobbed, clutching his only clean shirt and boohooing into it. He truly felt bad for the woman whose best quality was her closeness with her family. Her loyalty was one of the reasons Natalie Genovese liked her so much. That and she had a good job. For a few seconds, he patted her and let her cry it out.

Finally, she lifted her head. Mascara streaked her cheeks and her hair flew about her head, falling out of the bun thing she'd pulled it into. "Life is so precious," she whispered.

And then she kissed him.

He hadn't been expecting it, so his mouth was halfway open, which Angelina took full advantage of. He froze for a moment and then he pulled away, trying to remember Angelina was overwhelmed with emotion.

She stared at him with glassy eyes and a half smile. "I guess I shouldn't have done that, but I've been thinking about kissing you again. You've been so distant and I've tried so hard to get you to . . . like me."

Honesty was something he always appreciated, but at that moment after she'd kissed him—after she'd shown up for comfort—it was the last thing he wanted. Days ago, he'd tried to have an honest conversation with her about where he stood, but she obviously hadn't gotten the message. Friends didn't kiss friends like that.

Sighing, he shifted away. "I like you, Angelina. Our families have been friends for a long time, and this is a sad day for you, but I'm not sure kissing should be something we engage in, you know? You're dealing with the shock of your aunt's death."

She stared at him for a few minutes, a long few minutes. Finally, her shoulders sank and she swiped a finger under her lower lashes, stanching the tears. "You're right. Now's definitely not the time. It's just I'm human and I needed someone, you know?"

He nodded because what else could he do? He felt uncomfortable. Like a man in a room full of snakes. Not that Angelina was a snake. But he still felt like he couldn't step left or right without getting struck.

"I should go," she said, rising and pressing her hands against her skirt. "You don't mind my using your powder room?"

He had no idea how clean his bathroom was. Probably had underwear on the floor or towels hanging over the shower curtain. Might have left his deodorant out. "Uh, I'm not sure how clean it is."

Her mouth twisted faintly. "Well, I can't go to a showing like this. I need to wash up and fix my face." She picked up the designer bag she'd dumped on his couch.

"Right through there," he said, pointing to his right.

She went in the bathroom and closed the door.

Sal dug his cell phone out of his pocket and texted his father he'd be late. He added Angelina had shown up upset about her aunt, which would soften the ass chewing he'd get for coming in late. Then he set about picking up his place.

He'd planned on bringing Rosemary to Brooklyn to see some of the other parts of the city, so the place needed a good scrubbing. Maybe he'd call Merry Maids. And put fresh sheets on the bed.

A ding on his phone relayed a text from his pops.

Don't worry. Take care of Angie.

Of course his father would say that since Sal's mother had likely already selected his and Angelina's wedding china.

He managed to pick up the living area and toss the papers into the recycling bin before Angelina emerged, looking more put together, hair back in place.

"I took a little time to tidy up your bathroom for you," she said, rubbing her lips together. Fresh shiny gloss coated her lips and the pink matched the rims of her eyes, which still showed sign of grief.

"You shouldn't have," he said.

"You're out of cleaner so I had to use a damp washcloth. No problem. It was the least I could do for showing up here blubbering like a baby."

He felt the words stick in his throat. "It's okay. I'm glad . . ." He'd wanted to say he was glad to be there for her. That they were friends. Sort of. But he didn't want to lead her on, so he snapped his mouth shut.

"Thank you," she said, walking to him and taking his hand. "Will you come to Aunt Ginny's tonight? Everyone would love to see you and I already know your mother and father are bringing food. The wake's tomorrow, so it's just family and close friends tonight."

Angelina's lips trembled as she studied him. The morning light slanted in, like an unwanted reality. Here was his world knocking at his door. His family would be there, and if he didn't show, both families would take it as a mark of disrespect.

So what could he say?

That he had plans with another woman . . . a woman who was a temporary reprieve from his scheduled life? A woman who would be just a memory, leaving him here to live out the life already unfolding before him?

He had little choice. His mouth tasted sour with regret as he said, "Sure. I'll come by after work and pay my respects to your family."

"Thank you, Sal. You're a good guy." Angelina rose onto her toes and kissed his cheek. He followed her out the door, stepping out behind her and locking up.

"I'll see you tonight," Angelina said before clacking down the hall. Just as she turned to descend the steps, she gave him a tremulous smile, an I'm-so-brave-to-face-the-day smile that was a nail in the coffin of his familial obligation.

Yeah. He was stuck.

And it sucked. Because every hour, every minute was now precious to him.

He pulled out his cell phone and sent Rosemary a text.

Might not make tonight. Family obligation.

Somehow that was the theme of his life.

Chapter Fourteen

If trudging up a five-story walk-up was challenging, then walking up a five-story walk-up while carrying a rented sewing machine was grueling.

When Rosemary got to the top floor, she collapsed against the door and slid down, holding the precious (and expensive!) rented sewing machine in her lap. Beside her was a bag containing trim, spools of thread, and a Dr Pepper.

The weird lady in 5D poked her head out and stared at her questioningly. "Do you need me to call 911?"

"Uh, no. I"—pant, pant, pant—"think I will be okay."

The woman narrowed eyes behind horn-rimmed glasses that should have been chic, but the frizzy hair and patterned silk caftan said differently. "What are you doing with that sewing machine?"

"Being crushed by it," Rosemary joked, lifting the rented Singer off her. "Seriously, I'm going to piece together all the skin I've been saving from young boys and make myself into a man."

The woman drew back.

Rosemary pressed a hand. "I'm joking. *Silence of the Lambs*? No?"

The woman shook her head, still looking concerned. But then she stuck a cigarette into her mouth and lit it from a lighter in her pocket. "I worked for Karl Lagerfeld."

Rosemary struggled to rise, sliding the machine to the side. "*The* Karl Lagerfeld?"

"Do you know any other Karl Lagerfelds someone would say they worked for?" she drawled with a raspy voice that held a trace of exotic accent. She opened the door a bit wider. "You're Halle's sister?"

Rosemary shook her head. "Cousin."

"You want a cup of tea? I have chamomile."

Rosemary was intrigued. She'd seen the woman poke her head out a time or two, but Halle hadn't said boo about her neighbors. Merely instructions for the two uppity creatures who liked to sharpen their claws on anything squishy. Like her stomach. "I'd love a cup of chamomile."

The woman jerked her head and opened the door wider.

The place smelled like an ashtray, but it was wonderfully arrayed with bright colors and actual swaths of fabric. It was a feast of sensual delight, sans the cigarette smell. Huge beanbags resting on overlapping carpets surrounded by funky curved furniture and lamp shades with tassels. Rosemary didn't know whether she'd entered a sultan's harem or a decorator's crime scene. "Wow."

"Eh, I like color."

"That's an understatement," Rosemary said, setting the machine and her bag on the industrial table holding three vases of various flowers. "But I love it."

"I'm Gilda Besson."

"Rosemary Reynolds."

Gilda went into the small galley kitchen and put a kettle on. "So tell me what you're doing with a sewing machine. You a designer, too?"

"No," Rosemary said, eyeing the huge canvas that covered a good three-fourths of the far wall. She had no clue what it was, but the patterns were mesmerizing. "Well, not really. I have a fabric shop in Mississippi and I like to make pillows with vintage fabrics. Thought I'd piece a few together while I'm here."

Gilda arched a thin brow. "Hmm."

Rosemary spotted the workstation then. Beside the very small bed was a table holding a sewing machine. Shelves holding boxes of what looked like notions. "You still do design work?"

"I'm a milliner," Gilda said. "Of course, I've been lazy about it these few months. Had I known you were renting a sewing machine, I would have loaned you mine. It's gathering dust."

And then Rosemary noticed the high shelf that extended around the entire room filled with mannequin heads holding fantastical hats and fascinators. "Oh, look at that," she breathed spinning around. "I'd say you have good reason to be lazy. What a collection. Do you sell them?"

"I have a website," Gilda said, pulling down cups. "But I'm not interested in me. I'm interested in you. Tell me about Mississippi and these pillows you make."

Rosemary joined Gilda in the kitchen. She'd been sorely disappointed that she might not see Sal tonight, so she'd decided to plunge herself into another goal for the time she was in NYC. Designing pillows had always been a rewarding, stress-reducing task and she loved the results, as did her customers, who bought them for gifts. She'd gone out and scoured more secondhand shops for old pillowcases, sheets, and remnants so she could ship the materials back to Morning Glory. But that afternoon, she'd gotten an itch. The rented sewing machine would help her scratch it. "I love taking old fabric relegated to thrift shops and repurposing it."

"And you plan to make pillows while you're here?"

"Maybe a few," Rosemary said, accepting the thin bone china teacup. "But I'm not here for that. I'm doing other things while I'm here, too."

"Like that hunk?"

Rosemary felt her cheeks heat. "Uh, him, too."

"You have good taste in men," Gilda said, cracking a smile. The woman had a face that belied her age—she might be fifty or seventy-five years old. Hard to tell. Yet her youthful blue eyes sparkled with good humor.

Rosemary gave a self-deprecating laugh. "There's not much to choose from back home in Morning Glory, so I'm having a little romantic fun while I'm here."

"Is that why you came to the city?" Gilda asked, sinking onto a stool sitting beside the concrete counter. Something about Gilda was sage-like. As if the woman could be her Obi-Wan Kenobi.

"Good question," Rosemary said, taking the adjoining stool, feeling immediate kinship with the woman. Which was odd since they were nothing alike. Gilda had a horrible dye job and jewels sparkling on every finger. And Rosemary . . . didn't and never would. "Actually, I came because my best friend died."

Gilda's eyebrows rose but she didn't mutter any condolence. Just listened.

"I know that sounds weird, but Lacy wanted to see the world. She was full of life and had so many dreams. But sickness won. It wasn't fair."

"Life rarely is," Gilda said, glancing toward the sheer curtains muddling the sight of the outside world.

"That's so true," Rosemary said, contemplating the tea leaves swirling in the bottom of the cup. "So Lacy left me a letter essentially calling me out. She said I was in a rut, treading water, locked in a too-comfortable room of my choosing. And she reminded me of all the things I'd said I wanted to do . . . and so I'm doing them. Well, not all of them. But I grabbed an opportunity and I'm focused on being open to what life has to offer."

"Hmm," Gilda said.

Okay, so maybe Gilda was a poor substitute for Obi-Wan. No insight, no wise words. Just a hmm.

Rosemary shrugged. "So I'm in New York City all by myself. I'm going dancing with handsome Italians, having sex in showers—"

"You've never had sex in a shower before?"

"Nope. And I've never dated a guy with a tattoo or taken a subway—or a cab, for that matter. And I've never entered a fascinating stranger's apartment for tea. You're not a serial killer, are you?"

"Ha. You're the one making suits out of boys," Gilda said with a smile.

Rosemary laughed. "Lack of oxygen makes me delusional."

Gilda's lips twitched. And then they sat for several seconds sipping tea and enjoying what sounded like the indigenous music of New Zealand. Not that Rosemary knew what that sounded like. She just guessed.

"I know you," Gilda said, looking at her, eyes misty.

"Beg your pardon?"

"I was you. I'm from Minnesota."

Rosemary waited, because Gilda had a certain way of not explaining herself, it seemed.

"I came to New York when I was seventeen. Told my ma and pa I wasn't marrying no farmer. Met a costume designer and he took me to Paris. Taught me everything I knew. Wines, cheeses . . . and sex. All of it was intoxicating. I started hanging around designers and I learned how to make love, cry, wake up and wish I were dead . . . to fall in love. It was both painful and beautiful at the same time."

"And now?"

Gilda laughed. "And now I'm an old woman. But I lived. I lived well."

"I guess you did," Rosemary said, the chamomile tasting somehow more pronounced on her tongue. Something in Gilda's eyes told a story of heartbreak, loss, and no regret. Whatever it was, it sat heavy in her gut. Maybe it was a sense of rightness, that Rosemary hadn't been crazy as her mother suggested for coming to SoHo alone, for accepting Sal's offer to go dancing . . . for taking tea with Halle's odd neighbor.

"I'd love to see your pillows when you've finished them."

"Oh," Rosemary said, setting down the lukewarm tea. "Why?"

Gilda blinked. "Because I want to. Why wouldn't I?"

"Because you've seen the work of giants in the fashion industry. My pillows are a hobby."

"So?"

Rosemary shrugged. "I sent Halle a few for her birthday and I found them in the top of her closet. Guess the folksy, arts-and-crafts vibe didn't work with her midcentury modern look."

"Go get them," Gilda said.

Rosemary had no clue why Gilda was so interested in her damn pillows. "When I finish my tea?"

Gilda looked contrite. "Of course. I didn't mean to be rude."

Ten minutes later, Rosemary handed Gilda the pillows she'd made Halle two years ago. A mixture of ticking and a gorgeous quilt she'd found in a shop on a Mississippi back road, the matching toss pillows had been pieced into a cross pattern, edged in tatting Rosemary had found in their great-grandmother's hope chest.

"These tell a story," Gilda said, fingering the tatting. "Did you do the tatting?"

"No, I found it in my great-grandmother Pearl's trunk in the attic. It had been starched and wrapped around Coke bottles."

"Fascinating. May I keep these for a few days?"

Rosemary didn't know what to say. Though Halle didn't seem to want the pillows, they did belong to her cousin. But then again, Rosemary would know where they were. "Uh, sure. I'm certain Halle wouldn't mind."

"I don't think she would," Gilda said, stacking the pillows atop one of the beanbags. "Now, I'll say good afternoon. My program is about to come on."

"Oh. Of course. It was lovely meeting you. Thanks for the tea," Rosemary said, moving toward the door.

Gilda showed her out and then proceeded to lock what sounded like Fort Knox. Made Halle's dead bolt look like shoestring protection.

Just as she stepped into the hallway, her cell phone rang.

Her heart gave a leap as she imagined Sal on the other end telling her he was on his way. She pulled out her phone. Not Sal.

Jess.

"Hey, chickadee," Jess said when Rosemary said hello.

"Hi, I'm sorry I missed your call last night," Rosemary said, setting the sewing machine by her cousin's door.

"I'm sure you have a good excuse, and according to Eden he has a six-pack. Go, Rose," Jess said.

Rosemary laughed. "Hold on a sec. I have to unlock the door and then I want to tell you about the carriage ride I took in Central Park."

"I already know about those. My mom took me when I was a kid."

"Oh no. You've never had one like this," Rosemary drawled before pushing into the SoHo loft.

"Really?" Jess returned with a drawl of her own and a laugh. "Do tell."

If Sal thought sitting at his parents' dining room table jammed in next to Angelina was hell, then sitting at the Vitales' dining room table between Cousin Butch and the Vietnamese lady who lived next door to the Vitales was like swimming in a fiery lake of hell where flames singed his balls and bubbled his skin.

"Another cannoli, Sal?" Marianna Vitale, Angelina's mother asked, passing a laden platter his way.

"No, thank you. It's getting late and I—"

"Lou would have loved this," Marinna said, tears flooding her eyes. "If only we would have done this when she was here, you know? She always said she loved when our families got together."

Sal nodded. "Again, I'm so sorry."

Mrs. Vitale blew her nose into a lace hankie she withdrew from her pocket. Her brittle shoulders shook. "I know, I know. I'm so glad you're here though, Sal. Angie appreciates it so much. This has been so hard on her, being so fond of her aunt and all."

"Sure," Sal said, catching his mother's eye. She nodded at him, obviously pleased he had come.

Of course she'd sent him a text that said, "If you're not at the Vitales' tonight, you can find a new family." He'd like to think she didn't mean it, but he wouldn't put it past her. Natalie Genovese didn't shoot marbles. And she didn't put up with any of her children being disrespectful.

He turned away from his mother's direct stare because though he'd toed the line out of family loyalty, he wasn't happy about it. And he wanted his mother to know that. He'd already stayed late at the restaurant so his father could go home and change, and he'd been at the Vitale's house for at least forty-five minutes.

He glanced at his phone then stood and pushed his chair in, intending on taking his leave.

But Angelina appeared at his elbow, looking waiflike in a dress that covered all her assets for once. "Can I get you more coffee, Sal?"

"I'm not going to be able to sleep as it is," he said with a small smile. "I'll pass."

Angelina placed her hand on his arm and gave it a squeeze. "It's decaf."

"No, I'm good. I should probably—"

"My cousin Bella wanted to say hello to you," Angelina said, jerking her head toward a frizzy-headed woman who looked about forty pounds too heavy and twenty years past her prime. "Do you remember her from the YMCA? She was an aerobics instructor. Aunt Louisa loved aerobics."

Bella appeared with a wide smile. "So this is Sal?"

That shaky feeling in his belly grew. What had Angelina been telling her friends and family about him? But he knew. God help him, he knew.

"I've heard so much about you. Angelina positively glows when she talks about you and I see why," Bella said, raking him with an appreciative glance. "Of course, I've known your mother for ages. We went to grammar school together."

Angelina shot Bella a look, giving a curt shake of her head. "I glow when I talk about lots of people, Bella. Sal's just lucky he made the cut."

"It's nice to meet you, Bella," Sal said as the older woman shot Angelina a questioning look.

"And you. Terrible tragedy, but the upside is it brings people together." Bella gave him a nudge. Literally a nudge toward Angelina.

"Yeah," Sal said, glancing at the cuckoo clock hanging in the kitchen, where his parents sat with Angelina's father and siblings. Ten minutes past ten o'clock. It would take him at least thirty minutes to get to SoHo. Another five or ten minutes to walk to the block on Spring Street where Rosemary waited. It was foolish to keep her waiting. "Uh, I need to step out and make a call. Excuse me."

Sal nodded toward Bella and gave Angelina a tight smile before pushing past his brother holding his niece and slipping out the French doors that led to the small patio out back. Pulling his phone from his pocket, he dialed the number he'd added to his contacts only a few days ago.

"Hey," he said.

"Sal," Rosemary breathed. "Where are you? I thought you'd be here by now."

"I got hung up, baby. I'm sorry."

"Are you coming?

"I could make a joke about that," he teased.

Her throaty laugh made his balls tighten. Christ, he got hard just hearing her voice.

"Look, I'm going to be another hour or so. A family friend passed and I needed to be—"

"Oh, I'm so sorry. You have to stay. I can't be that selfish," Rosemary said, genuine anguish in her voice. "It's important to be there for your family, for your friends. I know."

"But I can still—"

"We can see each other tomorrow."

"Tomorrow's the wake. My parents have to go to that and Vincent has a final in his business class. So I have to run the restaurant tomorrow night. I'm going to be tied up all day and all night."

"Oh," she said softly. "Then I'll come have lunch at the restaurant. You'll be working, right?"

"Yeah. But it's not the same, you know?"

"I know but it's better than not seeing you at all."

He looked up at the stars winking at him. They seemed almost mocking. "I want to be with you."

"I want that, too," she said. "But I'll save the whips and chains for Wednesday night."

He chuckled and then caught sight of Angelina at the door. Her earrings caught the light of the full moon, and her grief-stricken face looked softer than normal. She made his stomach hurt, but he couldn't be harsh when the woman was in a bad place. Her family was her world, and Louisa had been one of her favorite people. Or so she'd always said. "Okay, that sounds . . . painful. But for you I'll try anything."

"Sweet dreams, Sal. I'll miss you."

"Yeah, me, too."

He hung up, frustrated, sad, and resigned to doing the right thing.

"Are you through with your call?" Angelina asked, stepping onto the patio.

"Yeah." He pocketed his cell.

"Sorry about Bella. She may have read into some things I said."

Sal wanted to chew Angelina out for misleading her family about him, but he wasn't sure the ballbusting beauty could handle the harsh truth about the way he felt at the moment. "Sure."

"Look, don't be mad. I had hoped things would be different by now."

"What? Like I'd roll over just because you decided I should?" he asked.

Her teeth flashed in the darkness. "I'm good at scratching bellies."

"Angie," he warned.

"Joking," she said, but he could tell she didn't mean it. "But why are you seeing me as the enemy? Because of your mother? Or do you not like me at all?"

"I never said that."

"I think this is about you defying your parents. It's one of those things a guy does. The more they push you toward something that makes sense, the more you dig in your heels because you don't want to be told to do something. Like reverse psychology or something. You won't give me a chance because that means you're giving in. And you don't like to give in. Maybe if you'd see the real me instead of this woman you think I am, things could be different. So I don't think it's me. I think it's you."

Maybe. He couldn't say that wasn't some of it. He knew this about himself, but that didn't mean he intentionally shunned Angelina out of spite. Angelina made sense on paper, and there was nothing wrong with her other than her being bold and cocksure. In fact, those were qualities he should desire in a mate, but for some reason Angelina came off as hard and manipulative. "I don't know, Angie. Maybe that's some of it. No one likes being managed. No matter what you say, it feels like you and my ma got together and decided we'd do good together. Nobody asked me what I wanted."

Angelina tilted her head, her eyes narrowing. "You're mad because when I saw you, I saw a future together? I want you. Why doesn't that flatter you? 'Cause I've turned down a lot of guys, you know. I'm not chopped liver or something the dog dragged up."

She made his protests seem absurd. But it wasn't that simple. "I don't fault you for going after what you want, and I know lots of guys want you. You're a beautiful woman."

"Exactly," she said, moving closer to him. "When I saw you across the fellowship hall at the church bouncing your niece on your knee, making silly faces at her, I knew I'd never seen a man as frickin' sexy as you. My knees actually got a little weak." She smiled.

"But you didn't know me. We hadn't talked since you were a kid."

"I didn't have to know you. I could see what I'd been looking for right there. Good-looking, kind, Italian, good family."

"You make me sound like a dog."

Angelina shook her head. "Oh, come on. You know that's not what I mean."

"Look, Angelina. You're a nice girl."

She ran a hand up his chest. "No, I'm not. We both know that. I'm ambitious—bitchy, even. I'm also smart and have tremendous upside. You shouldn't count me out because you didn't think of it first."

Was that what he'd done? Scratched Angelina off because she'd strapped on her hunting boots and grabbed an elephant gun to go after him? He'd always liked the chase. Or perhaps he'd always like the unattainable. Maybe that's what Hillary had been about. Maybe deep down inside he'd known she wasn't going to marry him and that made her safe. And now there was Rosemary. He'd chased her, wooed her beneath the stars to Nat King Cole. And she, too, was unavailable. Perhaps it wasn't about the chase. Maybe he was afraid to let himself get caught by the very thing he desired. Which made him one messed-up dude.

Angelina seemed to be waiting on him to say something.

He didn't.

So she did what she always did—took control. Raising up, she kissed him.

He let her. Because he needed to see if he felt anything this time. Maybe she deserved a chance, a clean slate.

Her lips were firm and tasted of cherries, as if she'd applied lip gloss before slipping out into the darkness. She wound her arms about his neck and he obligingly dropped his hands to her small waist. Her nails scraped his neck as she opened her mouth and devoured him.

No doubt about it—her kiss was hot, wet, and designed to make a man want her. Thing was, Angelina didn't do it for him.

He'd been fair, but no dice.

Breaking the kiss, he stepped away. "I need to go."

She frowned. "Will I see you tomorrow at the wake?"

"I have to run the restaurant so my parents can attend."

"But what if I want you with me? Would you deny me your support during a time like this?"

"I can talk to Pops if you want me to come. We can trade out."

"No. Don't come. I'm fine."

Guilt slammed him. He was being an ass. The Vitales were family friends; they were part of his community. He couldn't blow Angelina off if she wanted him to come to the wake. "I'll be at the funeral on Wednesday."

"I appreciate your taking time from . . . what is it you're doing? Going to strip clubs? Picking up whores?"

"Come on, Angie. Don't do this," he said.

"I can do what I want," she said, tears slipping down her cheeks. "My aunt died and you're standing here being a stubborn asshole. You won't even try with me. And we could be good together."

"Jesus, Angelina, don't you want a man who burns for you? Why would you settle for anything less?"

Her face crinkled and she wiped the tears from her cheeks. "You're so stupid, Sal. Love? And I guess you believe in Santa Claus, too? Life isn't about falling in love. It's about sex, power, and making your way. You don't piss away all that so you can chase rainbows and look for unicorns." Angelina looked at him with something akin to pity.

"You believe that? That marriage is business?" he asked, not believing she could toss aside the concept of love so easily.

"How can I not? The relationships that last between two people are based on mutual respect, compatible goals, and fondness. I don't need you to write me poetry or braid my hair. I want a man who knows what he wants—a family and a thriving business," she said, spinning on her heel and climbing the three steps that led to the porch. "So I'm not sure we're right for each other after all. Or maybe we're perfect. I can see the world as it is, and you can put on your rose-colored glasses. Funny—I never took you for a romantic."

He'd never thought he was, either, but he damn sure didn't see commitment the way Angelina did. Hers was a hard view, a joining of like-mindedness unaffected by emotion. Other than fondness. At least she'd mentioned that.

"I'll see you at the funeral. Thanks for coming, Sal."

And then Angelina disappeared back into the crowded kitchen, leaving him conflicted.

In all honestly, he'd never contemplated why a man made a commitment. When he proposed to Hillary, there'd been nothing logical about it. She'd consumed him and he'd wanted to please her at all costs. Hillary had wanted a diamond on her finger, a fluffy veil, and nine months later a squalling bundle of joy. So he'd gotten down on a knee and given her what she wanted. He'd never thought about what marriage should look like to him. Should a man take a common sense approach like his parents had suggested? Pick the girl who made sense? Maybe falling in love was something good for poetry and ballads, even if it seemed contrary to everything he'd ever believed. He'd always thought marriage was the joining of two hearts, but maybe it was better when it was the joining of intentions.

He shook his head and made his way back into the Vitale house, not sure about the concepts whipping through his mind, but very sure that he wasn't going to think about it until Rosemary went back to Mississippi and he was left to a world he'd always known.

Chapter Fifteen

Rosemary had just stepped out to go to lunch at Mama Mello's when Gilda caught her.

"Rosemary?" the woman said, sticking her head out the door and looking around wildly.

"Morning, Gilda," Rosemary said, turning to lock her cousin's door.

"I heard your rented machine going all night," Gilda said.

When Sal had called and said he couldn't make it, Rosemary had thrown herself into piecing together a new design. She'd cut the embroidered pillowcases into strips and finished with a light pink eyelet trim. She'd finished two pillows and had thought of a new design for a round pillow using vintage sixties poly blend she'd bought on a whim. "I hope it didn't bother you. It's a quiet machine."

"No, no." Gilda waved an arm holding seven or so bangle bracelets. "Where are you going?"

"I'm popping by a thrift shop I went to the other day to grab some red-striped ticking I saw on the clearance table and then I'm going to Sal's restaurant for lunch. Would you like to join me?"

The woman's face scrunched up. "I had hoped you didn't have definitive plans for lunch, because I called in a favor."

Rosemary walked over to the woman. "What do you mean, a favor?"

"Yes, and it was a big one. So I'm afraid you'll have to change your luncheon plans. Call your Italian and beg off. This is important."

Rosemary had not a clue what the woman was talking about. A favor? "What are you talking about?"

"I called Stanton last night and sent him some pictures of your pillows. Of course the photos on the phone don't do them justice, but Stanton liked them enough to show Trevor. And Trevor has a meeting on the West Coast on Wednesday, so the only time he has is today. So you're going to have to change your clothes."

Rosemary looked down at her shorts. "Why? Wait. Who's Stanton? And I—"

"Stanton's my son, of course. Didn't I tell you about him? No? Well, no matter."

"Oh no, you didn't tell me about—"

"Change," Gilda said, pointing a finger at the locked door over Rosemary's shoulder. "Trevor's a discerning man and short pants won't say what you need to say, dear. Go put on that fetching little seersucker dress you wore the day you arrived. It has the perfect branding of southern innocence and charm. Very authentic for your purpose."

"Uh, Gilda, I don't know what that purpose is," Rosemary said. She'd gleaned Gilda was eccentric the day before, but at the moment the woman seemed trapped in an alternate world only she understood.

"Your pillows, dear. They're charming as you are and Trevor has tremendous power in product placement. Unless you're not interested?"

Rosemary felt like she'd fallen down a rabbit hole. "Interested in what? Who is Trevor?"

"He's my son's lover and soon-to-be husband. They're getting married in the fall. In Sonoma. He's also Trevor Lindley."

"Trevor Lindley? The interior designer who has a show on HGTV? Are you joking?"

"Yes. And no."

Rosemary shook her head. "What?"

"Yes, he's that Trevor Lindley, and no, I'm not joking. Trevor also has several retail stores. Doing quite well for himself. Not that my Stanton doesn't do well on his own. He's an actor. Off Broadway, of course, but he's a solid performer."

"You arranged a meeting for me with Trevor Lindley?" Rosemary felt like someone else said the words coming out of her mouth. She'd watched *At Home With Trevor* for the past three years, loving the way the man had invented a rustic contemporary trend that had swept the designing world. She even had a bedside table done in chalk paint because she'd seen one on his show. "Why?"

"Because he loves fun pillows and yours have such authenticity. And they're very well made. I think he'd love to add them to his stores. Custom-made is such a desirable trend at the moment."

"You're joking," Rosemary said, reaching out a trembling hand.

Gilda laughed. "Dear girl, I never joke about design. It's at the very heart of the human condition. To create something beautiful is to be human. I'd say it separates us from the apes, but even apes can draw now. I've seen videos on YouTube."

"What? Why did you do this? I can't—" Rosemary shook her head and blinked twice. "I have to change."

"Yes. Wear what I suggested. Trevor will love it. He's always had a passion for all things southern. He and Stanton spent several weeks in Charleston last year while Trevor designed his tidal line. They even rented a town house there for a while."

Rosemary's body trembled as she turned back toward her cousin's loft. "I have to go back inside."

"Yes. And don't forget those lovely pearls. They're gorgeous with your coloring," Gilda said.

Rosemary turned back to Gilda. "What time? I don't know where I'm supposed to go."

"He'll send a car for you. He said it would be after one o'clock because he had a producer meeting or something such as that."

"Aren't you coming with us?" Rosemary asked, her voice small as the magnitude of the moment washed over her. She was having lunch with Trevor Lindley to discuss her pillows. It didn't even make sense. Not really. Why would he want to discuss the toss pillows of a small-town Mississippi girl who pieced them together for fun?

"I don't leave the apartment, dear. I suffer from agoraphobia. I don't deal well with the outside world."

Rosemary stared at Gilda, registering the reason why the woman never crossed her threshold. "I'm sorry. I didn't know."

"And why should you? But I'm perfectly happy where I am most days, especially when funny little girls collapse in the hall and then take tea with me."

"That's sweet of you to say," Rosemary said, "but this is crazy."

Gilda smiled and tapped the side of her nose. "Life usually is, darling. It usually is. Now off you go to prepare for Trevor. He's a dear man and you'll enjoy dining with him, regardless of whether you strike a deal or not."

"Strike a deal," Rosemary repeated weakly as she turned around and nearly bumped into the doorjamb. Total out-of-body experience. "Wait! Where do I meet him?"

"Out front. He knows where I live."

"Gilda, thank you for this opportunity," Rosemary said, turning around at the threshold. But Gilda had already closed the door. The sound of the three locks turning was the only sound in the hallway.

Rosemary dug her cell phone out of her pocket and texted Sal. She knew he was likely busy with the lunch crowd and wouldn't answer if she called. After she had lunch with Trevor Lindley—she pinched herself—she'd go by Mama Mello's and hope to catch him on a break.

As she shut the loft door, she looked at the two pillows she'd completed last night and the pieces she'd sewn together for the new design.

"Oh my God," she said aloud before squealing and clapping her hands. This was an opportunity of a lifetime tossed into her lap. And all because she'd taken a risk. This was how life happened, doors opened, windows shattered, and new places became hers.

Lacy had been so right.

"Thank you, Lace," she said, picking up the pillow top she'd stitched last night. "You knew what I needed. I miss you."

And before she could get misty, she shook herself.

Time to take life by the tail and give it a good shake.

Trevor Lindley.

Lord love a duck.

This time she woke to drums beating a steady rhythm. She cracked an eye and the number on the bedside clock glowed 12:23 a.m.

"What?" she groaned and rolled over. The room tilted. Her mouth felt dry, like it had been stuffed with cotton, and her head throbbed. Where was she?

Her fingers found material and vague images came back to her. One in particular. Champagne punch.

The thumping continued and she realized someone was at the door. So she struggled into a sitting position and immediately noted her right butt cheek throbbed as badly as her head. Nausea rose and she swallowed hard.

"Just a minute," she called, but damned if it didn't hurt to talk. She inched over to the table and switched on the lamp. The harsh light felt like knives stabbing her eyes.

She'd never had a hangover before.

Oh crap.

Standing up too fast, she nearly toppled over. The banging on the door commenced again. "I'm coming," she called.

Rosemary still wore the seersucker dress and her espadrille wedges nearly tripped her as she made her way toward the door. Peeking through the peephole, she saw Sal. He looked worried.

Unlatching the lock, she pulled the door open, wincing when her head snapped back and pain shot through her entire body.

"Rosemary," he said, looking relieved. "I was worried sick. You sent me that vague message about a lunch date and then you never stopped by like you said and I—" He stopped, squinting his eyes at her.

She hung on to the open door because she might possibly still be drunk. Could a gal be both drunk and hungover at the same time? She didn't know.

"Are you wasted?" he asked.

Rosemary swallowed the dryness in her mouth, noting the strong taste of cherry sewage. "I think so."

He drew back. "Huh."

"I had too much champagne punch with Trevor."

"Trevor?" His chocolate eyes turned to stone . . . or something really hard and dangerous and not so gooey. "Who the hell is Trevor?"

"Why don't you come inside before we wake everyone?" she asked.

But Sal crossed his arms and glared at her. "Did you go out with another guy today? And get drunk?"

She reached out and clasped one of his arms. "Don't worry. He's gay."

Sal looked at her like she'd undergone alien possession . . . and after four glasses of that delicious punch, she rather thought she had.

Tugging his arm, she pleaded, "Just please come inside. I'll explain."

Begrudgingly he stepped inside and shut the door.

"Lock it," she said. Or maybe she slurred the command.

He did.

"I need water." She padded into the kitchen and fetched a glass from the cabinet. Two glasses of water later she felt like she could possibly talk. Sal followed her into the kitchen and leaned against the counter, looking as disapproving as her father. No, her mother.

Rosemary took a deep breath, which somehow made her butt cheek hurt worse. What in the hell was causing that infernal pain?

And then she remembered.

"Oh my God." She hiked up her dress and jerked her pink panties down and screamed.

"What the hell?" Sal said, coming around the counter and seeing the paper covering her right butt cheek. He reached out and pulled the paper off. "You got a tattoo?" he asked.

"I—I—oh shit," Rosemary breathed running a finger over the actually quite gorgeous rendering of a compass rose on her butt. "Jeffery."

"And who's he?"

"The tattoo artist." Images came flooding back. At first the champagne punch had made her tipsy, not drunk. She'd left the restaurant, telling Trevor she needed the fresh air and a walk. And there had been a tattoo parlor on the edge of Chinatown. She'd told him to give her something that represented being bold and finding new direction. Give her something that had led her to Sal.

The tattoo artist suggested a compass rose. She'd said, "Perfect," and then gritted her teeth as the man swabbed her butt and subjected her to, on a pain scale of one to ten, a solid eight.

But Jeffery had told her she had a gorgeous ass. Which made her sorta smile through her clenched teeth. After all, the man had probably seen his fair share of bottoms.

"The view is nice," Sal admitted, his eyes taking in the red skin beneath the new tattoo.

Carefully, Rosemary pulled her panties over the tender flesh and dropped her skirt. Then she tried not to vomit.

"Maybe you better sit down," Sal said. He wrapped an arm around her waist, but when she leaned into him, she caught a whiff of tomato and garlic.

"I'm gonna throw up," she gasped and lurched toward the metal door, trying to push it closed before emptying her stomach into the thankfully clean toilet.

"Aw, jeez," Sal said, grabbing a washcloth and turning on the water. Rosemary assumed that's what he was doing since she heard the closing of the cabinet and the running water. She was too busy retching her guts up. The words of her father rang in her ears: "Beware champagne. It goes down like butter and comes back up like sewage."

"Here," Sal said, patting her back and handing her the blessedly cool damp cloth.

"Thank you," she breathed, brushing inadvertent tears from her cheek. "I'm so sorry. I've never had champagne before. It was so bubbly and sweet. And I was celebrating."

"Here, let's get you into something more comfortable."

"I want to brush my teeth."

"Of course," he said, helping her stand, pushing her sweaty hair from her cheeks.

A few minutes later, Rosemary was clad in her white lawn nightgown that covered her from head to toe. She sipped the ice-cold water Sal had poured her.

"Better?" he asked, sinking down onto the arm of the chair.

"Yes, thank you," she said, lowering herself on shaking legs into the cow-patterned chair. She felt horribly embarrassed at having tossed her cookies in front of the man she had the hots for, but at least she'd made it to the toilet. "I'm sorry you had to see that. Guess I'm not much for alcohol."

"So why were you drinking champagne with a gay guy named Trevor? And why do you have a tattoo on your ass?"

Rosemary launched into the tale about Gilda and her connection to Trevor Lindley. Sal had vaguely heard the name of the designer but seemed to glean from her excitement that lunch with Trevor was a big deal.

"So he wants to sell your pillows?"

"That's the thing, he wants prototypes and a marketing plan for them. Five different patterns that would be customized with reproduced vintage fabrics. He's doing custom work for bedding and drapery in his Nolita store, and if his team likes my pillows enough, he'll contract me to create more. He'll even feature them in his catalog. Once I create five prototypes, he wants me to bring them to his offices next week. This is like having a treasure chest buried in my backyard—totally unexpected, but I ain't complaining."

"That's a pretty incredible opportunity."

"I know. Thank goodness I rented that sewing machine and found some workable materials. But I need more. I'm going shopping in the morning."

"And the tattoo?"

Yeah, the tattoo. "I guess I'm not accustomed to drinking and Trevor kept ordering champagne punch. Weirdly enough, I couldn't taste the alcohol. I was a bit woozy when I left lunch, but not drunk. The champagne sort of snuck up on me. When I saw the tattoo place, it seemed like a good idea. You have a few, and they're so sexy. I wanted to have one, too. One that reminded me of you and how the wrong direction is sometimes the right direction. Or at least that's how I saw it in my drunken state." She gave a wry smile. Thank God she'd had it placed somewhere where her mother was unlikely to see it. She couldn't imagine the comments that would come out of Patsy's mouth about how trashy it was on an upstanding girl like Rosemary. Of course, she hadn't been standing when she got the tattoo. She'd been lying down, butt waggling in the air while Jeffery bit his own tongue in concentration.

"But it can be your secret, huh?" Sal asked, his dark eyes twinkling. "A forever reminder of your time here in SoHo."

"Or rather, Chinatown," she said, wishing she'd found a jewelry store instead of a tattoo parlor. Buying the charm for the bracelet would have been less expensive, less painful, and could be removed from her body. "And I'm sorry I didn't make it by the restaurant. Guess after the tattoo I was too out of it. It's a wonder I made it back here."

"You had a compass," he joked.

Rosemary shrugged. "True, and now I guess I always will."

"Tattoo regret?"

She twisted her lips and thought about having the reminder of this time with her always. "I don't think so. Just surprised by myself, that's all."

"It's late. I should go."

But she didn't want him to go. Of course, she had just puked her guts up and probably smelled like back-alley Chinatown, but those precious seconds ticked by, never to be gathered to her again. "You don't have to."

"But I know you don't feel well."

"We can just sleep."

"I wasn't suggesting otherwise," he said, giving her a smile.

"Stay with me," she said, feeling a little needy and a little emphatic.

"Okay," he said, turning off the lamp and unbuttoning his shirt. In the dimness she could still see how incredibly hot he was—the laser-etched abs, the broad chest with the more complex ink trailing down one shoulder. The belt came off and trousers dropped, revealing toned thighs and rock-hard butt encapsulated in the tight boxer briefs. Even though she still felt slightly nauseated, a hot flash of desire mixed with appreciation stirred in her gut . . . along with the remnants of too much champagne.

They were going to sleep together, but not *sleep* together. Totally new to her. Who was she kidding? This was all new to her.

The guys she'd dated in college didn't inspire any sort of domestic, I'm-comfortable-enough-with-you-to-traipse-about-naked-or-lose-my-lunch-in-front-of-you type of relationship. And the one guy she'd dated in Morning Glory, before he married a topless waitress from down in Mobile, had never stayed at her place. Sex with him had been like a drive-by shooting.

With a really small gun.

"You see what the thought of getting into bed with you does to me?" he said, gesturing to his crotch as they padded toward the bed. Rosemary caught sight of the hardness taking shape in his briefs. "And you're wearing a gown straight out of *The Waltons*."

Rosemary smiled. "This isn't off *The Waltons*. How do you know what the Waltons are, anyway?"

"I watch a lot of TV."

Rosemary pulled back the coverlet and climbed inside, choosing the right side of the bed. Sal did the same on the other side, switching off the lamp and gathering her to him.

"I'm not sure I've ever spent the night with a woman and not had sex. Other than my sisters."

"'Cause you're not from Mississippi?" she joked, curling into him, resting her head on his shoulder.

"Funny girl," he said with laughter in his voice.

"I so am," Rosemary said, though no one other than her closest friends would say that about her.

His warmth seeped into her, relaxing her, and she fell asleep in the arms of her Italian sex slave with the sounds of New York City in the background.

Chapter Sixteen

Sal had never felt as miserable as he had during Louisa Grimaldi's funeral. And it wasn't because the service was particularly sad, though there were plenty of tears. Nor was it because his wingtips pinched his toes. No, it was because everyone there treated him like Angelina's boyfriend. And it wasn't like he could come out and say, "This bitch be crazy."

Because it was a funeral and Father Pinada would have rapped his knuckles like a medieval nun if he'd dared to be so disrespectful.

Then when they went to the graveside services—which Sal had tried to beg off but failed—Angelina pulled him to her, wrapping her arm through his, rooting him to the spot with her family. He'd had to stand beside her while everyone in the community paused in front of her, paying their respects.

So, yeah, another nail in the coffin of his future.

His mother had beamed at him, giving him that nod again. *Good boy, Salvatore.*

The whole thing had made him feel like he couldn't breathe. He'd clawed at his necktie and tried to remember how lovely Rosemary had looked when he slipped out of her bed in the quiet dawn light. She'd snored like a lumberjack, but she'd looked like an angel. He'd left her with a soft kiss atop her head and a note for her to call him later.

She hadn't called yet.

"Sal," Angelina's father, Leonard, said, clasping him by the shoulder. "I'm so glad you were here with us today. It has been hard on my wife and daughters, but you have been a faithful friend to our family.

"Thank you, Mr. Vitale."

"I hear work on the deli is going well. Brilliant idea. You can catch the theater crowd. Your father has a lot of faith in you."

"That's the plan," Sal said.

"You've grown into a solid young man. I'm proud you are in my daughter's life. A bright future ahead, no doubt about it," Leonard Vitale said, his hand heavy on Sal's shoulder.

Jesus Christ. Even Angelina's father put pressure on him. Hadn't anyone realized he and Angelina weren't even dating? He'd yet to take her out to dinner. They saw each other only during prearranged instances. Not that Louisa Grimaldi's dying was prearranged or anything. "Thank you, Mr. Vitale."

"Come by the house more often. I'm surrounded by women and appreciate a little male companionship every now and then. You play poker?"

"No, sir."

"I'll teach you," Leonard said, slapping him on the back.

"My father likes you," Angelina said, her dark eyes softening, as her father moved on to talk to several other people. Her hand stroked his biceps.

"I better go. You have family to visit with and all," he said, feeling like he might hyperventilate. Did dudes even do that?

"Sal," his mother called, beckoning him with a hand. "Come ride with me in Brit's car."

He'd planned on taking the train back into the city. Using the leverage of the funeral and the extra hours he'd worked last night, he'd managed to get the rest of the afternoon and evening off. He planned on spending every single second with Rosemary. "I can take the train."

"No, come with me. I haven't had a chance to visit with you, and you know I need a good navigator when I drive."

"What about Pops?"

"He's going with Dom and Rachel."

Sal looked over to Angelina. "I'll see you later."

"Will you?" she asked, her hands crossing a chest accented nicely in the sleeveless classic black dress. Ironically a strand of pearls sat against her collarbone, giving Angelina a striking Audrey Hepburn look. Dressing for a funeral agreed with her.

He didn't answer and instead moved away. He had no more words for Angelina. He'd gone above and beyond the call of duty over the last several days and didn't owe her anything more.

The crowd dissipated and he joined his mother, who looked good in her dark pantsuit. Natalie Genovese preferred glitz and bold color, but she'd settled for sedate when it came to funerals, pulling her hair back with jeweled pins. The strands of gray embedded in the dark depths reminded him she approached sixty-five years.

"It's been a while since it's been just you and me, Sal," his mother said, dangling the keys. "You wanna drive?"

"No, you can," he said, sliding in the passenger seat of his sister's Honda, realizing it had been a while since he'd been alone with his mother. When he was young, she'd make a point to spend a day with each of her children every now and then. He'd loved being her sole focus.

A few minutes later they climbed the on-ramp of Brooklyn-Queens Expressway. "So what's this about?"

"What do you mean?" his mother asked. "I haven't seen you much. You've been preoccupied."

He wasn't fooled. His mother had a reason for asking him to ride with her. He knew it was Angelina. Just a matter of how long his mother would beat around the bush. "Okay."

"The deli will be finished by fall. You have any ideas about the grand opening?"

"Not really."

His mother sighed, pushing her sunglasses up her long nose. "You don't want to run the deli, do you?"

"I don't know what I want." And that was the truth.

"Your father thought you'd be pleased with the idea, but you're not."

Be honest or hedge? "It's a generous thing he's doing. But no one asked me."

"We have to ask you about giving you a gift?"

"When the gift determines my future? Yeah."

"And you have a plan for that future?" his mother asked, laying on the horn when someone tried to swerve into her lane.

"I don't know. Maybe."

"You can't go on working the way you are. Don't you want more? You're thirty years old. A man now."

Sal sighed. "This, I know."

"And Angelina? You're not buying into her, either, eh?"

"No. I'm not."

Natalie sighed. "Let me tell you something, okay?"

He nodded. She would say it anyway. His mother wasn't the kind to rest until all the wrinkles had been ironed, all the frayed edges trimmed.

"When you were with that Hillary, I thought, *Eh, he's different from the others and that's okay.*"

It was always *that* Hillary. As if she was subpar, which was ironic, since Hillary had thought Sal beneath her. Or so he assumed, since she cut off all contact and married a different guy the same day they'd chosen as their wedding date.

"Ever since you were little, I knew this. You were rebellious. If your siblings wanted macaroni, you wanted a meatball sub. It's your way. So I accepted that. But then that bitch broke you. I saw this, too. The way your shoulders slumped, the way you stopped fighting. That's what heart-break does. I understand."

"I didn't stop fighting," Sal said, flicking a piece of fuzz off his suit pants. "I hurt. But I got better."

"Yes, I remember the parade of women," his mother said, her red-painted lips tilting down in disapproval. "But we had a talk. You remember?"

"I wasn't serious when I said find me a wife."

His mother's eyebrows rose over the large sunglasses lens. "Maybe not." She allowed a pause to play out. "You ever have friends, and you can see they're about to slam into a concrete wall but they have no clue?"

"What?"

"Like people in your life, and you watch them make these decisions and you know they're not good for them."

"Sure, I've watched people make bad choices before."

"Well, that's how I feel when I hear you're running around with some tourist, when you brush aside the gift your father gives you, when you try to give a good girl the boot. I feel like I'm watching you about to hit a big wall."

"You're implying you know better than I do about my life."

She applied her brakes. Traffic had stacked up. "I'm not saying that. I'm saying I can see what's going to happen. You're chasing a life that won't work."

Sal felt anger gurgle inside him. His mother had stopped with the passive-aggressive manipulation crap and laid it out. "Why not?"

"Because you're a Genovese and that means you're stubborn, sure, but you have a place in this world, a spot at the table. Chasing women who don't complement you or understand you won't end well. Angelina might not be perfect, but she's already a part of your world."

"What if I don't want this world, Ma? There's a lot out there. The world isn't right here."

Her mouth turned down again as she honked and switched lanes, surging ahead. "You don't think about things, Sal. You act. And your impulsive nature always comes back to bite your ass."

The anger grew teeth and snarled inside him. "So what? It's my ass getting bitten."

"You think that, but when people love you, they hurt, too."

His mother had a point there. He knew his family loved him. They pressed, pushed, cajoled, and manipulated, but the intentions were always pure. They wanted the best for one another. But that didn't mean he had to give in to what they wanted for him. He had a say-so. "So you want me to fall into line, marry Angelina, and run a deli I never wanted so you won't hurt if I screw up. You want to treat me like a five-year-old."

"You make it sound like something it's not, Sal. I want you to be happy. You don't know what you need."

"End of conversation, Mother. Seriously, I'm done debating this. If it's not Dad, it's you. Hell, even Frances Anne jumped in on the disapproving of my life. As you mentioned, I'm thirty years old. I'm old enough to determine my own damn future." He crossed his arms and stared out a minivan with a plumber's placard attached.

His mother tsked. "You'll end up a delivery boy somewhere, still living in that cramped apartment with leftover furniture. That's what you want for your life?"

"Thanks for the faith you have in me," he said, the anger abating as hurt waded into the emotional war waging inside him. Wasn't a parent supposed to encourage? Breathe wind into his sails? Support her child's hopes and dreams?

"At some point, honesty's important. I can't lie to you and tell you I think you're making good decisions when I can see you're not." His mother shrugged. "But no matter what, I do love you."

"Well, that's a relief. And by the way, all of this is your opinion. Opinions don't make you right."

His mother shrugged again.

Thankfully, his mother didn't bring up the subject of Sal's crappy track record of decision making for the rest of the ride in. He had her drop him at the restaurant, telling her he had left something he needed.

When she drove away, he tossed a wave at Phillip, who worked the outside at the adjacent restaurant, and headed toward SoHo. Pulling out his phone, he dialed Rosemary.

"Hey," she said, the sound of the sewing machine humming in the background. "I missed naked coffee with you."

And like a curtain rising, his dark mood lifted. Her voice, the gentle teasing, even the sound of her working furiously on those pillows filled him with light. "We can have coffee when I get there. Start taking your clothes off."

She laughed. Joy. "Are you coming over? Now?"

"I'll be at the buzzer in five minutes."

"I'm already unbuttoning my shirt."

Desire popped him in the gut. "Make that three minutes. I'm jogging."

She hung up and Sal picked up the pace. He knew what he was doing with Rosemary was crazy. He'd allowed himself to fall into a protective joy-filled bubble that would pop in over a week, but damned if it didn't feel so good to live in that moment. His heart dangled on a thin string and he knew it would snap and he'd fall hopelessly in love with Rosemary. And that would be a mistake.

But he couldn't help himself.

Just couldn't.

So for the next nine days, he'd pretend that he and Rosemary were a happily ever after. He'd ignore the advice of his family; he'd silence the heavier voice of reason in his own head. His heart would fall and eventually it would splat onto the hard reality of life.

But he'd think about that tomorrow . . . or next weekend, after Rosemary went home.

Rosemary lay on her stomach bare-assed naked and traced the tattoo scrolling down Sal's arm.

"What are these?" she asked.

"The papal keys," he said, his eyes closed, as they lay on her cousin's bed, spent and lazy.

"You're Catholic?"

He cracked an eye. "I'm an Italian New Yorker. Of course I'm Catholic."

"I'm Methodist," she said, rising on her elbows. "I sing in the chapel choir."

"Are you a good singer?" he asked, twining her hair around his fingers. She loved the way she felt when he touched her.

"Not really. They needed some warm bodies and—"

"You have a very warm body," he said, pulling her to him and kissing her. Late-afternoon sun fell soft through the window, lending a hazy, contemplative mood. Melbourne hopped onto the foot of the bed, curled up and commenced purring. Moscow was nowhere to be seen.

"Sal?" she said, laying her cheek against his chest, threading her fingers through the hair on his chest. "I don't want this to end."

His head jerked toward her. "I don't, either."

"Why did I have to find you here? This was supposed to be fun, just sex, you know?"

He nodded, growing still.

For several minutes they lay there, tangled together. Her heart yearned for him, but she knew the reality of their worlds were too far apart.

"With this pillow thing and Trevor Lindley, would you consider staying here in New York City?" His words held hope, like a feather teetering on a window ledge, clinging but the inevitable ever near.

"I can't stay here. I have a store and my family and friends. I wish I were unfettered, but I'm not."

He let loose a sigh. "And neither am I."

She sank into him again, tears scratching her throat. This was all they'd ever have—a two-week love affair. They'd have to pack forever into the next few days.

But what if . . .

Impossible.

Sal had a life here and she had a life in Mississippi. Reality and romance were two different things. This wasn't a movie where against all odds, two lovers catch hold of forever.

"I need to work on my pillows, but maybe we can get some grub first? I'm starving," she said, shutting the door on the doubts, hopes, and things she could do nothing about.

Sal pulled her so she lay on top of his body, all the parts lining up where they should. "But first we work up an even bigger appetite with an encore performance?"

Rosemary wiggled her hips. "Nice refractory time, bud."

"Bud?" He laughed and rolled over, pinning her beneath him. Melbourne took an accidental kick and yowled his displeasure. Rosemary giggled. "He really hates you now."

"Eh, like I'd let go of you to soothe a stupid cat."

"Don't let Halle hear you say that. She thinks her kitties are little princes."

"Why are we talking about cats when we could be doing other, more pleasurable things?" he asked, nuzzling her neck. "You smell delicious."

"I showered."

He laughed against the column of her neck. "I adore you."

Powerful words to any woman. Rosemary had never thought she'd hear them. Oh sure—she had a grainy image of the man who would eventually adore her, a gentle hope that something such as mutual adoration existed, but she'd never expected it to happen at that very second.

She wanted to lock the moment in the shadow box of her heart, placing it carefully in the largest square to be taken out and admired when the days were long and cold. Those words were so precious to her. To be adored.

"I love you," she said, clasping him to her.

He froze, and she felt him swallow against her skin. "Don't say that."

Lacing her fingers through his hair, she felt tears prick her eyes. "Why not?"

"Because if you say it, it makes it real. And if it's real, we'll hurt when it's over."

"I can't—"

"No," he interrupted, his dark gaze finding hers. "Don't. We can't. Take it back."

Rosemary said nothing. Instead she cradled his face between her palms, shaking her head because she couldn't take the words back any more than she could deny she'd fallen in love with him. Next weekend they would be over, but Sal would always own part of her heart. He was the first man she'd ever loved, and like the scar on her knee from her first bike wreck, he'd always mark her.

"Oh, Rosemary. Don't," he said, his voice raspy with emotion.

Then he kissed her and she imagined the kiss held all he felt and all he would not say. That's the thing—you can't hide what you feel in a kiss. The unspoken words, the yearning, the anguish—all of it was in that kiss. She opened herself to him, teeth scraping teeth, tongues tangling. The sweetness emoting into passion.

"Don't love me, Rosemary," he begged, dropping his mouth to her breasts, his fevered breath hot against her skin. His hands slipped to her hips, anchoring her, pressing his will into her flesh. "Don't."

"Too late," she whispered against his hair. "It's too late."

And it was.

Chapter Seventeen

The week passed.

A beautiful week full of laughter, sightseeing, sex, and good food. Sal took her to all his favorite places to eat. They took the ferry to Staten Island and drank beer. Well, he drank beer. Rosemary pretended to drink hers. They walked the High Line, the elevated linear park on the unused railroad high above the city, stopping for lunch in the Meatpacking District. He wiped Rosemary's tears when they visited St. Paul's Chapel of Trinity Church, across from the Sept. 11 memorial, and he watched her marvel at George Washington's pew, which he hadn't even known existed. Through her eyes, he saw his city.

He took as many days off as he could, ignoring his father's stink eye each time he put in for vacation. On the days he had to go in, Rosemary worked on her designs. She spent one entire day at the Metropolitan Museum of Art using the art hanging in their galleries as inspiration for her own designs.

Twice they took tea with Gilda, who freely gave her advice but was careful not to overstep Rosemary's artistic vision.

"The idea of naming them after the boroughs is interesting, but not ideal," Gilda said, examining the five pillows propped up against the huge mural on her wall. "Manhattan and Brooklyn aren't bad. But who wants to lay his head on the Bronx? Connotation is everything, dear."

Rosemary tilted her head, her ponytail swinging, making her look younger than her twenty-seven years. "Good point."

Sal shifted in the beanbag and tried not to spill the tea. He wasn't much of a hot tea drinker anyhow, but he didn't want to scald his balls. "Why not something that fits you, Rosemary?"

She looked over at him with a question in her eyes. "Me?"

Gilda snapped her nicotine-stained fingers. "What I said all along. You are part of the sale."

"I don't see how—"

"You're old-fashioned, southern, and small-town. Use that," Sal said, lurching from the beanbag, struggling to look graceful. Failing.

"I'm not old-fashioned. Not really," Rosemary said.

"It's not a bad thing. Let's tie it in with your pillows—vintage, retro, yesteryear. Why not Yesteryear by Rosemary Reynolds?" Sal suggested.

"And I could name the pillows for southern cities. Or places in southern cities. Like this one." Rosemary lifted the pillow with the tiny yellow and black brocade bees paired with deep purple, green, and red. "Vieux Carré. Or French Quarter."

Gilda clapped her hands together. "What about this one?" She picked up the pillow quilted with Wedgwood blue ticking, gray flannel, and deep-green sprigged muslin.

"Low country?"

Gilda nodded. "I don't know what that is, but I like the sound."

"It's the lower part of South Carolina and Georgia. I can add a nice linen braid as trim, which will give a coastal feel," Rosemary said, excitement in her voice. "I love this idea and I bet Trevor will, too."

"I'm going to buy the first one. I like this one," Gilda said, lifting one that had brighter color blocks. "What are you going to call this one?"

"It looks like this place," Rosemary said.

"South of SoHo?" Sal said.

Rosemary bit her lower lip. "No."

"No?" Sal asked.

"I think that's the perfect name for my pillow collection. Way better than Yesteryear." She beamed at him, running to him to throw her arms around him. "You're so brilliant."

He kissed her and Gilda made a snorting sound.

Rosemary had spent the rest of the evening in her cousin's loft, sewing and humming a song he'd never heard before but that sounded suspiciously country. He'd sat on the sofa and watched the Yankees lose to the Texas Rangers, perfectly content to pretend such domestic bliss.

And that's how the week went—moments of sweet rightness with the darker shadow of reality chasing them. There were moments of silliness and even more poignant were the moments of naked vulnerability. Like when Rosemary told him about her friend Lacy.

"This is what she left me," Rosemary had said, opening the drawstring of a small ditty bag.

"A bracelet?"

"She prized this thing. Her grandmother gave it to her on her tenth birthday and then took her to New Orleans to the zoo. That was her first charm—this little alligator."

"But why did she leave it to you and your friends? I don't get it. I mean, it's nice and all."

"Like I said, she wanted us to do something she couldn't. Travel, take a class, buy something . . . as long as it was something we'd dreamed about doing but had never gotten around to."

"And you dreamed about coming to New York City?"

She shook her head. "Not really. My cousin called me a few weeks afterward and asked me to do this. I'd once told her I'd love to come visit. I didn't mean when she wasn't here." Rosemary gave a laugh, sighing when he took her foot and started massaging her instep. She set the bracelet on the coffee table. "But I knew it was an opportunity to experience a world I'd never tasted. It was a chance to be someone other than who I was."

He understood more than she knew. "So what are you supposed to do? Wear the bracelet?" he asked, sliding his thumbs up the sole of her foot. She had an elegant foot, thin with cute toes painted the same ladylike pink she wore on her fingers.

"I could, but that doesn't feel right. It's like she gave it to me to help complete. I'm supposed to find a charm and put it on once I've completed my part. Then I pass it on to Eden or Jess."

"Interesting bequest," he said, moving his hands to her trim ankles and then up to the pretty calves.

"It's so Lacy. She loved romantic notions and quests."

"Like you?"

She had closed her eyes but now she sat up opening them. "You can see that about me, huh?"

"I like that about you. Some people would have taken the seed money she left you and put it in the bank or spent it on something that wouldn't lead to adventure. You were willing to chase a dream."

"Because Lacy couldn't. I owed her that much." Rosemary's eyes took on a sheen. "Life's not fair. I know that. I mean, we're living that right now. We found each other, but—"

"I've been meaning to ask you—what kind of job can I get in Morning Glory?"

Rosemary laughed. "Don't tease me that way."

But part of him wasn't teasing. Why did they have to wait for Sunday like a death row inmate awaited his date of execution? It didn't have to be an ending. Sunday could be a beginning . . . if he had the guts to pursue it. "Maybe I'm not."

She sat up and took his hand. "We agreed on a two-week love affair. Are you saying you're trying to change the rules?"

Did he? Maybe.

He'd given a lot of lip service to his parents about making his own decisions. But the thing he didn't want to admit was the truth hanging around in much of his mother's words. He didn't make good decisions. From using his college money on a truck to dropping out of culinary school to Hillary, he had a track record for fucking up. When he'd met Rosemary two weeks ago, he'd been running from growing up, looking for someone or something to help him forget the confusion of his life, to stave off the inevitable. Rosemary was supposed to be temporary, a vacation from reality. He hadn't expected her to change him.

And what about her?

She said she loved him, but was it sustainable? He knew enough to know she hadn't much experience with men. Falling in love was all good and well those first few weeks when everything was sloppy kisses, hand-holding, and happy smiles. But he'd seen firsthand how the glow wore off. So many of his relationships had started the same way—hot, passionate, but cooling as real life elbowed its way in. And that's something he and Rosemary hadn't had—a pin to prick the bubble of make-believe they'd been floating in. Real life threw punches and pushed you down.

From the beginning they'd known the score.

Just a few days ago while they were eating in Washington Square Park, watching people walk their powder-puff dogs and take drags on their cigarettes, she'd told him she would always remember these two weeks, storing them in her memory as precious as a baby curl or prom corsage. That some days she would take out the memory of his smell, the feel of his hand in hers, and she would roll around in it. Poetic words, but words that stuck to their unwritten policy. What he and Rosemary shared wasn't about a lifetime. They were about a moment.

"Sal?" she asked, jerking him from his contemplation.

Her eyes had gone from sleepy contentment to alert concern. Auburn hair framed her pretty face with its peony-pink lips and jeweled eyes, brushing the tops of breasts hidden by a T-shirt that had something to do with grits.

"Sorry. Guess with Sunday looming, I'm having some—"

"Don't say regrets," she said.

"No, not that. It's just hanging there over us, ready to fall. I hate the way this feels."

She bit her lower lip, her eyes sad. "I know."

He wanted to say, "And . . ." to see where she'd let the conversation go, but he didn't. Because he didn't trust himself. To make a good decision. To not beg her to stay. To not throw away everything that lay before him. He'd been pissed at his ma, but she'd planted the seeds she'd intended to plant. He wasn't sure he knew what was right for his life, so he couldn't toss his life and chase a whim. Not even for love.

If it was real love.

How did he know what love was anyhow?

So he decided to avoid the question. Such was his way. "You hungry? 'Cause I could eat."

She nodded. "You know what I've been craving? The meatballs I ate at Mama Mello's the first night I was in town. Want to take me back there?"

He didn't. He didn't want Rosemary anywhere near the censure of his father, his sister, hell, even the waiters. Rosemary was his escape. Mama Mello's and his family were the anchors that held his feet to the ground. "I have to go in tomorrow for the lunch shift. You can come eat and then we'll go to that club I told you about. Or we could go to my place in Brooklyn. You can stay with me for once. I cleaned up and even bought flowers for the table."

"For me?" she grinned, leaning forward to kiss him. But then she pulled back. "What about Moscow and Melbourne?"

"They're cats. Feed them, give them fresh cat litter, and pack an overnight bag. Saturday morning we're going to the Brooklyn Flea."

"What's that?"

"It's only the best flea market and artisan marketplace in the city. Very hipster. You'll love it."

Rosemary launched herself into his arms, covering his face with kisses. "You're the greatest sex slave in the history of sex slaves."

He caressed the ass beneath the shorts, thankfully not eliciting a hiss from the still tender tattoo site. Though he was perfectly willing to kiss it better again. "Which reminds me, I've been remiss in my duties." He started tugging up her T-shirt.

Rosemary laughed against his lips. "We had sex this morning."

"I thought you needed servicing every six hours," he said, placing all his doubts, concerns, and expectations on the mental shelf where he was apt to place things that had no solution, and instead lost himself in the salty sweetness of her neck.

"Every six hours sounds about right," she said, sliding her hand down to clasp the erection suddenly straining his gym shorts.

And so he made love to her, reveling in her body. The taste of her, the scent, the way she made mewling noises when she came, the way she looked deep into his eyes while he moved inside her. He memorized Rosemary, immersing himself in every sensation.

He couldn't have known as he lay there on the couch afterward, watching her shimmy back into her panties, that the fairy tale they'd woven with threads of desire, make-believe, and hope would start to come unraveled the next day. Because Sal had forgotten reality did more than throw elbows and head-butt. Reality wore sly stilettos, had brash red lips and an Italian temper.

Yes, reality could be vicious.

Because reality didn't play fair.

Friday morning came with Sal up early, taking the train to Brooklyn. Rosemary spent the morning and early afternoon completing the five prototype pillows Trevor Lindley had requested. She was still in disbelief he was interested, but overall, she could say she'd done her best with the designs. Extra time poking into secondhand stores and antique malls had netted some lovely bright embroidery for the Graceland pillow. And some of the trims and notions from Gilda's huge supply lent a finished look. Her nerves jangled when she thought about Trevor and his team looking over them and finding them lacking, but she'd done all she could to create authentic, vintage throw pillows that portrayed who she was . . . who so many women were. Not every woman sipped cosmos, wore designer shoes, and partied until the wee hours. There were some who liked eyelet, old wood floors, and lemonade from a mason jar. Her pillows were for both kinds.

Sal had surprised her with some custom tags stamped with "South of SoHo." She used old-fashioned diaper pins and twine to secure them to the pillows' trimming. Afterward she placed the pillows in two large shopping bags. Gilda had said her son would come to visit like he did every Sunday afternoon and she'd send them with him. No need to go to Trevor's offices. No need to waste one more precious second of her time here in New York City.

Rosemary sank onto the couch, her mind tripping back to what she'd almost blurted out last night. Yep, she'd come a cat's hair from breaking down and begging Sal to keep her. To stop her from going back to Mississippi. To make what they had real.

But that would be insane.

Of course, everything about the past weeks in SoHo had been crazy, so why would her changing the rules be any different?

But she knew the answer.

Because though she loved Sal, they weren't meant to be. No matter how lovely the dream she'd whipped up for the past few weeks, the fluffy clouds and sunshine were a netherworld of her own making. Sal didn't love her. He'd implied as much almost week ago when they were making love.

But she'd given her own heart anyhow. How could she not and be true to who she was? She might have gone sans undies, gotten her butt tattooed, and gotten snockered on champagne punch, but she was still regular ol' Rosemary. Pretending the world away for a little while was one thing, but she'd never lied to herself. Truth waited like a winged creature sitting sentry. It would not stay content to watch her run away much longer.

So she had a come-to-Jesus meeting with herself. Sal would stay here. She would go. And their time together would be stitched on her soul, marking her for always. Rosemary had accepted this was the way of it.

Two more days until she left.

She got up and got on with it.

Friday afternoon was busier than normal on the streets of SoHo. But wasn't that always the case? Even in Morning Glory people started the weekend on Friday.

"Hi, Michelle," Rosemary said to the cashier at Golly Gee Willikers, a small café with good bagels and wonderful jams and jellies. "Do y'all ship?"

Michelle smiled. "I love when you say *y'all*. And, yes, we ship in the continental US."

"Perfect. I'm going to mail home some jams for gifts. Don't want to pay overage on my bags for the flight home."

"Smart girl," Michelle said, pulling the jars she pointed to off the shelves behind her. The café resembled an old-fashioned general store. Which was probably why Rosemary liked it so well. Old-fashioned. Wasn't that what Sal called her? "You going back home soon?"

"Sunday." Saying it made it so real. So final.

"Well, I'm glad you came by. And don't forget to send me that— what was it?"

"Mayhaw jelly. My mama makes it every year. I'll mail you some."

Michelle handed her a card and rang her up. "'Bye, Rosemary. If you come back to the city, come see me."

Rosemary waved and as she stepped out into the SoHo sunshine, her phone rang.

Jess.

"Hey, stranger," Jess said, her voice hoarse.

"Hey," Rosemary said, moving to the side as a group of tourists passed her. "Are you fighting a summer cold or something?"

"No. I went to Tanner's T-ball game. He scored two home runs. Well, of course, everyone scored a home run. Fielding is not a priority for four-year-olds. But picking dandelions and noses is. Go figure."

Something warm edged out the desperate feeling she'd been carrying around for the last day and a half. "Oh my gosh, he's already four?"

"I know, but my sister-in-law keeps feeding him for some reason."

"So how are things?" Rosemary asked, knowing the impending divorce weighed on Jess. Personally, Rosemary believed her friend was better off without her high school sweetheart turned lunatic.

"They're going. I'm sorry I had to get off the phone the other day before you could tell me about your New York fling. Someone from a staffing firm called and I had to get paperwork in to them. I'm signing up to do contract nursing. So finish telling me about the carriage ride."

"Wait, what staffing firm?" Rosemary asked.

"Just a way I can get out of Morning Glory every now and then. Most jobs are only a month or two, but it will be nice to not carry a shooter's mirror to check around corners. Benton and whatever slut he's dating seem to pop out of nowhere. I need a break."

"I heard he's dating a bartender from Jackson. It almost makes me feel sorry for Brandy. Almost."

Benton had left Jess for their florist, Brandy Robbins. Silly Brandy thought Jess's ex-husband and son to the mayor would marry her. Ha-ha. He'd moved on to a string of women.

"Yep. Been dating this one for a couple of weeks."

"Ugh, but good for you. Applying with that agency is a good way to get over Benton and the divorce. Of course, I'll miss you like crazy when you're gone, but you need some time away."

"And money," Jess drawled before giving a sigh. "Enough about me. Last time you were telling me about the carriage ride. And since Eden has such a big mouth—"

"She's already told you about my Italian stallion?" Rosemary teased.

"Only that he's romantic and hung like a horse."

"Jess," Rosemary hissed even as she laughed. "Yes and yes."

"Oh, sister, I'm so glad. You needed to go somewhere wonderful and have hot, no-strings sex with, well, obviously a guy who could satisfy your inner slut."

"Oh my Lord, Jess," Rosemary said, nearly choking.

"I'm kidding. Sorta."

"This *has* been good for me. Lacy was right."

"And wouldn't she love to hear you say so?" Jess said, humor gone.

"She would," Rosemary said, before telling Jess about Trevor Lindley and the opportunity to sell her pillows to his company.

"That's so awesome, Rosemary. Just all the stuff is happening for you," Jess said, sounding almost as if she was about to cry. Which was very un-Jess-like.

"Yeah," Rosemary said, her feet leading her toward Little Italy. Funny how she now knew the way. Maybe it had something to do with the man waiting for her. Or maybe she'd stopped worrying so much about the scary stuff, no longer fearful of the world around her.

"You sound sad," Jess said.

"A little," Rosemary admitted, stopping to admire a cute strapless maxi dress in the window, one she never would have contemplated buying before because it showed too much skin. "It's going to be hard to leave. I mean, I miss Morning Glory and I could never live here really, but—"

"The Italian?"

Tears scratched her throat. "Yeah. My Italian sex slave."

"You're making me blush, Rose," Jess laughed, before sobering. "You didn't fall for him, did you? I mean, you were supposed to go up there and be a wild, modern woman who used men, drank hard liquor, and owned the Big Apple."

"You didn't think that would really happen, did you?"

Her friend sighed. "No. You're just not that kind of girl, are you?"

"Nope," Rosemary admitted, putting her hand on the handle. The dress would look good on her. "But I did get a tattoo."

"What the hell?"

Rosemary couldn't stop the laughter. "I love shocking you."

"Oh, whew. You're joking."

"Oh no, I did get a tattoo."

"Great Lord have mercy, what has this man done to our Rosemary?"

"I could tell you but then I'd have to kill you," Rosemary joked, opening the door and stepping into the boutique. "I've got to run, but I'm glad you called. I'll see you next week." If she didn't die of heartache first.

"Okay, enjoy your last two days, slut."

Rosemary laughed. "I love you, too, Jess."

And then she hung up, strode into the store, and asked the clerk to pull the dress in the window in a size eight. If she had to endure the pleasure/pain of saying good-bye to the man she loved, she could at the very least do it in a cute maxi dress. Two more days to be bold, sexy, and smitten with a hot Italian boy from Brooklyn. Two more days to own the new Rosemary, the girl who'd spread her wings and couldn't image folding them up never to be used again just because she would go back to her hometown.

Okay, so she wasn't going to go braless at the church picnic or let a guy get to third base in the back of a pickup truck. But she wasn't going to be the woman she'd been before. Everything she'd done thus far in New York, from the cab ride to taking a business lunch with Trevor Lindley, had fashioned a more self-confident, self-aware woman . . . a woman who believed in her abilities both in and out of the bedroom.

Lacy hadn't just given her a gift of adventure. She'd given her the gift of herself.

After trying on the dress and loving it, she handed the clerk her Visa and decided to wear the new dress to meet Sal at Mama Mello's. She didn't have a strapless bra, so she went without one. Another first, but damned if her boobs weren't perky enough to look fine beneath the gathered elastic.

Ten minutes later, she stepped into Mama Mello's and found Sal sitting at the bar with one of the most gorgeous women she'd ever seen.

And that's when she got a wriggly feeling that wouldn't leave her.

Chapter Eighteen

When Rosemary walked into Mama Mello's their last Friday together, time stood still. As in Sal could almost hear the tinny seconds tick off from the clock keeping track of the few moments he had left with the southern girl who'd rocked his world.

Angelina moved beside him, her dark hair swishing past his face as she turned to look at what had captured his attention. Out of the corner of his eye, he saw a V form between her eyes; he heard her measured breath, felt her register the situation.

"You know her?" Angelina asked, her blood-red fingernails scraping the bar.

He didn't say anything, which seemed to annoy Angelina, because she gave a slight huff. But he didn't care because once again Angelina sat uninvited in the middle of his world. Like a bad penny, she'd cropped up, contrived reason tumbling from her glossy lips. This time, his mother had asked Angelina to stop by Mama Mello's to pick up Frangelico for a recipe. Supposedly his mother had graciously volunteered to teach

Angelina to make Italian pastry. The thought behind the action made Sal's skin crawl, but he'd complied, sliding behind the bar to hunt for the liqueur.

Angelina had taken his maneuver for an invitation and plopped her rounded ass down on a stool and started asking questions about culinary school, of all things.

"Was the school hard?" she'd asked.

"Not really. For a while I enjoyed it, but then it started seeming like the same thing every day—a bunch of stuff I already knew. I figured I could learn what I needed from Pops, so I quit going. Probably a stupid move because I find I use techniques they taught me all the time. Some of the menu items we've done well with evolved directly from a few of the classes."

"But you won't go back?"

He shrugged. "I've taken some specialty classes, but you know I like making pizzas. Guess some people find it stupid to limit myself to something like pizza, but I like the challenge of making an American staple complex and interesting."

"I like them," Angelina said, latching on to the passionate subject. "Especially the sauces."

"Took me a while to find the perfect balance between sweet and tangy for the tomato base," he said unscrewing the top of the bottle. "Why? You thinking of going to culinary school? Real estate a bust?"

She shook her head. "No, I wondered why you didn't stick with school is all. You seem to like cooking so much. Like it's a true passion."

Sal shrugged, filling the clean sauce jar with the liqueur his mother had requested, wondering about this new tactic of Angelina's—interested chitchat. Was this another ploy to get him to lower his defenses, or had she accepted the fact he wasn't interested? "I do. I feel more myself when I'm creating new pies. Probably the same way you feel when you show a place and sell it on the same day, right."

"Real estate isn't creative. Not really."

"Yeah, but accomplishing a goal is," he said, wondering why he told her this. But something in his own words resonated within him. He felt more himself when he was creating a dish . . . not running a restaurant. Not that he couldn't run his own place, but he longed to do his own thing. He'd always be a Genovese, but that didn't mean he couldn't break out of the box a bit.

"So you doing something fun this weekend?" she asked, pointing at the zinfandel sitting behind him. "I'll have a glass of that before I go to your mother's."

He shook his head when the bartender started for the bottle. "No worries, Kyle. I got it."

Pulling out a clean stem, he poured Angelina a glass. Then he tilted his head and poured one for himself. He was off the clock and wouldn't mind something to mellow him. "I've got plans tonight and Saturday, if that's what you're asking."

"Oh," she said. "I'm going to Bloomie's with some girls tomorrow. Maybe hit a few clubs tomorrow night. If you're out, you should text me and come hang with us."

He didn't say anything, because meeting up with Angelina sounded as fun as going in for a prostate check . . . and likely just as uncomfortable.

Dreading this Sunday had become a hobby, but he hoped to give Rosemary and their short-lived love affair a perfect send-off by dinner at Tavern on the Green, the one place she'd mentioned wanting to dine at. Then they'd go dancing at the Hotel Morey rooftop bar. They'd started on that dance floor and he wanted to finish there. Full circle.

"Frances Anne and Bobby split, huh?" Angelina asked.

Had they? He hadn't paid attention. His spare thoughts had been occupied and he hadn't engaged his sister in much conversation since she'd been so judgmental about Rosemary. He knew Frannie knew he was miffed. He didn't really care, because he'd been avoiding anything that reminded him of the reality of his world, which included skipping Mass and Sunday lunch last week. "Huh."

"You didn't know?"

Sal shook his head as a flash of guilt hit him. He'd call Frannie later. His sister had been pretty damn good to him when Hillary had broken his heart, bringing him his favorite beer, refusing to say she'd told him so. Frannie had liked Hillary, so when Sal got dumped, she'd taken it personally. Which was probably why she'd been so overly protective when she met Rosemary. Sal owed his sister the same commiseration. Once Rosemary left, he and Frannie could drown their sorrows together.

He glanced at his phone, noting the time. Rosemary would be there in ten minutes. He needed to get rid of Angelina, but the woman was too busy yapping rather than drinking the expensive vintage she'd requested. "You like the wine?"

Picking up the glass, she sipped, wrinkling her nose slightly. "It tastes like cherry cobbler."

"That's why I like it," Sal said, pulling Angelina's glass away and sliding the jar of liqueur she'd come for over to her. "Here you go."

"I wasn't finished with the wine, you rude ass," Angelina said, her brown eyes flashing.

"You said you didn't like it. Figured you weren't going to finish it," he said.

"That didn't mean you could take it from me and pour it out." Her face grew as tight as the skirt she wore. The blouse she wore was sheer enough to show her bra. Wasn't very professional to him, but the yahoos she sold real estate to probably ate it up.

"Thought my ma was waiting on you? It's nearly five o'clock and the train will be slammed."

"You're right," she said, snatching the jar and shoving it into her purse. She didn't look happy.

Yep, friendly as a viper, and nothing in her demeanor suggested she had the hots for him. Hopefully, she'd turned a corner. Because after this thing with Rosemary, he'd decided while he might give in to some things life pushed him toward, he wasn't letting anyone pick a woman for him. No damn way. And he didn't give a rat's fart what anyone thought, Angelina would never be the woman wearing his ring, bearing his children, and sitting in the rocking chair with him fifty years from now. If he even got married.

Running a deli and living in Brooklyn wasn't a bad life. He could negotiate the menu with his pops so that he had more control of the Mama Mello's uptown. And one day, maybe he'd fall in love again. Hey, he'd fallen twice before. Surely, he could do it again.

But as Rosemary walked in, his heart shattered against his ribs and he forgot to breathe.

Yeah, he wasn't sure he'd ever feel this way again.

And the thought of her walking out of his life made him feel desperate.

Rosemary looked at Angelina and he saw the suspicion in her eyes.

"You should get going," he said, ripping his gaze from Rosemary and glancing at Angelina.

"You know her?" Angelina asked, narrowing her gaze. He could almost see the cogs of her mind turning, inputting the situation, analyzing the emotion, and drawing the conclusion. "Wait. You've been seeing *that* woman?"

Angelina spoke the question like his interest in Rosemary was an insult to her, as if she thought Rosemary far beneath her. But women like Angelina—with her fake boobs, tight clothes, and gym-honed body—never understood the attraction of fresh, natural beauty . . . and would never get the concept that Sal thought Rosemary was the most desirable woman he'd ever seen. Hillary included.

Sal pulled away from the bar. "Later, Angie."

"Seriously?" she called.

He ignored Angelina and made his way to the door. The guys who'd hit on Angelina a few weeks ago spilled in, loosening their ties, looking ready for Friday night.

"Rose," he said, taking her elbow and spinning her back toward the open door.

"Hey," she said, craning her head to look at the empty tables that would soon be filled with a Friday night crush. "I thought I was having the meatballs."

He'd forgotten she wanted to eat. "I'll grab some from the back and we'll go to my place. You said you wanted to see where I live, right?"

"Well, yeah, but I thought we were going to go to that club you'd tried to take me to that night. The one with the good cocktails?" Rosemary didn't look upset about his scrapping the plan that had sounded good the day before. Merely confused.

"If you really want to go we can, but I'd much rather spend time with just you." Some frantic feeling drove him to squire her away, hiding her from anyone who would demand a crumb of attention. Ticking seconds.

"No, I'd rather do that, too," she said with a smile, her gaze once more flickering back toward the bar. The tip of her tongue touched the arched bow of her top lip as she nervously looked around. Probably waiting for Frances Anne to pop out and karate chop her or something.

He wanted to kiss her, but something held him back. Maybe it was Frances Anne, who passed them, sending him a look as she brought water to a couple sitting near the window. Or maybe it was Angelina, no doubt staring daggers at them. Or maybe the truth was he didn't want everyone seeing how vulnerable he was . . . how much he'd fallen for Rosemary. He felt naked, anxious for more time, dreading the end of them. Made him feel protective of himself.

"Good. Let me go back in the kitchen and grab some dinner."

"Want me to wait at the bar?" Rosemary asked.

He glanced back and caught Angelina watching them. "No. Why don't you run across the street and get dessert? Don't tell my ma, but Joey Cigar makes the best tiramisu." He didn't want her anywhere near potential drama with Angelina. No telling what the dark Italian woman would do to his sweet southern girl.

Rosemary glanced out the large window and pointed toward the bakery kitty-corner from Mama Mello's. "That place?"

"Yeah. Oh, and get one of their raspberry tarts, too."

He watched her go and then grabbed Jean, their newest waitress, as she passed by. Giving her his order, he jogged back toward the bar. He ignored Angelina, who still sat there with her mouth half-open, and grabbed a bottle of white zinfandel.

"Sal, you're joking, aren't you? She looks like a child and she's not even—"

"Don't say it, Angie. This is none of your business," he warned before showing the bottle to Kyle so he'd mark it off inventory. Kyle made a face like he couldn't believe he wanted white zinfandel.

Didn't Kyle know he'd do anything to please his Rosemary . . . even drink sweet pink wine?

"I'll be back on Sunday afternoon," Sal said, giving his sister a slap on her rear as he rounded the bar.

"You owe me for taking your shifts," Frances Anne called.

"I gotcha. And we'll share some beers. My treat," Sal said, taking the bag and pushing out the door into the late afternoon of Little Italy. His sunshine girl waited for him in the bakery across the street and for the next thirty-something hours he wasn't going to think about anything but her.

Rosemary ran her finger over the curve of the white rose in the bouquet on Sal's table and took another bite of the delicious meatballs over spaghetti. The plates and silverware didn't match and the table had seen better days, but the pressed tablecloth and earnest expression on Sal's face warmed her heart.

"Sorry about the glasses. I had some nice ones, but they went missing during a Super Bowl party I threw a few years back. I usually drink beer from the can and rarely have anyone over." Sal waggled the iced tea glass filled with the pink wine.

"It's fine," she said, spearing an Italian sausage–stuffed mushroom from the foam container sitting between them. "Who was that woman you were sitting with at the bar?"

"What woman?"

Rosemary wrinkled her nose. "The one who was drop-dead gorgeous and somewhat irritated you left her for me."

"Oh. She's a family friend. I've known her forever."

"She looked upset."

"That's her problem," he said with a shrug. Sal didn't look concerned about the woman. "You want more wine?"

"I'm good."

Rosemary fell silent, something pressing uncomfortably on her. The woman had looked possessive, like Sal belonged to her. And he'd been talking to her, sharing a glass of wine. Not to mention, he'd hustled Rosemary out of the restaurant quick as spit, sending her on an errand rather than risking her sitting at the bar. Like wanted to hide her.

He hadn't even kissed her hello like he had for the past couple of weeks. So odd.

It had never occurred to her that Sal might be seeing someone else. During their first date on the rooftop of the hotel, he'd asked her point-blank if she had a boyfriend, but she'd never asked him. She'd gleaned from his comment about the difficulty of finding the right girl in Manhattan, paired with his availability to take her out on the town, that he was totally single. But something about that woman and the way she'd looked at Rosemary was unsettling. Of course if Sal was dating the woman, it would have been a different scenario, right? He wouldn't have left with Rosemary. He wouldn't have even acknowledged her. He'd left the sophisticated brunette to come to her, so there was that.

But still, the woman weighed heavy on her mind.

"You don't have a girlfriend, do you?" Rosemary asked, setting down her fork.

He jerked his gaze up. "No. That's nuts."

"Well, there was this weird vibe with that woman at the bar."

Sal shook his head and picked up his empty plate. "I don't know what you're talking about."

"It's just that woman—"

"Are you trying to pick a fight or something?" he grumbled, running water over the plate.

"No." Rosemary stood up and took her plate to the trash can in the corner of the tiny kitchen, sliding the remaining food into the depths. "It was a question. Not an accusation."

Sal's shoulders sank. "Look, I'm sorry. I'm a bit on edge."

"Why?"

"Because you're leaving Sunday and we're spending the last few days together and I'm not ready for . . ." He trailed off. Grabbing the half-filled bottle of wine, he said, "Want to go up to the roof?"

"The roof?" she asked, wanting to continue the conversation they were having, but unwilling to let something unpleasant in to stomp on their evening. She should leave it alone. Sal said he was single. End of story.

"Yeah, there's a patio that overlooks the city. It's why I rent this dump. In the summer it's fun to go up, take a beer and hang."

"Can I sing 'Up on the Roof'?" she asked, trying to put aside the heavy stuff and enjoy the evening Sal had created for them. His small apartment smelled like Pine-Sol and he'd taken extra care to buy flowers and pull out his great-aunt's napkins. In a few days she wouldn't have to worry about Sal and gorgeous women. She'd be back in Morning Glory. Back to being Rosemary Reynolds, owner of Parsley and Sage, alto in the church choir, and chair for the Junior League Fall Bazaar. Her two-week fling would be over.

Her heart throbbed like an open wound, but she shut the door on it and followed Sal out the door and up the stairs. After climbing the five stories to her cousin's loft for fifteen days straight, she didn't need an EMT to climb the three flights.

The sultry night had nothing on Mississippi, but the sparkling view took the breath away.

"Whoa," she said, walking toward the edge of the small patio clustered with potted plants. Fat lemons hung on one of the plants, and someone had strung up Christmas lights. "This is so cool."

"Yeah," he said, following her to the edge, placing his hands on her bare shoulders. And like every other time he touched her, tiny chill bumps appeared and warmth curled round her heart. "Here is where I appreciate living in the city."

She turned to look up at him. "Have you always wanted to live here?"

He shrugged. "When I was a kid, my parents sent me to a camp upstate. We canoed, shot arrows, and roasted weenies over a fire. The woods were so scary to me, unknown and full of things that had teeth. The first year I hated it. But funny thing, after I stopped being so scared of bears and snakes, I liked it. Begged my ma and pop to go every year. I ended up being a camp counselor until I was twenty. Made me want to live somewhere up there. But I never did anything about it."

Rosemary didn't say anything, because she knew what he meant. When she was in college, she'd planned on living in Jackson. Felt like it was close enough to Morning Glory but would give her more things to do . . . more guys to date. But after graduation, she couldn't find a job. She moved back home after her dad renovated the carriage house. Two months later, she got the financing for the fabric store. She never thought about moving away again.

Because she'd bloomed where she'd been planted.

But Sal's words made her wonder.

Was love enough of a motivator to give up all she knew?

Could she look at the Manhattan skyline every night?

"So you went to work for your father and never looked back?" she asked.

Sal stepped away. "I don't know. At one point I had a different plan, but that was over a year ago. There was someone—" He took a deep breath. "Well, I was engaged, and things didn't work out."

"You were engaged?"

He gave her a sheepish look. "*Was* is the key word."

"That woman I saw tonight?" That would explain the peculiar vibe.

"No," Sal said, his hands gripping the ledge. She could tell this was hard for him to talk about—his knuckles grew white. "Water under the bridge, but the short of it is she married someone else. Lives in Connecticut. Plays tennis and hosts parties. I was a break from her snooty world . . . or her last attempt at rebellion before settling into the life she was born into."

His words were an uppercut, snapping back her head.

Wasn't that what she'd been doing? Using Sal for her wild fling?

But then she saw Sal realize what he'd made it sound like. "Oh, I don't mean to suggest that—"

"But that's what I've been doing, right? Taking a break from my narrow world, making a last-ditch effort to do something more than watch the grass grow in the town square. Do you feel used?"

His dark eyes said it all. "No. I don't feel used. From the very start I knew the score. You knew the score. This wasn't a repeat of what happened with Hillary. Don't think that."

Rosemary turned away, emotion plugging her throat. She could see the hurt in him. Bitch Hillary had broken his heart and perhaps that's why he wouldn't let himself crash into love with her. He'd been there, done that with another woman. She couldn't blame him for protecting his heart. "I'm sorry that woman hurt you, Sal. You deserve to be loved. You shouldn't be anyone's fling."

He gathered her into his arms, setting his chin atop her head. Words weren't spoken. They were content to hold each other, wrapped in thought, unable to say things they wanted to say.

So much bottled up. So much left on the table she'd walk away from in a few days.

But such was life.

Her entire life her mother had protected her from mosquito bites and unwrapped Halloween candy, but no one could protect her from the broken heart she'd go home with. Not even Patsy Reynolds could save Rosemary from heartache.

"Let's go back, get naked, and do things to each other that could be illegal in twenty states," Rosemary said.

He shook with laughter. "In only twenty states?"

"Well, I know it would be illegal in Mississippi. God-fearing people and all," she said into his shirt. Which smelled like him—woodsy cologne, fresh-baked bread, and Sal. Wonderfully delicious Sal.

He pulled back and looked down at her. The city sat behind him, twinkling against the obsidian sky, horns honking, traffic swooshing. His world moving around him. But Sal's face was in soft contrast to the hard angles.

Brushing a stray strand of hair from her eyes, he kissed her much as he had the night they met—sweet, reverent, and somehow fixed with all his intent.

And for a moment she believed he loved her.

Chapter Nineteen

This time a horrid buzzing woke Rosemary.

She opened her eyes and blinked, not knowing where she was, but noting the ceiling had a two-foot crack near the whirring fan. She rolled over and caught a specific scent. Sal. She reached out to find she was alone in his bed.

The buzzing was as incessant as a woodpecker, so she sat up, looking down to find Sal's imprint on his pillow and a note propped against the lamp.

Out for coffee and bagels. BRB.
XOXO,
Sal

A rose from the arrangement on the table lay beside it. White with a pink center. Innocence blushing.

Rosemary struggled to free herself from the tangled sheets. They'd spent a lot of time making sure the bedding got good and twisted last night, causing Sal to pull a soft, worn quilt over their sated bodies before they fell into sleep. Pulling on the maxi dress she'd left crumpled on the floor, she hurried to the door, thinking Sal likely balanced coffee and bagels so was unable to fetch his key from his pocket.

Throwing open the door, she pasted on a sunny smile. "Hey . . ."

Her mouth dropped open when she found the woman from the bar, clad in a perfectly tailored linen pantsuit. Her dark hair had been pulled back in a messy bun that looked somehow glamorous and the silver-blue silk tank she wore beneath the suit clung spectacularly to her breasts. Her makeup was flawless, her jewelry a bit over-the-top, and her perfume overwhelming. Burgundy lips tilted down as her amber eyes crackled. She took a step toward Rosemary. "You."

Rosemary stepped back. Mostly because the woman didn't give her any room to do anything else. "Uh, I'm not sure I'm supposed to let—"

"Where's Sal?"

"He went out for coffee."

The woman turned, crossed her arms, and raked Rosemary with a cold glance. "You know, I should have expected as much. This is typical of him."

"Typical?" Rosemary repeated, the niggling feeling that had bothered her yesterday back full force. This woman meant something to Sal. This woman barely held her anger in check.

"Bringing home one-night stands just to irritate me," she said. "I can't believe it."

"Irritate you? Wait, I'm not a one-night stand. I'm—" She snapped her mouth shut because she'd been about to say *a two-week stand*. Wasn't like she could say she was something more. They were, after all, no strings and all that. "Wait, who are you?"

"Angelina Vitale," the woman said, her lips curving in an unpleasant manner. "He didn't tell you about me, did he?"

Nope.

"Why would he?" Rosemary asked.

Angelina gave a fake *ha-ha-ha* laugh. "Only because I'm the woman he's going to marry."

Rosemary felt her stomach hit her toes. "Marry? He's not engaged."

Was he? Rosemary felt like she'd been tossed off a ship into shark-infested waters without so much as a how-do-you-do.

"Yet," Angelina said, walking into the kitchen and setting the bag she'd been carrying on the small counter beside the sink. "But he will be."

Rosemary's mouth went dry. "He never said anything about you or marriage."

"And why would he? He was interested in getting in your pants . . . or under your skirt. He wasn't going to tell you he had been contemplating settling down with me, now would he?"

Angelina had a point. If Sal were engaged or heading toward engagement, he likely wouldn't have told Rosemary. He'd made a comment about having his life planned out for him. So was this what he meant?

She'd assumed he referred to the pressure from his father regarding the deli, not settling down with the beautiful woman standing before her, looking as if she might slap Rosemary silly. Still, Rosemary couldn't reconcile the Sal she'd known and loved for the past few weeks as some philandering, mustache-twirling villain who lied to a dumb-ass country girl in order to land her in his bed. "So you're saying you're his girlfriend?"

Angelina didn't say anything. Just looked at her as if Rosemary was the biggest whore this side of the Hudson River.

"If that's true, why didn't you say something yesterday afternoon when I came to the restaurant? I saw you there, drinking with him at the bar," Rosemary said.

Angelina shrugged. "I assumed you were a friend from culinary school. Sal said he had a friend who wanted to go over the menu and make some suggestions. Now I feel ridiculous. After all, you weren't exactly dressed for business." She looked down at Rosemary's rumpled dress.

"He told you I was a friend from culinary school?"

"Why would I lie? Especially to the woman who just fucked my fiancé."

Rosemary clutched her stomach and tried not to choke on nausea. "But you said y'all weren't engaged yet."

Angelina sniffed. "Semantics."

Crazy thoughts ballooned in her head. Sal agreeing easily to her two-week affair verbal contract. Sal begging her not to say she loved him. Sal practically shoving her out of Mama Mello's to fetch tiramisu. So many things he'd done to allay his guilt and hide her, including staying almost every night at her place and avoiding Little Italy if she suggested going there. Rosemary hadn't seen his true motivation because she hadn't been looking for it.

Shame burned inside her. She was the other woman. Sal had cheated on Angelina with her the same way Benton had cheated on Jess. Rosemary had spent many a night calling Brandy Robbins a slut, a homewrecker, and a fat-tittied cow. And now *she* was Brandy Robbins.

Her stomach rolled over.

"So why are you so matter-of-fact about this?" Rosemary whispered, tears springing into her eyes. "I *slept* with him."

Angelina shrugged a shoulder. "How do you know I'm not crying inside? Like I would give you the satisfaction of knowing you hurt me?"

"Oh my God," Rosemary whispered as she looked past Angelina to the still-rumpled bed where she and Sal had made love into the wee hours of the morning. She felt like she was going to be sick.

"Even so, I can forgive Sal. He's always been a sucker for a pretty face. I wouldn't say you're his usual type, but you *are* pretty. And besides, he forgives my flirting. When we get married, things will change, of course, but for right now, we're a bit more open in our relationship. Suits us both until we make our vows before the church."

Rosemary grappled with the idea of having an open relationship. Sure, she'd known some couples who weren't exclusive. She'd even heard of married couples who were swingers. Heck, there were shows on TV about all sorts of strange relationships. But she couldn't see Sal living that way.

Angelina tapped the bag she'd set down. "Tell Sal I've left him some of the tart I made with his mother. It's his favorite and now so appropriate, don't you think? Tart."

Her words were meant to confirm who Angelina was in Sal's life. She cooked with his mother. She obviously came to his apartment. Angelina was in his life, that much Rosemary could be certain about.

"Why don't you wait for him? Sal will be back soon," Rosemary said, searching for her purse. For some reason she couldn't breathe. She needed to go back to Halle's place. She needed to think. She needed to cry. Vomit. And cry some more.

"I have an appointment. Tell him I'll catch up with him tomorrow at lunch."

"Lunch?"

"We always eat at his parents' after Mass," Angelina said, walking toward her. She stopped in front of Rosemary, lifting a hand. Rosemary flinched, but Angelina merely tucked a strand of hair behind Rosemary's ear. "Poor thing. I know this is shocking, but this is Sal. The man has such a weakness for a sweet face, but truly, you don't belong in his world, now do you?"

Rosemary batted at Angelina's hand and stepped away, trying to hide the tears trembling on her lashes. Pain roared in, flooding her, washing away common sense.

Angelina dropped her hand. "I understand. He's a gorgeous man, full of soft words. But he belongs to me. So go back to wherever you're from and leave Sal to a woman who understands him, to a woman his family already trusts and loves."

Rosemary wanted to refute the ugly words that spilled from the woman's lips, but she couldn't. Because no matter what, Angelina was right. Sal belonged here. And Rosemary didn't.

Without another word, Angelina walked toward the open door. Before she disappeared, she turned and gave Rosemary a small smile. "Perhaps it would be best if you left now. Anyone can see you're already half in love with him, and that can only end badly for you."

Then she shut the door, leaving Rosemary's heart in ribbons on the floor.

"Oh my God," Rosemary said to the empty apartment with its stupid flower arrangement and fanned sports magazines on the chipped coffee table.

Sal wasn't who she'd thought he was.

But what did she expect, showing up in New York City acting like she was a worldly woman who had crazy flings with guys all the time? She had been such a blind fool. A big fat sucker.

Sal had used her desire to be bold and wild for his own purposes. She was a dumb rube who'd been easy pickings for a guy like him.

And the cherry on top of the disaster was her mother had been right—Rosemary hadn't known enough about Sal for intimacy. Instead, she'd trusted untried instincts and jumped in without looking. And look what had happened.

She hurried into the bedroom and rooted around for the sandals she'd kicked off last night when Sal had tossed her onto his bed and beat his chest, doing a crazy Tarzan yell. Once she found them, she hurriedly pulled them on, shouldered the bag she'd stuck her change of clothes into, and finger combed her hair.

Then before she fled Sal's bedroom, she grabbed the pretty rose he'd laid across the note. Tossing it to the floor, she ground her heel against it and whispered, "You effing bastard."

Childish, but somehow it appeased the anger rising alongside the pain.

Soon to be engaged.

Oh, Lord Jesus, what had she done?

Rosemary ran to the front door and slipped into the hall. Banging down the stairs, she said a silent prayer she wouldn't run into Sal.

Please, God, don't let me see him. Don't let me throw up. Don't let me fall apart until I get back to Halle's. I know I've been a sinner. I know I've been a fool. Just do me this solid, God.

The prayer partially worked, because she made it down the street and to the metro stop without seeing Sal. Or his effing fiancée.

Now she had to make it back to SoHo.

Then back to Morning Glory.

Back to the Rosemary who was sensible, safe, and not apt to get her heart torn from her chest and danced upon because she wanted to play *Sex and the City*.

Rosemary knew where she belonged and it wasn't in the Big Apple. And it wasn't with Sal.

Sal opened the door, frowning at the lock. He was certain he'd locked it on his way out to grab breakfast. He'd never leave Rosemary so vulnerable even if his building had never had issues with crime.

"Rose?" he called, setting the coffee on the counter. "Breakfast, baby."

Then he noticed two things at once—the Feinstein Realty bag sitting by the sink and the smell of Angelina's perfume.

Alarm snaked through his body.

Oh shit.

"Rosemary," he called, rounding the corner and entering the bedroom.

The bed was still a snarl of twisted sheets and the bathroom lay open and dark. No Rosemary.

Irrational fear swept over him. Had Angelina hurt Rosemary in some way?

No. That was ridiculous. Angelina could be a manipulative bitch, but she wouldn't stoop to anything violent. At least he didn't think she would.

"Rosemary?" he called one last time as he walked around the side of the bed and lifted the note he'd written, thinking maybe she'd left her own note. But then his gaze snagged on the crushed rose.

"Oh shit," he said, crumpling the note in his hand.

Sliding his cell phone from his pocket, he dialed Rosemary's number. He drummed the seconds off on his fingers until it went to voice mail. He hung up. Called again. No answer.

Then he tried texting.

```
Where are you? Brought back bagels and
cream cheese.
```

He waited a few seconds. No response.

So he dialed her number again. She didn't answer, but he left a voice mail telling her he was worried and asking her to call him back.

Next on the list was Angelina.

"Angelina Vitale," she answered, sounding very businesslike and very innocent of wrongdoing. Like she didn't know it was him calling.

"Hey, did you come by here?"

"Oh, Sal. Is that the way you greet people? How about, 'Good morning, Angelina'?"

"I don't have time for this shit, Angie. Were you here or not?"

"Where's here?"

"My place."

"I stopped by. Thought you might like some of the hazelnut tart I made with your mother last night. They came out nice. You're welcome."

"What did you say to Rosemary?"

"Oh, is that the whore's name?"

Hot anger grabbed hold of him. He was going to kill Angelina. Shake her until her teeth fell out. "What did you say to her?"

"Just to tell you I brought the tart by."

"What else?" he asked through gritted teeth.

"Are you implying something, Salvatore?" Angelina asked, an air of superiority in her voice. "If so, spit it out. I have an appointment at nine in the Village."

"Did you tell her you were my girlfriend or something?"

"Why would I do that? I'm not."

"Okay, so did you imply something that wasn't true?" he asked, grabbing his keys and his MetroCard. He also snagged his coffee. Something told him he'd need to be bright-eyed for the conversation that was about to go down.

"Not to my knowledge," Angelina said, the sound of traffic swishing by in the background. "Look, if she inferred something between you and me, that's not my problem. That's your problem. If she runs out because I pop by, she's definitely not the girl for you. A real woman fights for her man. A real woman doesn't run like a frightened puppy."

"Only because you said something to scare her away," he said, heading out the door, locking it while juggling his coffee. "You like to tell people that we're together, or let them think it, when we're not. And it's gone on far too long."

"Oh, well, thank you, Sal. It's so nice of you to turn my feelings for you into something sordid. I chat for a few minutes with your half-dressed slut and suddenly I'm the villain?"

"You told her something."

"Maybe I told her the truth. That she doesn't belong with you. That you belong with me. And what's wrong with that?"

"I'm not with you."

"Oh, come on. Stop pretending to be something you're not. When will you accept reality, Sal? You're a stupid greaseball with no education and a family who supports you. You ought to be glad any woman wants to go out with you."

Sal wanted to throw something. Punch something. Crush the nearest object with his bare hands.

"Maybe so. But you know what's really sad? I'm all that and I still don't want you. So what does that make you?" He pressed the END button and shoved the phone in his pocket, feeling no regret. Angelina had intentionally set out to rip him and Rosemary apart. Yesterday at the bar, he'd known Angelina was angry and he hadn't protected Rosemary from her because he hadn't wanted to talk about his family, his problems, or the crazy bitch who thought he belonged to her. He didn't want to acknowledge the issues in his life. Instead he'd carried on with the foolish daydream that he wasn't Sal Genovese . . . that the problems in his life didn't exist. He'd allowed this to happen by keeping the Angelina problem far away so he could live in his bubble of happiness.

But his ass had been bitten.

He ran for the train, not caring he looked like a lunatic, lurching around people taking leisurely Saturday morning strolls. He had to get to Rosemary. Had to make her understand Angelina was crazy, vindictive, and delusional all rolled into one dangerous package.

Christ, didn't Rosemary know how he felt?

Didn't she know him . . . that he'd never do something so low, so despicable? How could Rosemary believe he was the kind of man who would use her? The kind of man who would cheat on a woman?

His feet slapped the concrete, rat-a-tatting down the steps to the metro, his heart thumping hard time to the rhythm of despair.

Forty minutes later he stood before her cousin's walk-up. Pressing the button on the call box, he waited.

No answer.

He pulled out his phone and dialed her number again, leaving a message when she didn't answer. "Rose, I'm downstairs. Buzz me up. We have to talk."

For several seconds he paced, praying one of the tenants would arrive and he could slip inside. Nothing.

Gilda.

He pressed the older woman's button.

"Yes."

Thank God. "Gilda, it's Sal."

"Oh yes. Can't let you in."

He sucked in a deep breath. "Gilda, please. I have to talk to Rosemary."

"Sorry. She told me you'd do this. No. Go away."

"Please."

No response.

"Fuck," he said and kicked the side of the building. Turning, he caught sight of a woman pushing a stroller. She shot him a dirty look before telling her toddler the man had said a really bad word and that she should never repeat it. Probably had to tell the kid that often in New York City.

Sal sank onto the steps and cradled his head in his hands. He had to talk to Rosemary. If he could explain everything, she'd be okay. He could tell her about how his family didn't like Hillary, how they hadn't supported the engagement and how he'd jokingly told his mother he'd marry whoever she picked out. He could make her see that he'd habitually made bad decisions, that he'd considered Angelina at one point only because he didn't trust himself. He could tell Rosemary he loved her. He could beg her not to ruin what they had by believing the worst of him.

Again he called. Again no response.

So he texted her.

```
I know Angelina told you some things. But
they're not true. She's a friend of the family.
Please talk to me. You know I wouldn't cheat.
```

Sal felt near tears. He'd planned such a lovely night for them, and now everything was ruined.

His phone buzzed.

```
Leave me alone.
```

He tapped quickly.

```
Let me in.
```

She replied:

```
No. It's better this way. I'm leaving anyway.
We're done.
```

He typed back.

```
Don't say that. We still have tonight. Please
don't end us this way. Not on a lie.
```

He waited several seconds.

Nothing more from Rosemary.

Another thirty seconds passed with no response, so he texted,

```
Please talk to me. Let me in.
```

```
Go away or I will call the police!
```

He set the phone down on the stoop and looked out at the cars moving down Spring Street. Everyone was going about their normal everyday business while his world fell apart on the stoop of a SoHo walkup. How could they smile? How could they window-shop? How could they sip coffee and read papers and be so stupid?

He typed the only thing left to type.

```
I love you.
```

A few seconds later his phone buzzed.

```
You're a fucking liar. Don't call me again.
```

Sal felt his heart break into small pieces. So much for protecting himself from heartache. He'd tried to stay away from love, but it had thrown a net over his head anyway. Held captive by heartbreak. Sounded like a romance novel.

Rising, he winced. Not only did he hurt inside, but his legs felt achy, as if he'd run a marathon. Sal could hang around the building, hoping to gain entrance, but Rosemary was too angry with him to talk at the moment. She'd actually used the F word, something he'd never heard her say. Hell, she rarely used any profanity. Rosemary was a good girl and he'd unwittingly turned her to the dark side.

And not in a sexy, kinky, good way.

In the worst of ways. He couldn't stand the idea she might feel used or cheap.

Thanks to Angelina, Rosemary thought he was the lowest of low. What if Rosemary questioned everything she was? What if she regretted the entire time he had spent with her? That thought hurt him as bad as the actual heartache. He didn't want her to regret the time they'd had together. It had been the best two weeks of his life, a beautiful, wonderful time he'd never forget. He'd fallen in love with her and would savor every touch, kiss, laugh, and moment they'd spent together. But now a cloud of shame and betrayal covered the memory for Rosemary.

Looking up at the top floor, he stuck his hands in his pockets and closed his eyes.

I'm sorry this happened, Rosemary.

I love you.

Be happy.

And then he walked away, feeling lower than the dog crap some moron hadn't picked up on the sidewalk.

Game over.

Chapter Twenty

Rosemary stared at the four walls of her cousin's loft and felt so incredibly alone.

So heartbreakingly alone.

Thirty minutes ago she'd taken Gilda the pillows and told her to not, under any circumstances, let that no-good, cheating Italian into this building.

"Which one?" Gilda had asked, smoking a cigarette.

Rosemary made a face. "Sal."

"No," Gilda had said, shaking her head. "He seemed like such a nice boy. But they all do, don't they?"

Her temporary neighbor wore a shiny fuchsia unitard that looked straight out of a 1980s Jazzercise infomercial. She even had a braided headband. She looked ridiculous but somehow comforting.

"Well, I'm a stupid girl," Rosemary said, handing her the two bags.

"You're not stupid. Being open to life doesn't make you stupid. It makes you incredibly brave, dear. You're not standing on the sidelines.

You're playing the game. Sometimes you lose. You get knocked down, kneed in the testicles."

Rosemary made another confused face.

"Oops. It's the standard speech I've given to Stanton all his life. Sorry. Sometimes you get kicked in the, uh, shins. Hurts. But you're out there. You can't win if you don't play. I'd say suck it up, buttercup, but it's too fresh. Go have yourself a good cry and don't worry—he'll get into Fort Knox before he'll get in here. I'm calling Herman in 4A and telling him to let Caesar out if he sees the Italian. That dog hates men and if he bites Sal, well, he deserves it."

Rosemary thought Gilda a little too bloodthirsty, but maybe that's what she needed. "Thank you, Gilda. For everything."

Gilda tilted her head, her dyed hair sticking out like wings beneath the headband, making the woman look like one crazy angel. "You're not saying good-bye, are you?"

Rosemary shrugged. "I'm not fit company. Won't be for a while. Thank you for the opportunity you've given me with Trevor. Thank you for siccing Caesar on Sal. You're a perfect Obi-Wan."

Gilda smiled. "He was a generous lover."

Rosemary looked confused again.

"Alec. You brought him up, dear. I'm merely paying the man a compliment," Gilda said with a shrug.

Rosemary didn't feel much like smiling, but how could she resist in this instance? Impulsively she leaned forward and kissed Gilda on her leathery cheek. "You're one of a kind, lady."

"It's what I've always strived to be," Gilda said, pressing her hand to Rosemary's bare shoulder. "Now, I have to go watch National Geographic. It's that crazy vet who's always sticking his arm up cows' hoo-has. For some reason, I *have* to watch."

Then Gilda had shut the door, leaving Rosemary to wonder what in all that was holy the woman talked about. She went back to Halle's, plopped on the couch, and got a semi-nuzzle from Moscow that essentially meant, "Feed me, human."

And finally the tears came.

Like a felled tree she slumped over and gave in to the horrible emotion she'd dammed up in front of Angelina. Once unleashed, she couldn't seem to stop.

Her phone chirped and she felt for it in the bag she'd dumped inside the door.

Sal.

He had lots of excuses. Lots of platitudes. Lots of begging. But she wasn't going to be suckered again. In the words of Sissy Spacek in *Coal Miner's Daughter*, she might be ignorant, but she ain't stupid. No matter what she professed to Gilda. Too many things added up, including how eager Sal was to keep her from his family, from his normal life.

He didn't want anyone to know he was a lying dirtbag.

Kitty cat paws dug into her back.

"Okay, okay. Jeez," she said, pushing the cat off her. Struggling to her feet, she staggered toward the kitchen. The phone kept chirping.

Finally, she picked it up and told him to go away. She threatened the police though she knew she wouldn't involve them. No way would she have some police report and court date. Not after Patsy Reynolds had predicted such disaster.

"You'll probably end up in a hospital or police station," her mother had said right before Rosemary climbed into the car to the airport.

So, no. No police report. But if it got Sal to give up and go away, she'd threaten it.

She poured the cats some food and they went right to work, crunching and smacking.

The phone buzzed, rattling on the table.

She looked at his platitudes and when she saw the final text, she wanted to throw the phone across the room.

`I love you.`

Anger blanketed her. Oh, so now he loved her. Couldn't say it to her face. Begged her not to say it to him. He wanted nothing to do with love, but he'd use it to get to her?

No. Effing. Way.

She tapped her response, throwing in the never-to-be-used-unless-really-pissed-or-dropping-a-can-on-her-toe F word.

Then she pressed SEND.

Emphatically.

Like she pressed it so hard she dropped her phone and the screen shattered.

"Gosh darn it," Rosemary said, tears leaking from her eyes, making the last text from Sal a blurry blue stained-glass window. So Rosemary shut her phone off and lay down on the couch. She had to figure out what to do.

Her first inclination was to grab some ice cream, climb into her cousin's bed, and turn on a movie. Ride it out. She'd be home tomorrow afternoon and she could lick her wounds in her own bed.

But part of her wanted to leave now.

Go to the airport. Buy a ticket. Just get back to her world. Away from any possibility of seeing Sal again.

She rose, grabbed her phone, and called the airline. Moving her flight cost a small fortune, but she could swing it. She didn't want to be in New York any longer. Since Halle was coming home on Monday afternoon, she could leave the cats extra food and water and a clean litter box. They'd be fine for forty-eight hours. She'd send Halle an e-mail, tidy up, pack, and get the hell out.

Pulling her suitcase out, she started packing. Tears spilled down her cheeks as her mind tripped through the past two weeks—images of the carriage ride, of making love as droplets of rain plinked against the windows. The crazy staircase striptease. Her mother in rollers. Sal's hands, his ruffled hair, the sound he made when he came, arching his head back, pure pleasure on his handsome face. The way he laughed, did funny voices, and made the tags for her pillows.

She expended the grief for what she'd lost.

And it hurt like a razor slicing through skin.

But she had to do it. She knew this because this was how it was to lose Lacy. Finality. Never going to see them again. Cry a river and get over the hump.

When she packed Mimi's vintage black dress from the fifties, new tears appeared. She had planned on wearing the cocktail dress tonight, to dance at Luna on the top of the Morey Hotel. The skirt was full enough to swish and she'd planned on wearing her pearls and the Louboutin pumps she'd splurged on. She'd even searched on the Internet for a vintage hairstyle, planning on being Sal's old-fashioned glam gal.

But not anymore.

Something popped into her head as she carefully folded the dress.

Breakfast at Tiffany's.

The charm for the bracelet.

She had to get a charm to signify her very big-girl attempt to live and love in NYC. Or rather, her failed attempt.

Hurriedly, she shoved all her things in the suitcase, not worrying if she accidentally forgot something. She could always have Halle send it later. She had to hurry because if she was lucky she might have just enough time to do what she'd promised.

Zipping the suitcase, she left her cousin a note, petted the cats (who didn't seem to give a flip that she was saying good-bye), and locked the door. Placing the key in an envelope, she slid it under Gilda's door so Halle could pick it up.

She knew not to interrupt Gilda when she was in the middle of watching a program.

She pressed a hand against her cousin's loft door. "Good-bye, SoHo."

Then Rosemary walked down the stairs for the last time, her suitcase bumping behind her.

Once Sal had walked away from Spring Street, he realized he had nothing to do for the entire day. He canceled his reservation at Tavern on the Green and started walking north with no particular destination in mind. Just a walk. To clear his head. Regroup. Try to forget about how shitty his life was.

In his mind the sun had been extinguished.

But what? He had already known this would be the end result. Just hadn't expected it to happen with ugly words and unstated accusations. And for it to be at the hands of such a scheming woman.

Still, he couldn't put all the blame on Angelina. By nature, she was a woman who stopped at nothing to get what she wanted. Aggressive and smart, Angelina used what was at hand to make her path easier. In this case, she'd used lies to dispense with her competition. If he hadn't wanted to choke her, he might admire the cool way she'd played it off. She'd actually made it sound like his fault.

As he'd walked, he thought not only about his heartache but about everything. Like a bottle tossed in the ocean, he'd allowed himself to be flung about, never landing anywhere. He'd dropped out of culinary school and contented himself with working for his father. Doing so was easy. He made decent money, he could shift his schedule to suit him, and he could spend his evenings hanging with his friends, picking up girls, and watching whatever the hell he wanted on his TV. The path less traveled was hard, the life he led now, easy.

Yet where was his passion for living?

Sure, he'd fallen in love with Hillary and thought he'd build a life with her. Her parents had money and she'd convinced him to open an upscale pizza place out in the Hamptons. For a few months, he'd been obsessed with finding real estate there . . . or at least real estate he could afford. She'd planned their wedding while he designed menus in his head, daydreamed about write-ups in the *New York Times*, and delved into market research. For a month, he'd been consumed with the possibility of Sal's Downtown Pizza.

But then he and Hillary split and he'd shoved the dream of his own place into a cubbyhole, never letting it back out into the light. And he'd gone back to being the Sal he'd always been.

He disgusted himself.

Passing an elderly lady coming out of Macy's, he was reminded of the person who always shot straight . . . and put liquor in his tea. So he'd hopped a train and headed out to the Bronx and her small garden, where life seemed better.

Sal's grandmother Sophie Mello Genovese had been thirty-eight when she'd given birth to his father, her only child. So she was ninety-one years old and wizened like a raisin. Still, she had a razor-sharp wit and a feisty disposition. Her old dog was missing an eye, and she spent nearly every day in her patio garden with the mutt. Every square inch of the garden was covered with blooms, herbs, and interesting shrubs, but the highlight was the weeping cherry tree that when in bloom was showstopping. Sal loved being with her.

"The last time you looked this way, that bitch married the investment banker," his grandmother Sophie said, handing him a delicate bone-china cup full of brandied tea.

"Yeah."

Her eyebrows were still dark, though the rest of her hair was a stiff white mushroom. Her beauty operator—that's what she called the old hen who took clients in a small beauty shop in the back of her house—believed in heavy hair spray. "That's all you have to say, eh?"

His grandmother smiled and crossed her legs. She wore elastic-banded pants and a flowered Hawaiian shirt and didn't seem to be in a rush to say things. He appreciated that about her. His mother could learn a thing or two from her mother-in-law.

After several minutes of watching small sparrows hop on the branches of the cherry tree, he said, "Ma is set on me marrying Angelina. Pops is set on me opening the new deli off Times Square."

"And what are you set on?" his grandmother asked.

Sal shrugged.

Grandma Sophie tsked. "Well, that's your problem. You don't set on anything, Salvatore Genovese."

"Ma's already lectured me on my poor decision making."

"I'm not lecturing," she said, taking a sip of tea, again falling silent.

"Maybe I need a lecture," he said, setting his empty cup on the scrolled iron table. His stomach felt warm from the brandy . . . or perhaps it was the sunshine striping the patio with its heat.

"No one needs a lecture when they're hurting. I can see this is more than confusion over what your parents have planned for you."

"There's this woman."

"Ah," his grandmother said, holding up a finger crooked from arthritis. "The best and worst stories start with those words."

He managed a smile. "But she's from a different world. It won't work."

"What world would that be?"

"Mississippi," he said.

"Oh yes, very different. I went down there when your grandfather was in the navy. I couldn't even understand what those people were saying half the time."

Sal smiled. "They say weird things like 'It's hotter than a billy goat's butt in a pepper patch' or 'He's useless as tits on a boar hog.'"

That made his grandmother giggle. "So what's wrong with Mississippi?"

"What do you mean?" he asked, confused about her intent.

"I mean if you love her and she loves you, you have to meet her halfway. You're not happy here, so what's wrong with Mississippi?"

Sal looked hard at the old woman. "You're suggesting I go to Mississippi?"

Her mouth turned down, and she tilted her head in the age-old expression that meant, "That's what I'm saying, dumb ass."

"But I can't live in Mississippi. I'm a New Yorker."

"And that's why you're working for your father and considering marrying that cow Angelina? Because you're a New Yorker? And I suppose you'd cut off your nose to spite your face, too."

"Angelina's not a cow. She's actually very slender."

"Cow," his grandmother said, jabbing a finger at the ground. "I don't like her. Never have. Spoiled rotten. Her mother should have whipped her ass when she had the chance. If you marry her, I won't be at the wedding."

Sal shook his head. "I'm not marrying her."

"Good. Maybe you're starting to find your balls."

"Grandma Sophie," he said, trying not to laugh.

"What? It's the truth. That's what I liked about your grandfather. He never let me walk all over him. He was a man who knew what he wanted. He wanted me. I danced in the chorus line and he was the boy who pulled the curtain, you know?"

He nodded, because she loved to talk about her dancing days.

"But that Anthony's eyes burned with fire. He wanted more than what life had given him. He didn't know my papa owned a restaurant. He thought I was a little songbird of no account, but he knew he wanted me. Smart man to take what he wanted and gain a restaurant in the process. My papa loved Tony like a son, and he loved him even more because he loved me. Tony was never afraid to roll the bones and see what came up."

Sal didn't say anything because his mind was glutted with too much to think about.

"Why don't you stop holding your dice, Sal?" his grandmother said, reaching for the brandy she'd set on the table and pouring herself half a cup. "You don't want the life you're living. Give them a roll."

"But . . ." Sal started to say that everything he knew was here, but he couldn't. Because the one person who made him happy had shut him out of her life and would board a plane for the South tomorrow. What would life be if he settled for the life he'd had before? Where was his passion? His challenge? His reason for getting up every morning?

He looked down at his hand and opened it.

Stop settling. Roll the dice.

"Years after Tony and I were married, he told me that he'd spent his last two dollars to take me for ice cream. For three days, he ate scraps so I could eat ice cream and fall in love with him. Ah, his smile and the way he looked at me. If they could bottle that, we'd all be rich, you know?"

Sal nodded. His grandfather hadn't been afraid to disappoint or to fall on his ass. He'd rolled his dice, spent his last dollar on love.

"I'd like to say the apple doesn't fall far from the tree, but your father, *ay-yi-yi*. He has a romantic bone somewhere in his pinkie, maybe. Hard to tell. And your mother is from a forward family. She has always pushed, pushed, pushed. The woman must be exhausted. But you—you I've always had hope for. You're a dreamer, though they would beat it out of you. But the dreamers are always the ones who win big. Or they go home." His grandmother drained her brandy and rose, creeping across the garden much like the snails she'd drowned in the small containers of beer sitting round the patio. Picking a lovely rose from a thorny shrub, she carried it back to him. "See how beautiful?"

He nodded, taking the deep-pink blossom.

"Soon it will wither and fall away. Admire it now."

Determination and revelation uncurled inside him. "You're so smart. Thank you for telling me all of this. For using this to get your point across."

His grandmother made a face. "Using this? It's just a rose."

"Yeah, but somehow you knew. You knew what I needed to hear."

"I picked it to take to Betsy next door. She's taking Tom Tucker to the senior citizen dance and asked me for a rose for his lapel. You read too much into things. See? Just like your grandpapa Tony." His grandmother smiled, chuffed him on the chin, and toddled back into her small town house.

Sal wanted to leap up and get to it, but instead he remained sitting, soaking up the scent of lavender, suddenly lazy at the drone of the bees buzzing about the sage. A large rosemary bush sat in one planter, as subtle in its beauty as his Rosemary. And like her, one touch and it stayed with him, permeating his skin with the evocative scent. Not easy to wash away.

Today had been both tragic and jubilant. He didn't know his future, what would happen, even exactly how he'd go about changing all he'd been. He just knew he would be bold the way Rosemary had been and step outside his comfort zone. The thought of letting go, rolling the dice, and letting fate decide his future was freeing. If he crapped out, he'd live with it. But he wouldn't be a coward anymore. His soul felt fifty pounds lighter.

Rising, he went over to the rosebush and clipped a similar bloom. He lifted it to his nose and sniffed appreciatively then slid it into his shirt pocket. And then he snipped a piece of fragrant rosemary, sliding it in beside the rose.

He was a new man.

Now all he had to do was shut down his life here in New York City, move to Mississippi, get a job, and win Rosemary back.

Easy peasy, lemon squeezy.

He shook his empty hand and pretended to roll the dice.

Game on.

Chapter Twenty-One

"This is gorgeous, Rosemary, and way too much," Eden said, lifting the silver necklace from the depths of the signature blue box from Tiffany's. A small songbird hung on the end of the chain.

"Every girl should have something from Tiffany's, right?" Rosemary said, sliding the next box to Jess. "This is for you."

Jess looked at the box and then glanced up at Rosemary. It was Monday afternoon and they sat at their regular table at the Lazy Frog coffee shop. "You didn't have to bring us gifts. You're supposed to bring us stories, lots and lots of stories. We need some vicarious living, sister."

But she took the box, sliding the white ribbon from the top.

"I have stories," Rosemary said, swallowing the emotion that popped up at weird times. She'd been home for a week, but had made excuses every time Eden or Jess suggested coming by. Things had felt too raw and there was something about falling in love with a man she was supposed to use for sex and then finding out he was using her for sex that was embarrassing. So she'd spent the week working with her head down, sewing more pillows in case she landed a contract with Trevor Lindley. She didn't want to think about Sal or New York City. In fact, she'd tried to delete the picture of them smiling on the top of the Empire State Building a dozen times, as if erasing it could erase what a fool she'd been. But she couldn't do it. Instead her heart would break into a million pieces all over again and she'd toss her phone away.

Rosemary figured Eden had sensed as much. Rosemary had gone to Penny Pinchers to pick up some storage bags for her mother. Patsy was in the process of freezing things for the long cold winter she was certain they'd have. If her mother believed in anything, it was Jesus, good manners, and the *Farmer's Almanac*. Eden's gaze had lasered through the forced cheerfulness Rosemary had cloaked herself in and Rosemary knew she'd run out of excuses for not meeting her friends. So here she was pretending to be happy.

Jess pulled off the lid and smiled. "Holy crap. You got me a Tiffany pocketknife."

Eden started laughing. "That's hilarious. And so perfect for her."

Rosemary said, "If you're going to carry a pocketknife, it might as well be a silver Tiffany Swiss Army knife."

Jess looked up. "I love it."

After Benton told Jess he was leaving her, she'd come to Rosemary's house, tears streaming, which was atypical of the hard-ass Jess. When Rosemary answered the door, Jess had started bawling. Rosemary pulled her into a hug and after her friend had told her what had happened, she made a comment they'd laughed about for the past year. She'd said, "Now how am I going to open beer bottles or cut the tags off stuff? Benton always had his pocketknife with him." It was such a bizarre thing to say and even Jess laughed about it . . . now.

"I wouldn't want you trying to open beer bottles with your teeth. You have such a pretty smile," Rosemary said.

Jess shook her head. "So tell us more about your Italian guy. I haven't had sex with someone for almost a year, so I need some vicarious orgasms."

Rosemary had known she'd have to bear this. She didn't want to admit to having her heart broken, though her mother had been saying things like, "Maybe you should try some new eye cream," and "Are you still jet-lagged?" Because a one-hour time difference always made a gal jet-lagged. Nope, it was Patsy's way of prying. Or making Rosemary feel bad about the bags under her eyes.

"He was great. We did a lot of fun things. Um, we went dancing—y'all already know that, though—and we took a carriage ride in Central Park. Jess, you know how that one went. Um, we ate at lots of different restaurants. Oh, we also saw Kirstie Alley at—"

"Yeah, but what about him? You're not telling us the good stuff," Jess said, tapping on the table.

"He was—" How could she put everything Sal had been to her in words?

Impossible.

Ever since she climbed off the plane in Jackson, she'd been going over and over that last morning in New York. Maybe she should have let Sal up to explain. Maybe she shouldn't have allowed a perfect yet supercilious stranger define Sal for her. She'd not given him a chance to defend himself. Instead she'd acted on emotion. When Angelina implied she was Sal's fiancée, mortification had swept through Rosemary. Like a snap of fingers, she'd gone back to being an uncertain, gauche country mouse come to the city who didn't know champagne from soda water. Pairing that with the thought Sal had taken advantage of her lack of experience had erased any chance for reasonable examination. The idea he'd lied to her had petrified her emotionally, and because she felt inferior to someone like Angelina, she'd allowed her emotions to sweep her into a tailspin.

But what if she'd been wrong?

In the long run, would it have mattered? She'd told Sal she would give him her heart and body for two weeks. She'd dance, try naughty things, drink wine, and go without underwear. She'd give blow jobs, eat caviar (which, by the way, she thought disgusting), and listen to Gilda's weird Scottish music. She'd allow herself to sample new experiences with him, but they'd both known it would end when she went back to Mississippi. Clean break. No regrets.

Perhaps the way they'd ended things had been for the best. Maybe letting him upstairs wouldn't have changed anything. She'd still have been mourning the loss of Sal.

"Rosemary?" Eden prodded, placing her hand over Rosemary's. "Are you okay? 'Cause you don't seem like the same Rosemary who left Morning Glory. You were supposed to enjoy using Lacy's money."

"I did. I even bought a pair of those ridiculously expensive Christian Louboutin shoes because she always wanted a pair. It's just . . ." She sighed.

Jess narrowed piercing eyes and tucked her curly brown hair behind her ear. "Uh-oh."

"What?" Rosemary asked, glancing up at her friend.

"Well, butter my butt and call me a biscuit, you fell in love with him."

Eden jerked her gaze to Rosemary. "Did you? You said you wouldn't."

Lie to her friends?

Or spill her guts.

"I got a little attached is all. But things didn't end well anyway. And it's not like anyone can have a long-distance relationship."

"Why not? These days it's easy. With Skype and texting and—what's that called on your phone?" Eden asked Jess.

"FaceTime."

"Yeah," Eden said, her pretty blue eyes plaintive. "And Snapchat. You can see him on the web all the time and then fly up there every now and then. And you can bring him down here."

"Here?" Rosemary smiled, thinking about Sal going fishing with her daddy or listening to her across-the-street neighbor Mrs. Simpson gossip about the Pentecostals down the road who don't watch their kids or sitting on the pew with her listening to Reverend Hyde preach about the Sermon on the Mount. Lord, would the choir be atwitter. "I don't see Sal wanting to come down here. Lord, what would we do all day—watch the grass grow?"

"Oh, I could think of some good ways to pass the time, Rosemary Marie," Jess teased.

And damned if she didn't blush. "Hush your mouth, Jessica Anne."

"Ugh, don't call me that," Jess said. "Why can't you have your Italian?"

"Because he may belong to someone else . . . and it wouldn't work. End of story."

"Belong to someone else?" Jess pressed her slender fingers on the table. "Let's go back to that."

"No. Look, the last day I was there, this woman came to his place. She told me Sal was going to marry her. She's like this old family friend and they've known each other forever."

"So?"

"Well, he was all secretive about things. Wouldn't let me get around his family and stuff. I don't know. I felt like he hadn't been totally honest with me about this woman."

"Wow," Eden breathed. "You think it's true?"

"I don't know," Rosemary said, feeling the press of tears for the tenth or twentieth time that day. Every time she thought about the way things ended, she got weepy. "It wouldn't matter, though. I live here. He lives there. Long distance wasn't going to work anyway. Guess I wish things hadn't ended on that note."

"I know what you mean. Life's a bitch sometimes, huh?" Jess said, covering Rosemary's hand with her own and giving her a squeeze.

"Let's not talk about it right now," Rosemary said, pulling out the paisley ditty bag with the charm bracelet inside and setting in the center of the table. Almost two months had passed since the little bag had last sat on the table.

"The bracelet," Eden breathed. "I had almost forgotten about it."

"So, kid, what charm did you get?" Jess asked.

Rosemary set a tiny box on the table. Opening it, she withdrew a silver charm.

"The Empire State Building." Eden grinned, taking the little charm from Rosemary. "It's so cute."

"So even though things didn't work out with you and Sal, you're calling it a win?" Jess asked, opening the paisley bag, allowing Lacy's bracelet to spill onto the table.

"I drank champagne punch, had lunch with Trevor Lindley, got a tattoo, and fell in love. Most of it was wonderful, even if the ending was crappy. But I lived it. And I don't have any regrets."

"Wait a second, Trevor Lindley? The Trevor Lindley who has a TV show and a bunch of stores and crap?" Eden asked.

Rosemary looked at Jess. "You didn't tell her about the pillows?"

Jess's eyes widened. "It wasn't mine to tell."

"What about the pillows?" Eden asked.

"It's a long story, but let's just say I'm going to be busy with a side project that could turn into something bigger. My new design label South of SoHo is officially being courted by the Lindley Group. If they buy my designs, my pillows will be sold in his New York, Chicago, and LA stores."

Eden squealed and everyone in the coffee shop turned to look at them. "You're gonna be famous. And rich. Well, richer," Eden said.

Rosemary laughed. "I'm not sure about that, but it's way more than I bargained for. I took a bite out of the Big Apple even though it took a bite out of me."

Eden laughed. "That's one way of putting it."

"So hand me the bracelet so I can do my duty," Rosemary said to Jess.

Jess slid the bracelet toward Rosemary, but her gaze was centered beyond Rosemary's shoulder. A small V had gathered between her brown eyes.

"What?" Rosemary asked.

"It's just—hold on a sec." Jess rose and walked toward the large glass window portraying a frog relaxing on a lily pad.

Eden shoved the bracelet at Rosemary. "Are you going to put it on? Isn't that part of the whole thing Lacy wanted? I think you have to do it."

"I guess."

"Hey, Rosemary," Jess called, interrupting them.

Rosemary held the charm clasp open but looked over her shoulder. "What?"

The owner of the Lazy Frog, Sassy Grigsby, had walked around to look out the window, too.

"What's Sal look like?" Jess called.

"Huh?" Rosemary hooked the charm on the bracelet and wondered if her job was done. Lacy had written some mumbo jumbo that made the thing sound magical. Which was plumb silly. "Why?"

"Well, Fred Odom is talking to this really hot guy and they're pointing at Parsley and Sage," Jess said.

Sassy nodded. "Jeez, he could eat crackers in my bed any ol' night. Hotter than a two-dollar pistol."

Rosemary handed the bracelet to Eden and pushed back her chair. "What are you talking about?"

When she stepped up to the window, her knees nearly buckled.

Sure enough, Fred Odom pointed toward her store, his sweaty bald head shining like a beacon. He'd been delivering mail for more than thirty years and his cheerful disposition made him a Morning Glory favorite . . . and the perfect person to know everything in town.

And he was talking to Sal.

The man she'd pined for over seven straight lonely nights wore a pair of jeans and a graphic print T-shirt. Sweat streamed down his face as he nodded to whatever Fred was telling him.

"Oh holy shit," Rosemary whispered.

Jess turned to her and took her by the shoulders. "Good Lord, Rosemary. That man has come for you."

"No, I can't imagine why . . ." Rosemary's voice faded as she tried to grasp the words Jess had spoken. Had he come for her? Or was he really intent on apologizing? But that would be ridiculous. No one flew to Mississippi just to apologize, did they?

Eden craned her head around Rosemary. "Ooh, he's cute, Rose."

"Sexy," Sassy said.

Jill Crabtree and her two teen daughters got up from their table. They all nodded.

"Go out there and save him, Rosemary," Eden said, giving her a little push. "Someone has to save him from Fred. No one can get away from him when he starts talking. No telling what he's saying about you."

"I look terrible," Rosemary said, tucking her hair behind her ear. Why hadn't she washed it this morning? And put some concealer beneath her eyes?

Jess turned. "I don't think he cares. Rosemary, he came for you. Go."

Numbly, Rosemary pushed out the door.

Sal stood across the street on the edge of the town square. The courthouse and old jail were the only two buildings in the middle of the square. The rest of it was covered with live oak trees, large flower beds, and curlicue iron benches. Sal stood beside one of the old-fashioned lampposts, wiping his hand across his forehead.

"That sounds really cool, Mr. Odom. I'm looking forward to seeing his Boy Scout patch collection."

"And don't forget to ask him about all the World War II stuff. The man could open a museum with the things he has in that old barn," Fred Odom said, not even registering that Sal looked as if he might pass out from the heat and humidity. "Oh, here she is now. Rosemary, this young man has been looking for you."

Rosemary waved her thanks and then had to wait as three cars went by. She jogged across the street. "Hi, Mr. Odom."

"Hello, Rosemary," Fred said, digging in his bag. "I was just about to deliver your mail to you and now you can save me the trip."

"Oh, well, could you take it to the shop, please?" she said, waving off the stack of mail.

"Course I can. Hey, did you see Rita Harmon's new gazebo?" Fred asked, leaning close. "Told everyone in town she special ordered it from some fancy place in Jackson, but everyone knows she got it at the Big Lots."

"Oh, I haven't seen it. Uh, can you excuse us, Mr. Odom? I need to talk to Sal privately."

"Oh sure. I'll see you in church on Sunday." Fred ambled away, leaving her and Sal standing in the middle of downtown Morning Glory.

Sal panted. "It's like really hot, Rosemary. How do you people do it? I might be having a heatstroke."

"Come on," she said, taking his elbow and heading toward her store. She'd taken her lunch break at the Lazy Frog, and Lorraine, the lady who worked with her, needed to take hers. That should give her and Sal some much-needed privacy.

"Where are we going?" he asked.

"To my store. You need water and air-conditioning."

"You want to call me a pansy New Yorker, don't you?" he joked. He acted like he hadn't flown down to Mississippi. Or driven. Or whatever. He acted like it was any other day.

"What are you doing here?" she asked.

He stopped by the bench she often sat on to eat lunch when the temperature wasn't near one hundred degrees. "What do you think I'm here for?"

She turned, thankful they at least stood in the shade of a huge oak tree. Sal's face resembled a beet and his shirt was damp. Of course, that was a good thing, because it clung to his chest. "I don't know."

"I'm looking for real estate."

Rosemary felt her heart drop into her stomach. She clasped her belly beneath her thin navy dress. "What?"

"I did a little research and found out that the only pizza places y'all have are national chains. Did I use 'y'all' correctly?"

Rosemary blinked a couple of times and then she shook her head. "Wait, you're looking for . . . you are opening a pizza place? Here? In Morning Glory?"

He nodded. "Sal's Downtown Pizza. Or Sal's New York Pizza. Not sure. What do you think?"

Rosemary sank onto the bench, mostly because her knees finally buckled. "I think I don't understand what's happening."

"What's not to understand? I fell in love with the most amazing woman and I'm unwilling to be a thousand miles away from her." He looked around. "I like your town. The weather? Not so much."

She glanced up. "You're moving here? Because of me?"

He dropped down beside her. "Rosemary, I'm not in a relationship with that Italian witch. I never have been. She and my parents had an agenda that contained her, the deli, and, I don't know, a mortgage and kids. But that's not what I wanted. For a while, I thought I should go with it. I've never had a great a track record with things working out in my life, but I met you and . . ." He spread his hands out.

"You're a New Yorker."

"Yeah, that's what I thought," he said, a wry grin appearing. "But I'm thinking I'd like to give the South a try. I've been practicing my y'alls, and Mr. Odom has already invited me over to his neighbor's house to see some Boy Scout stuff. Oh, and the lady at the gas station right outside town already invited me to visit her church. I think I'm going to fit right in."

Rosemary started laughing. Because Sal with his Brooklyn accent and Bronx bar T-shirt collection would never fit in. "You're going to visit a church."

"Sure. Of course, I'm Catholic and it was hard enough on my parents when I told them I was moving here. I had to get a map of the US to show them where it was. So I'm not sure if I can go Baptist on them or anything." His smile was like Manhattan. Blinding. Seductive. The most exciting thing she'd ever experienced.

Rosemary shook her head.

"What?" he said, spreading his hands. "I can fit in. I'll get some plaid shorts and knot a sweater around my neck. Oh, and some cowboy boots. And a spitting cup."

Rosemary laughed harder. "You're crazy."

"Yeah, well, I ain't got a tattoo on my ass, do I?"

"Shh!" Rosemary said, pressing a finger against his lips and looking around. A bit of a crowd had formed. Lorraine had come outside Parsley and Sage, and her friends, Sassy, and the Crabtrees stood pressed against the Lazy Frog's window.

"Okay, but what I'm trying to say, Rosemary Reynolds, is that I love you and I will go wherever you go. If this is where you belong, it's where I'll belong."

Rosemary's laughter turned to tears. "You're serious."

"You're damn right I am."

She pressed a trembling hand to her mouth. "This is—"

"How love works. You roll the dice, you take the chance, and you hope like hell it pays off." He paused, his brown eyes pleading. "Is it going to pay off?"

Rosemary swallowed and shook her head. Emotion overwhelmed her at the thought of this man giving up his life in New York City so he could move to Morning Glory . . . so he could love her.

"'Cause I gotta tell you, it's gonna be uncomfortable with both of us living here. I read there's only six thousand people, so we're gonna run into each other at the market sometimes and I can't be responsible if I follow you around and cry and stuff."

"Sal, I can't believe this," she said, reaching out to touch his sweaty face. "You love me?"

"More than I ever knew I could love anything. This past week away from you was hell. Not to mention I had to tell my parents I'm leaving Brooklyn and that's why I needed the map. My ma cried, but I promised to bring you up for Thanksgiving or something. Then I cleared out my apartment, packed my junk, and bought you a car." He dangled a set of keys. "I was going to go with an engagement ring, but then I saw this perfect car outside Jersey."

He pointed to a pink Cadillac convertible and then he got down on one knee.

Rosemary stood up and looked at the car. "Is that a 1959 Series 62 in Elvis pink?"

"Yep."

"You bought me the Elvis convertible?" Her voice reflected how stunned she was at what sat across the square from them.

"Yep. Now I know a ring is a typical engagement gift, but when I saw this, I knew this was perfect for my old-fashioned Mississippi girl."

"You bought me a pink convertible?" she repeated, looking at the vintage beauty gleaming in the sun. How she'd missed it before she didn't know. Probably because all she could look at was the gorgeous New Yorker planted in the middle of her world.

Sal made a face. "Damn it. I told you I'm not great with decisions. I should have—"

Rosemary launched herself into his arms, knocking him back onto the very green grass, and then she kissed him in front of God and Morning Glory.

He started laughing as she covered his face with kisses. "I'm hoping that's a yes."

"Yes, yes, yes!" she shouted, rolling onto her back and laughing.

Then Rosemary heard Lorraine start yelling, "Someone help Rosemary. That man is attacking her!"

Rosemary sat up and waved her hands. "No, no, Lorraine! I'm fine. I'm more than fine! I'm getting married!"

And that's when she heard Eden and Jess whooping and hollering. Her nosy besties had cracked the swinging door of the Lazy Frog and had been listening.

Nothing like making a spectacle of oneself in the town square. Rosemary figured her mother would be aghast, but she didn't give a good damn. She'd never been so happy in her entire life. Sal loved her.

Sal. Loved. Her.

Sal sat up and blinked. "Not even been here two hours and someone is trying to have me arrested. Nice welcome," he said with a smile.

Rosemary took the keys from his hand. "I'll drive the getaway car."

"To where?"

"Well, it's time to introduce you to southern living. Hmm . . . you ever been skinny-dipping?"

"Yeah, I'm a New Yorker," he said, puffing out his chest.

"In a pond with gators?"

"Now that sounds like a challenge."

Rosemary leaned over and kissed him. "Thank you for loving me this much. I promise to spend the rest of my life making it worth your while."

He pulled her into his lap. "Oh, baby, it already is."

And as Rosemary kissed Sal, she could have sworn she smelled Lacy's signature perfume—Beautiful. Which was crazy, but maybe not. After all, Lacy had set all this in motion. Her last gift to her friend had been something way more than taking an art lesson or experiencing being a SoHo girl for a few weeks. No, Lacy did things big. She'd given Rosemary a love of a lifetime.

Acknowledgments

A warm thank-you to Phylis Caskey, Jennifer Moorhead, and Winnie Griggs for their support and advice. Also, I'd like to thank my talented editors—Kelli Martin and Melody Guy—along with the Wisconsin wonder, Michelle Grajkowski. I'm surrounded by strong, intelligent women who have big hearts. What a blessing you all are.

Sneak peek at

Perfectly Charming

The New Morning Glory Novel from Liz Talley

COMING IN FALL 2016

Chapter One

Jess Culpepper, formerly Jess Mason, stared at the envelope sitting in the center of her table and then slid the final documents inside, sealing them with the double prong. In her craptastic handwriting, she scrawled "Divorce Papers" across the front. There. They were now ready to be added to the filing cabinet beside her cramped desk, filed somewhere between business receipts and federal income tax returns. Just another chapter in her life relegated to a file.

"That's it. Finished," she said to the apartment she'd occupied for the past six months. Her austere apartment didn't answer back. She'd never added any homey touches to the place, preferring the white walls and utilitarian carpet over anything that might look like she gave a damn. She hadn't wanted to live here anyway. Sky Oaks Condominiums. A romantic name for a bunch of boxy, plain apartments.

She picked up one of the salt and pepper shakers Lacy had brought back from New Orleans when they were fourteen. A comical gift typical of her late friend. The pepper shaker was a frog groom; the salt was the bride. When lined up properly, the pair kissed.

Silly like Lacy.

Her friend had laughed and said they reminded her of Jess and her boyfriend, Benton. Lacy had wiggled her eyebrows. *Maybe he'll kiss you finally.*

No one had thought it strange that Jess had used the cheap ceramic shaker set atop her wedding cake. She even had a cute picture of her and Benton kissing behind the cake, mimicking the frogs. People had loved the personal touch, the fact that two childhood sweethearts had married each other. Till death do them part.

Or rather, until someone changed his mind and screwed their florist.

The doorbell rang, the door opening immediately after. "Yoo-hoo?"

Eden.

"Hey," Jess said, rising from the table, catching the swish of Eden's black pageboy from the corner of her eye. "What are you doing here at this hour?"

Eden scooted inside the apartment and shut the door. "You shouldn't leave your door unlocked, Jess."

"We live in Morning Glory. The biggest crime wave we've ever had was when those high school kids came over from Jackson, knocked down mailboxes, and left a dead cow carcass on the high school football field." Jess went to the fridge and grabbed a bottle of white zinfandel and waggled it. "Vino?"

"God bless you," Eden said, tossing her flip phone on the coffee table and dropping onto the plush couch, toeing her sneakers off and wiggling her toes. "I'm not sure how much longer I can work at Penny Pinchers."

Jess smiled. Eden said that every day. Seriously. Every day. The woman had been working at Penny Pinchers since she was sixteen. She was now the manager at twenty-eight. "Youngest manager in Mississippi," her regional manager liked to crow as he ogled Eden's boobs. "So quit."

"You know I can't," Eden said, accepting the glass of sweet, cold wine and curling her feet beneath her. "Mama's with Aunt Ruby Jean. We had the annual Voorhees reunion at the church today. Honestly, we're lucky lightning didn't strike when we stepped in the place. It was a potluck and Aunt Ruby took Mama home and gave me the evening to pretend I'm a normal person."

Eden Voorhees had been Jess's first friend, smiling at the new girl who was tall, skinny, and slightly bucktoothed as she balanced her lunch tray and looked desperately around for someone to sit with that first day back in fourth grade. Eden had patted the round stool attached to the lunch table and told Jess to sit down. Jess had adored the shy Eden ever since.

Her friend wore her crappy life like a backpack, strapped on and never complaining. Well, at least not much. Bless her pea-pickin' heart. Since her mother was a stripper/crack addict and her stepfather was in prison for armed robbery, it was a bloomin' miracle the girl had blossomed into the kind, hardworking, beautiful woman she'd become. Eden liked to credit her surviving hell with the friendships she'd made with Jess, Rosemary, and Lacy early on. But Jess knew goodness such as Eden possessed didn't fade away under the duress of hardship. Goodness like Eden's was a flower in a bed of weeds, stretching up toward the sun, refusing to be choked out.

Presently, Eden worked at the local Penny Pinchers and took care of her now handicapped mother. She'd missed out on frat parties, keggers, and beach trips to stay home and mark down cheap crap from China and change her mother's diapers. Eden deserved a medal. Or at least more than what she'd been handed.

"So it's final. Are you okay?" Eden asked, eyeing Jess with concern.

"I'm not suicidal, if that's what you're asking," Jess said.

"Why would anyone be suicidal over that jerk face?" Eden responded, picking up the remote control. "You talk to Rosemary yet?"

"Yeah, but she's busy having fun in NYC. I don't want to piss in her punch," Jess said, frowning when Eden settled on reruns of *Bones*. She was so not in the mood for gore. But then the idea of rom-com made her want to hurl.

"She's never too busy for you. You know that. But I'm so glad she's met someone fun. She got a tattoo," Eden remarked, hooking an eyebrow inquiring about her programming choice.

Jess shook her head. She didn't want to watch TV or talk about the fun Rosemary was having with a certain Italian guy in SoHo . . . even though she was truly happy for her. And she damned sure didn't want to look at that envelope sitting on the table like a knot on a log. And she didn't want to drink last night's wine.

No, Jess wanted to forget about the reality that was her life.

"Let's ditch the flesh being dumped in a tub of worms"—she gave a shudder—"and go to the Iron Bull."

Eden blinked. "I'm not exactly dressed for a bar. I'm wearing tennis shoes."

"So? You look cute."

"I look like I work at Penny Pinchers."

"I'll loan you a shirt. And some hoop earrings. Hoop earrings always make a gal look stylish." Jess rose and walked toward her lonely bedroom. It looked like the rest of the apartment—uniformly uninteresting, the antithesis of the three-bedroom cottage she'd shared with Benton for six years. Their house had been adorable. Everyone said so. Three months after Benton left, she sold it to a man who worked for the paper mill. The new buyer was divorced and had let the flower beds go to weeds. She could barely bring herself to drive by the place.

"I don't have big enough boobs for your shirts," Eden called out.

"I have some clingy things that will work," Jess said, opening the closet, feeling determined to do something about the depression she'd been courting for almost a year. So Benton didn't want her anymore? So he'd divorced her? Said he needed to experience life . . . whatever. So did she. The divorce was done. Over.

About the Author

Photo © 2009 Kara Lee

Liz Talley is the author of sassy contemporary romances, including the RITA-nominated *The Sweetest September*. A finalist for the Romance Writers of America's Golden Heart Award in the Regency romance subgenre, she made her debut in contemporary romance in June 2010 with *Vegas Two-Step*. She went on to publish eighteen more titles. Her stories are set in the South, where the tea is sweet, the summers are hot, and the men are hotter. She lives in northern Louisiana with her childhood sweetheart, two handsome children, three dogs, and a mean kitty. Readers can visit her at www.liztalleybooks.com to learn more about her upcoming novels.